FORGOTTEN MEMORIES

FORGOTTEN MEMORIES

CECILIA AGETUN

Forgotten Memories (Freya's Legacy, book 1)
Published by Cecilia Agetun
www.ceciliaagetun.com

ISBN: 978-1-7396488-0-0 (ebook)
ISBN: 978-1-7396488-1-7 (paperback)
ISBN: 978-1-7396488-2-4 (hardcover)

Book design:
Brittany Evans, https://bedesigns.ca/

Editor:
Chelsea Lauren, https://representpublishing.com/
Catherine Dunn, https://catherinedunn.co.uk/

To Tage Andersson

For showing me the beauty of nature growing up

ACKNOWLEDGEMENTS

There are so many people that I would like to thank for helping me make this book come to life.

A massive thanks to my critique groups; Mila, Jordan, Noah, April and Trena, Breea, Robin. I am extremely grateful to Trena for her emotional support and encouragement throughout this journey.

I want to thank Ann, Mathew, Michael, Charlotte, Victoria, Samantha, Megan, Branan, Faye, John and everyone else that provided feedback that helped to improve my story and my writing. I'd also like to thank Jo for sharing her publishing journey with me and answering all the questions I had regarding it.

A special thanks to Lewis, for providing visuals for some of my characters, even if they rarely got past the initial mock up.

I want to thank Brittany, my cover artist, for creating an amazing cover and my editors Chelsea and Catherine.

I'd also like to thank my other half, David, for the love and support, and for giving me the time and space I need to do my 'bookstuff'.

And last but not least, A massive thanks to you, the reader, for allowing me to share my world with you.

FORGOTTEN MEMORIES

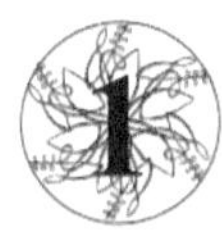

A Favour For A Friend

I soared above the treetops, appreciating the scenery while enjoying the warmth from the sun and the sensation of the wind between my feathers. Flying always helps me find my inner peace.

I descended towards the forest floor. Greenery covered the ground, and large oak trees cast shadows across the vegetation. I let my instincts guide me as I navigated through them.

The leaves rustled in the wind, and the creek flowing nearby created a soothing melody. I landed on a branch by the stream and breathed in the wonders of nature. Here, in my crow form, I could forget about everything – forget what I was and just be.

A deer and its fawn made their way over some rocks for a

drink. I watched them for a while. A sense of longing echoed in my chest as I thought about how my own parents had abandoned me. Not wanting to dwell on the past, I took to the sky again. I followed the stream as the landscape opened up, giving way to a lake. Sunlight glittered peacefully on the surface. I used the rising currents of warm air to boost my height, making me feel weightless as I drifted effortlessly through the sky.

While I glided over the lake, an invisible force tugged at me, pushing its tendrils into my mind. My breathing became rapid as I fought against it. I scanned the area, scared whoever had caused it would imprison my mind. My heart pounded and black dots clouded my vision as I struggled to break free. But it was no use. The force became stronger the more I fought it, causing me physical pain. The world spun and I struggled to stay upright. I swiftly looked for a place to land as the force pushed me towards another location.

What was going on? Wait ... was I being summoned?

The only person who could summon me was Nick. But why was he summoning me? He had never done it before. Maybe he was in danger. Instead of fighting against the force, I tuned in to it, allowing it to fully enter my mind and transport me to Nick's side. I wasn't completely sure where I would end up or what I would walk into, only that my best friend needed me.

I emerged in Nick's old house and instantly scanned the room to determine whether there were any imminent threats. When I didn't sense any, I took a deep breath and let my body relax. Nick seemed lost in thought, pacing back and forth in the living room. He didn't acknowledge me until I transformed into my human form.

A chill ran down my spine. I inspected my surroundings, trying to figure out why. The house hadn't changed much. The two leather sofas were still there, facing the fireplace, as was the enormous bookcase that engulfed an entire wall. Even the Persian rug, which almost completely covered the wooden floor, was still there. But something felt off. Different. I was still searching for a clue when Nick cleared his throat.

He gave me a smile, but it didn't reach his eyes. 'Jax. It's good to see you. I'm sorry about summoning you like this. I realise how degrading it must be to be forced somewhere against your will, but I didn't know any other way to reach you.'

I took a step towards him and met his gaze. I wasn't bothered; I knew he must have had his reasons. 'It's okay. What's going on?' I studied him more closely. Even though I hadn't seen him for a long time, he still appeared to be in his mid-twenties. Dark circles hung under his ice-blue eyes, which seemed to have lost their brightness. His beard was scruffy and unkempt, and his brown hair was put up into a bun. It looked like he hadn't showered for days.

Nick evaded my gaze and took a seat on the sofa, gesturing for me to do the same. He stared into the fire. I crossed my arms and uncrossed them, waiting for him to speak.

He took a deep breath but didn't move. 'I need a favour from you. You're the only one I can trust,' he said, his gaze still on the fire. A moment later he clasped his hands together in his lap and glanced at me with a pained expression. 'I never told you how Lily died.'

Nick broke eye contact and moved his gaze back to the fire. Silence followed. I ran my hand through my dark tousled hair, not sure whether to say something or wait for him to continue talking. Nick looked like a shell of what he had once been. The death of his wife had hit him hard. Guilt tore at my insides. I hadn't been a very good friend. The last time I'd seen Nick had been shortly after Lily had died. He hadn't wanted to talk about it then, and I had respected his wishes, telling him I'd be around if he needed me. Maybe I should have pushed harder?

'She was killed by a shadow demon.'

My eyes went wide. 'What?' I blurted out. 'Why?' It didn't make any sense. Shadow demons could only be created by upper demons. What would they have achieved by killing her? 'Do you know who made him?'

'Them.' Nick clenched his fist. An aura of raw power shot out from him, causing me to move back in my seat, worried that the demon inside him had temporarily taken over. It's hard to hold on to our humanity at times. It's something I've been fighting my entire existence. I fear what I might become if I let the demon inside take over again. That's why I prefer being a crow; everything is less complicated.

His voice brought me back to reality. 'If I did, he'd be dead already,' he said in a hard, hostile voice. He closed his eyes and sighed, reeling in his anger. 'I think I was their target.'

I opened my mouth to ask more questions, but he cut me off, shaking his head. 'It doesn't matter. I can take care of myself. But I have a daughter, and ...' He drew a shaky breath, despair filling his voice. 'Lily died protecting her.'

I shifted in my seat. This was news to me. He hadn't mentioned a daughter, but I hadn't seen much of him since he'd married Lily. And after she'd died, he had gone completely off grid.

'Her name is Cassie. She lives in the human world.' He took a deep breath. 'I had to hide her away. No one can know she is my daughter.' A sour expression came over his face as all the emotion drained from his voice. 'Not until I've killed every single one of the beings responsible.'

My muscles tensed up and I observed him for a moment. 'What do you need me to do?'

He let out a sigh. 'She's turning seventeen soon. My source could only guarantee her safety until her powers manifest.' He continued to stare into the fire. 'She doesn't know what she is. She doesn't know about this world. If anyone tried to get to her, she would be an easy target.'

'What do you want me to do?' I asked again, watching the reflection of the flames in his blue eyes.

He turned away from the fire and acknowledged me. 'I want you to keep her safe. Watch her, befriend her if you must, and help her understand her abilities like you did for me.'

'I'm not sure I'm the right person for the job.'

He stared into my hazel eyes. 'You're the only one I trust. I may be overreacting. Maybe no one is after her, but I made a promise to Lily to make sure that she's safe.'

I nodded in response. Nick was like a brother to me, and even though I would have preferred to go back to the forest, to the simple life, I owed him my life.

'So where can I find Cassie?' I asked.

He stared into the fire again. 'She lives in a town called Stonefield.'

'Where?'

He shrugged. 'I'm not sure. I can't tell, but it's a small town. Let me show you.' He used telepathy to send the images of the town over to my mind along with an image of Cassie. 'Sorry I can't be more helpful.'

'No worries. I should be able to find her based on this. Can't be too many Stonefields about.'

'Thank you. This means a lot to me.' He got up from the sofa and I followed suit.

'I guess I should be off,' I said, giving him a pat on the back. I tried teleporting away. Nothing happened. I tried again, this time closing my eyes and really concentrating on the task at hand. Still nothing. My mouth went dry. Beads of sweat formed on my forehead as panic rose inside me. I gave Nick a fleeting look. 'Why can't I teleport?'

'We're in Surtr's realm.'

'What?' I froze. My vision closed in on itself and flashbacks of my imprisonment swamped my mind. Bile rose from my stomach. 'Why would you do something this stupid?'

Nick winced and placed a hand on my shoulder. 'It's okay. Just breathe. My father doesn't know we're here. My house is concealed.'

My eyes went to his wrist. Partly hidden by his sleeve was a scar – a claw mark. A scar I had caused. Surtr's imprisonment had caused my demon to take over, so when Nick had finally found me, I was so far gone, I hadn't recognised him. Thinking he was out to cause me harm, my demon had lashed out. Unwilling to give up on me, Nick had bound me to him to get me out of there. The next few years were a struggle as I learned to take back control and suppress my demon, and I'd made a promise to myself never to let it take over again.

I took a deep breath and pushed the memories aside before glaring at him. 'How? Why?'

Nick let out a sigh. 'It's a long story. Short version, I grew tired of being attacked.'

'Who attacked you?'

'Demons. Lily's death broke something inside me. My powers aren't contained. They're like a beacon telling everyone where I am. Can't you feel it?'

I sent out my energies again, but I couldn't feel anything different about him. I shook my head. 'You feel the same as always.'

Nick furrowed his brow. 'What about when you came by the cemetery all those years ago?'

'I could sense you, just like now. I thought it had to do with me being bound to you.'

'Was it like that after we escaped Surtr?'

I shrugged. 'I don't know. I've done my best to forget about it all.'

Nick became thoughtful.

I scanned the room. The weird feeling I'd had made much more sense now. 'How do I get out of here?'

'Let me show you out.' Nick gestured towards the hallway.

I followed him to the front door and braced myself as he pulled the door open, expecting smoke and fire mixed with the sounds of war cries, but the world beyond the doorway looked exactly like the view from Nick's house in the human world – an English suburb consisting of brick terraced houses with bay windows. I rubbed my chin and blinked a few times. 'I don't understand. Why can I see the human realm?'

Nick chuckled. 'I would have thought you'd know a portal when you see one. Just step through and you'll be in the human world.'

I shook my head in shock. How had Nick managed to build a portal? He really had come a long way since we'd first met. I gave him a pat on the shoulder. 'Look after yourself.'

'As long as you make sure nothing happens to Cassie. I made a promise to her mother to keep her safe.'

'I will protect her with my life.'

Nick gave me a nod.

I stared at the door for a moment and ran my hand through my hair. I hoped Nick was right and that I wouldn't remain in Surtr's realm. Taking a deep breath, I closed my eyes and stepped through. My body vibrated from the energy of the portal. When I reached the other side, I let out a relieved sigh and turned around. Nick gave me a cheeky grin as if to say 'I told you so' before closing the door. I transformed into my crow form and took to the twilight sky. The wind caressed my feathers, soothing my body and mind. Nick had given me a lot to think about.

Back To College

I inserted the key and unlocked the door to my new house. It had taken me a long time to find this cottage, and even though it wasn't anything special, the land surrounding it had pulled me in. The house had a large garden with a forest at the back, bordering a nature reserve. The forest would provide me with the privacy I needed to come and go as a crow. The only downside was the wolves, but having the shifters on my doorstep wasn't necessarily a bad thing as long as I stayed out of their territory.

I walked into the living room. I hadn't lived in a house in a long time. Having spent most of my time as a crow, I hadn't needed one. But this mission was important, and the house was needed if I wanted to keep up appearances.

I sat down on the floor and tapped into my powers so I

could set up protection barriers around the house to make it safe. I visualised a dome of energy that had certain abilities and imagined it covering the area that needed protection. When I had a clear picture in my mind, I pushed the energy outwards until it left my body and created a wall of protection. I repeated this process several times to make sure I'd covered all my needs. The different layers provided various types of protection. Some were to keep supernatural beings out unless specifically invited. Others were to retain the energy within. A spell was only as strong as the person wielding it, but luckily for me, I'd had a lot of practice over the years, as I never really stayed in one place.

The next morning, back in my crow form, I circled the campus Cassie attended, looking for a place to land. I descended to a sheltered area beyond the car park and changed into my human form. It was a good thing immortals aged slowly; my appearance would fit right in.

As I approached the tall brick building with large windows, I passed a sign stating that it was Stonefield Sixth Form College. My heart thumped in my chest as I climbed the stairs leading to the entrance. It was almost half a human century since I'd last hung out with mortals. Would it be similar to the last time I'd masqueraded as a student?

I rubbed the back of my neck and entered the building. It had a spacious hall with stairs at the back and doorways to the sides. A group of teenagers stood talking amongst themselves; they glanced at me but paid me no further attention as I made my way to the reception desk on my right.

A woman with grey hair and warm, friendly eyes sat behind it.

Letting out a deep breath, I flashed her a smile. 'Hi. I'm new. I have a meeting with the head teacher. Would you mind telling me how to get there?'

The woman returned my smile. 'No worries, dear. What's your name?

'Jax'

'And your surname?'

'Smith.' I didn't really have a surname. It was a human invention, but I learned a long time ago that Smith was as common as could be and wouldn't raise any questions.

She nodded and made a call to let them know I was there before turning back to me. 'Let me show you the way. It's a big place and we wouldn't want you to get lost on your first day.' She stepped away from the desk and talked about the campus and its history as she escorted me along a few corridors consisting of white walls and rows of lockers with classroom doors between them. The sounds of lockers opening and closing, along with people walking around and talking, made it hard to hear what she was saying. Eventually the students disappeared into the classrooms and the corridors became quiet. We continued up some stairs and reached a small waiting area with chairs.

The receptionist gestured towards them. 'Please have a seat. The secretary will come and get you shortly.'

'Thank you.' She gave me a smile before departing.

I sat down on the chair closest to me. My eyes moved to

the window and the cloudy sky outside. I could've been out there feeling the wind between my feathers. I was lost in thought, imagining myself flying through the sky, when a female voice brought me back to reality. 'The head teacher is ready to see you now.'

I looked up and a woman with curly hair and dark-framed glasses was standing next to me. I wiped my hands on my trousers and got up to follow her to the head teacher's office.

As I stepped inside, a middle-aged man with a trimmed beard and grey hair stood up behind his desk. 'Hi, Jax. Welcome to Stonefield College. I'm the head teacher, Mr Ryder. Please have a seat.'

I sat down on the chair in front of the wooden desk. 'Do you have the enrolment forms with you?' Mr Ryder asked.

I tapped into my powers, focused on the thoughts I wanted to convey and visualised them being absorbed by Mr Ryder, making him believe I had already sent all the paperwork I needed. This way, if anyone came snooping, there would be nothing to find. 'I emailed them over a couple of days ago.'

Mr Ryder checked on the computer. 'Unfortunately, we don't seem to have received them. Did you bring the originals?'

I adjusted my seat and nodded, pulling out some blank papers from my bag. Sometimes my suggestions needed a bit of a push. I could have tried to fill in the enrolment papers, but there would have been too much information missing. It was safer this way. I handed them over and focused on my ability to convince him that these were the papers he needed.

He took them and reached for his glasses. The intense look on his face as he reviewed the paperwork had me on edge. What would I do if this didn't work?

'Thank you, Jax. I believe everything is in order.'

I let out a relieved breath and my muscles relaxed. Mr Ryder started typing on the computer in front of him. 'Let's get your timetable sorted so you know which classes to attend.'

With a lightness in my chest, I used my ability again and visualised him pulling up Cassie's timetable and creating an identical one for me.

Mr Ryder got up from his chair and handed me a copy of my timetable along with some other information about the college. 'I believe that's everything you need, but if you have any questions, please come and see me.' He checked the time. 'It's almost lunchtime, so your first lesson will be period four.' He ushered me towards the door and opened it.

'Thank you, Mr Ryder,' I said as I walked out.

I inspected the information I had been given, which included a map of the campus and the location of my locker. I followed the directions and ended up in a corridor filled with teenagers. They were walking in the opposite direction to me, making it challenging to navigate around them. Eventually I found my locker. As I opened it, someone slammed into me from behind.

'Oi, watch it, new guy.'

I turned around to find a broad, muscular guy with short ginger hair and a stern facial expression staring back at me for a moment before he continued down the corridor as though nothing had happened.

I clenched my fists to stop them from shaking. Who did he think he was? Despite his build, I knew I could take him. He was only human. If only he knew how effortlessly I could break him, he wouldn't dare treat me like this. I shook the tension away and pushed down the rage of the demon inside me. This was going to be harder than I'd thought.

I made it to my new class in the afternoon without any more incidents. The classroom had a teacher's desk at the front and four rows of two-seater tables. I walked to the back and slid into a plastic chair. Letting out a yawn, I inspected the other people filling up the classroom. A girl with long brown hair walked through the door. Something about her made me straighten in my seat. She scanned the room, and when her ice-blue eyes landed on me, warmth flooded my body.

Everyone else faded away. Every part of my being was entranced as she made her way towards me. There was something about her I couldn't place. A sense of familiarity. I studied her more closely. The energy radiating from her was similar to Nick's. This had to be his daughter.

The scent of spring flowers reached my nose as she sat down in the empty seat next to me. Her scent reminded me of my safe place, the forest. I wiped my hands on my trousers and mustered up a nervous smile. Why was I nervous?

She returned the smile. 'Hi, I'm Cassie. You must be new.'

I nodded and met her gaze. 'I'm Jax.'

She sorted through her belongings and pulled out a book and a notepad from her bag. I ran a hand through my hair, trying to come up with something else to say, but my brain had temporarily stopped working. I'd never been good at small talk.

The teacher walked into the classroom and started the lesson. It passed in a haze as I tried to get my brain to work again. I needed a plan. I'd promised Nick I'd keep her safe and help her control her powers. The best way to do that would be to spend time with her.

Peeking over at Cassie, I opened my mouth to say something. Anything. But I found myself tongue-tied.

Luckily Cassie spoke first. 'Did you just move here?'

I nodded. 'Yes. I got here a couple of days ago.'

'Cool. Whereabouts?'

'On the outskirts of the nature reserve.'

'Near the old settlers?'

I scratched my face. 'I don't know what that means.'

Cassie gave me an apologetic smile. 'Sorry. They're a group of people that live in the nature reserve. Some say they lived there before the town was built. They mainly keep to themselves, and most of them are home schooled. But a few of them go to college or have jobs around the town.'

I nodded. She must be talking about the wolves.

The bell rang and Cassie turned away to collect her stuff

from the desk. An uncomfortable silence followed. I shifted, wishing I could come up with something to talk about. Failing that, I took my timetable out of my bag to see where my next class was.

'What's your next class? Maybe I can show you how to get there.' Cassie leaned over to look at my timetable. Her hair brushed my shoulder. It took everything I had to remain unaffected. The smell of her shampoo didn't help. For a moment, I closed my eyes and imagined what it would be like snuggling up to her. I shook the picture out of my mind.

'My next class is maths with Mr Pine.'

'Mine too. Let's walk together,' Cassie said with a smile. She got up and exited the classroom. I followed her. She greeted other students with a warm smile as we made our way down the corridor to our next class.

When we arrived, Cassie excused herself and walked over to sit with some girls who had saved her a seat. Some of them glanced my way and whispered something to Cassie.

I took a deep breath and made my way to an empty seat. I wondered what they were talking about. If I wanted to, I could figure it out, but not without drawing attention to myself. As far as I could tell, they were humans and therefore not a threat, so it wasn't important. Besides, Nick had said Cassie would be safe until her birthday.

When class finished, Cassie left with her friends. I walked behind them as they made their way to the car park, hoping I would get another opportunity to talk to her. After she'd said goodbye to her friends, I took a step towards her, hoping to catch her up, but she got into a car with another girl. I let out a sigh and scanned the area for a sheltered area so I could follow them in my crow form.

They arrived at a detached brick house with a surrounding garden. I recognised the house from the images Nick had shown me. Cassie lived there. I landed on the roof and placed a protective barrier around the house. There were still a couple of weeks until her birthday, but I didn't want to take any chances. Better to be safe than sorry.

The Shock

I woke up to the morning sun shining through my window. The clock on the bedside table showed that I had a couple of hours to spare. I got up and took a shower, humming to myself as I got ready for the day. Hopefully I'd be able to talk more to Cassie today. There was still plenty of time before classes started. I stepped outside. The warm breeze danced on my skin and a wide grin emerged on my face.

I turned into a crow and spent some time flying around in the forest, listening to the birds chirping while taking in the earthy smell of nature. After some time, I slowly made my way to college. The forest gave way to roads and buildings, and the peaceful sound of nature was replaced by the noise of traffic and construction.

I landed at the far end of the car park and transformed

back to my human form behind the shelter of some trees. I entered the building and walked to my first class. A few students had already arrived, but Cassie was not among them. I scanned the room before sliding down onto a chair and dropping my bag on the empty seat next to me while I waited for her to arrive.

With a pounding heart, I inspected the students trickling into the classroom. When Cassie arrived, my heart skipped a beat, and I straightened my back and gave her a wide smile. She met my gaze and returned the smile. I wiped my hands on my trousers before removing the bag from the empty seat next to me. When I looked up again, Cassie was walking over to an empty seat on the other side of the room. My smile faded and I slouched in defeat. Why did she not want to sit next to me? My heart ached from her rejection. The next couple of lessons followed a similar pattern, though I had been discouraged from saving her a seat.

After a pep talk to myself over lunch, I decided to approach Cassie at the end of the next lesson. When the bell rang, I pushed myself to my feet and marched up to her. 'Hi,' I said with a smile.

'Hi,' she replied.

'How are you?'

She gave me a nervous smile. 'I'm fine. You?'

I nodded. 'I'm good.'

An awkward silence developed. She tucked her hair behind her ear and glanced over at her friends.

I scratched my neck. I wanted to ask her about this

morning, but I didn't know how. I considered using my ability, placing a thought in her mind to make her believe we were friends, but if it didn't make logical sense, it was unlikely to work. Besides, free will was sacred, and I didn't want to mess with that. No, I would have to befriend her the normal way. I opened my mouth to say something, but no words came out.

She looked up at me with an apologetic smile. 'I'm sorry, Jax. I need to go.'

'Okay. I'll see you around,' I said as I watched her walk away. I let out a sigh. How would I get her to become my friend when I couldn't even talk to her?

As the days passed, I kept trying to approach her. We smiled at each other and exchanged pleasantries, but I didn't seem to have much luck befriending her.

I spent the weekend as a crow, trying to come up with a plan. I scouted all the popular places to go, hoping I could invite her out somewhere. Maybe we could go bowling or go to the cinema?

Cassie's birthday was less than a week away. I could keep her safe without being involved in her life, but it would make things more complicated, and I wouldn't be able to help her with her abilities. Maybe I should just approach her and tell her the truth?

I made my way to my locker to get the books I needed for the day. My mind was preoccupied with thoughts of Cassie when someone bumped into me from behind. The books in my arms scattered on the floor.

I turned around and came face to face with the person who had slammed into me on my first day. He gave me an intense stare and bared his teeth. 'Didn't I tell you to watch it?'

I wiped small droplets of his spit off my face as several students stopped what they were doing and glanced at us. Rage flushed through my body. I hated bullies. I clenched my fists and took a deep breath. My throat constricted. If I didn't get this anger under control, my eyes would turn red.

I hid my red eyes by scanning the floor, pretending to look for the books. I hadn't come here to get humiliated. It would be easy to shut him up, but people talk, and if anyone found out what I was and why I was here, Cassie would be in even more danger. I couldn't take that risk.

I bent down to pick up the books, but every time I reached for one, he kicked it away. The other students laughed. This was just great.

I was waiting patiently for the bully to move away so I could retrieve my books when Cassie came up to me. She glared at the guy. He shrugged and continued down the corridor.

'I'm sorry about Mark. He can be such a dick sometimes.' She bent down and picked up the books. When she handed them to me, our hands touched, and an electric shock travelled up my arm, causing an intense tingling sensation. It ignited something inside me – something that had been locked away. It brushed the surface, but I couldn't reach it. Cassie jumped back with a yelp. Her face turned ashen, and she looked up at me with wide, frightened eyes. Before I had a chance to react, she turned and rushed down the corridor. I stood there frozen, staring after her. What the hell had just happened?

The bell pulled me back to reality and I made my way to the classroom. When I arrived, I scanned the room for Cassie, but she wasn't there yet. I moved over to an empty seat at the back so I could keep an eye on the door. My anxiety was getting the better of me, and I fidgeted with a pen as I waited for her to arrive. After what felt like ages, the teacher turned up and closed the door. Cassie still hadn't arrived. Where was she? She hadn't missed a single class since I'd enrolled, so why now? Did it have something to do with what had happened when we'd touched?

Knots formed in my stomach, and I asked the teacher if I could be excused, as I wasn't feeling well. The need to make sure nothing had happened to Cassie overwhelmed me. My gaze darted back and forth as I frantically searched the school without any luck. I took a deep breath, attempting to calm my erratic heart. Where could she be? I smacked my head. Her energy. Why hadn't I thought of that earlier?

I closed my eyes, homing in on Cassie's energy and allowing myself to drift towards it. An image of her house emerged in my head. I let out a sigh. She had gone home. Technically she should be safe there with the ward around the house, but I needed to talk to her. I needed to figure out what had happened between us. I had never come across anything like it before, nor had I heard of it happening to anyone else. Had Nick got her birthday wrong and this was somehow related to her powers, or had the spark between us been caused by something else?

I teleported over to Cassie's neighbourhood. A nervous laugh escaped my lips as I marched up to the front door. How would she react to me being there? I shook my hands to relieve some tension and rang the doorbell. My heart raced as I waited for the door to open.

Cassie opened the door and the pain in my stomach eased. She'd changed into black leggings and a big white top. Her hair was pulled up into a ponytail. My eyes wandered over her, taking in every little detail. She appeared to be fine. I let out a sigh of relief.

Cassie tensed up and grabbed hold of the door, ready to close it. 'What do you want?'

I ran a hand through my hair and cleared my throat. 'I wanted to make sure you were okay.'

'I'm fine.'

'Can I come in? We need to talk.'

She stared at me in silence, shifting her weight from one foot to the other. 'No.'

Rubbing my neck, I contemplated my next move. How could I get her to talk to me? I reached into my pocket and pulled out a piece of paper with my mobile number. 'It's important. I really need to talk to you. Just pick a time and place where you feel safe, and I will tell you everything.'

Cassie shook her head. 'This is crazy,' she muttered to herself before carefully taking the paper from my hand.

Would there be another spark if we touched?

'Thanks.' She gave me an unsure smile and closed the door. I stared at it, unsure what to make of this encounter. Hopefully she would text and meet up with me so I could explain everything.

I did a quick sweep of the neighbourhood as I walked away from the house before turning into a crow. I flew towards my house, but halfway there I changed my mind. Freya might have some answers.

Two Parts Of A Soul

I teleported to the forest where Freya lived. The shield around the area made it impossible to teleport directly to her cottage. I had to make the rest of the journey the old fashioned way, which involved flying.

The bright and colourful landscape gave the forest a magical glow, every shade of colour clearly visible. The seasons didn't affect this place like they did the human world. Even though the leaves on the trees changed colour, a warm breeze was always present.

When in the mood, I would fly through the trees, enjoying the nature and wildlife. Sometimes I would check on the other magical beings that lived in the forest. Today, I flew high in the blue sky, appreciating the beautiful view of the treetops blending into each other in different shades of green. Every now and again the trees would give way to a lake, and the water would mirror the sky and give a nice contrast of blue amongst the green. Even though the flight wasn't too bad, I was conscious of the fact that time moved differently here.

When I arrived at Freya's house, I took in the familiar view: a simple dark wooden cottage with a large veranda. Birch trees grew next to it, covering part of the view but intensifying the earthy atmosphere.

Freya has always been my rock. She took me in after I was abandoned at birth and raised me with love and kindness. She taught me that nothing good comes from hatred and jealousy and reminded me that I had a choice – that I could overcome the darkness inside me and choose my own path. 'Always have love in your heart, for it will defeat the darkness,' she used to say, and that's the mantra I've been trying to live by ever since.

I landed on the veranda and changed back into my human form. Freya was sitting on a wooden chair with a large grey cat cuddled up on her lap. I glared at it as I walked closer until it got the message and left. I scanned the area for its twin but couldn't see them. Freya's two familiars were loyal to her, but it didn't mean I wanted them to know about my problems.

I leaned down and kissed Freya's cheek. 'Your hair seems whiter every time I see you,' I said with a cheeky grin as I took the seat next to her.

'Nonsense.' She waved a hand in front of her as a smile

escaped her lips. 'Have some tea. It's freshly brewed.' She picked up the second cup from the small table between the chairs and handed it to me before taking a sip of her tea. 'What can I do for you, my child?'

I studied the wooden decking. I wasn't sure where to start or how much detail to give her. 'There's this girl,' I said a bit hesitantly before meeting her eyes.

Freya gave me a warm smile. 'I see. Would you mind telling me about her?'

I shook my head. 'I can't.' Based on my knowledge, Freya probably already knew about Cassie, but Nick had gone to a lot of trouble to hide her and make sure no one knew about her existence or connection to him, and I'd promised him I wouldn't tell anyone. I shifted in my seat. 'It's not really about her but about the electric shock that occurred when we touched.'

Freya gave me a knowing smile before she zoned out. Her blue eyes glazed over, and her breathing became slower. I took another sip of my tea as I waited patiently for her to come back to the land of the living.

Even though I'd grown up with her, I had no idea what type of being she was. She never talked about it. She had been around for several thousand years, and she somehow seemed to know about everything that was going on in one capacity or another. I'd asked her once if she could see the future, but I never got a proper answer; instead, she told me it changes nothing. When I got older, I realised asking someone about their abilities was very personal. I didn't want to disrespect

Freya, as she'd given me so much. I accepted that I might never truly know for sure. All I knew was that I could always count on her, even if it wasn't always in the way I expected. She was a strong believer in free will. Adamant about letting me form my own path and learn from my own mistakes but providing me with guidance when I needed it.

Freya came out of her trance and her eyes became clear again. She spent a few moments collecting herself. 'An electric shock happens to wake up two parts of one soul that have known each other before.'

Unsure what she meant, I waited for her to say something more, but she reached for her tea – a clear sign that I wouldn't get any more information out of her.

I got out of the chair and started pacing. 'That's it? That's all you're going to tell me?'

She placed her hand on my arm. 'Some things we need to figure out for ourselves.'

'But—'

She cut me off. 'No buts. Have faith and you will find the answer you seek. Just remember to look through your heart instead of your eyes. The reality you see is not complete.' She released her grip.

My gaze followed her as she strolled back into the house. I stood there for a moment, staring at the closed door, before I shook my head and sighed. I'd been hoping for a decent answer, but I should have known better. She'd never been very forthcoming with information. Why should this time be any different?

Despite the short time I had spent at Freya's, it was already past midnight in the human realm. I checked my phone to see whether Cassie had texted me, but I wasn't that lucky. Should I seek her out tomorrow and tell her who she was and why I was there? I shook my head. She wouldn't believe anything I told her if she didn't trust me, and trust had to be earned. Hopefully she would talk to me when she was ready. I just hoped it would be before her birthday.

CASSIE'S BIRTHDAY

When I saw Cassie in our class on Tuesday morning, she pretended I wasn't there. Every now and again I could feel her eyes on me, but as soon as our eyes met, she looked away. Maybe she just needed time? I waited for her to come around, but several days passed without her making any attempt to talk to me. If anything, it was almost like she was avoiding me.

I kept away from Mark as much as I could. Every time I saw him, he would slag me off or slam me into the lockers. It pissed me off. What did he have against me? When my anger boiled over, I clenched my fists and took a few deep breaths, reminding myself why I couldn't stoop to his level.

When I woke up on Friday, my stomach felt empty. Cassie hadn't texted me and I didn't know how to proceed. I paced the room. Today was the day when everything would change. Her powers would start manifesting, and according to Nick, she would no longer be safe. From what, I wasn't sure. Nick hadn't specified what might come after her. I don't think even he knew. Either way I would be on high alert, ready to step in and protect her as needed.

I teleported to the college early, before any students arrived, and made a quick stop at Cassie's locker. In my hand was a small black box with a silver bow. The box contained a talisman for protection – several knots surrounded by a circle in the form of a necklace. I hoped she would like it enough to wear it. Freya had given it to me when I'd first ventured into the human realm. It would dampen Cassie's magical energy and make it harder for anyone to detect what she was. It would also help her control her abilities. In my case it had made it easier to suppress the demon inside. I hadn't worn it in a long time, and even though it held sentimental value to me, Cassie needed it more.

After I'd placed the box in her locker, I made my way to our first lesson and took a seat at the back. It would be easy enough to keep an eye on Cassie during class, but what about the breaks?

The first part of the day went smoothly, but halfway through, Cassie stared down at the table in front of her and rubbed her temples.

I got up from my seat and approached her. 'Are you okay?'

She jumped and turned around, her eyes struggling to

focus. 'I'm fine.' She turned back and placed her head in her hands.

She obviously wasn't fine. I wanted to ask her what was bothering her, but considering how she'd been acting towards me, I doubted she would tell me anything. I reluctantly went back to my seat but kept an eye on her throughout the lesson.

When class finished, I followed her at a distance but lost her in a sea of students. I made my way over to the next class, hoping she'd beat me there. She hadn't. As the students trickled in, a chill went through me. My chest became heavy, and I struggled to breathe. Something wasn't right. I ran out of the classroom just as the teacher arrived.

I took a deep breath, located Cassie and teleported to her side. I'd deal with the consequences of anyone seeing me later. Cassie was more important. Besides, everyone was supposed to be in class.

She was sprawled on the floor, her bag and its contents scattered around her. With a pounding heart, I rushed to her side. Seeing her chest rise and fall decreased my panic. There were no obvious wounds, but her face had lost all its colour. I wiped some sweat from my forehead as I attentively scanned the area for threats. My senses were on high alert, my sword seconds from being summoned. I wasn't taking any chances.

When I didn't see or sense anything out of the ordinary, I gathered her belongings and scooped her up in my arms. When I touched her, another shock coursed through me, causing a disjointed collection of images accompanied by the smell of grass. It was too fast for me to make sense of, and as I teleported us over to my house, I questioned whether it had even happened.

I placed Cassie carefully on my bed and extended the energy in my mind to double check the protection spells were working, just in case someone was after her, and added a few extra for good measure.

With my breath still caught in my chest, I examined her more thoroughly. I couldn't detect any injuries or supernatural interference. As far as I could tell, there was nothing wrong with her. So why wasn't she waking up? I grabbed a chair and positioned myself next to the bed, determined not to let her out of my sight.

I sat there watching her for a while until she stirred. Her body tensed and she clutched her head, mumbling something incoherent. Seeing her in pain intensified my need to protect her. I wanted to take her away and keep her safe from all the supernatural dangers in the world. I silently cursed Nick for the target he'd unintentionally put on her.

Her voice got louder and she shouted for someone or something to shut up before passing out again. I scanned the room for anything that might have caused it. Nothing should be able to get into the house without my knowledge. Despite this, I sent my energy out to be certain, but I couldn't sense anything unusual. What was going on? I'd never felt this helpless, not even when Surtr imprisoned me. I thought back to when Nick's abilities had manifested. Could this be related?

Nick had the ability to read minds. His voice echoed in my head. 'If these voices won't stop screaming and shut up, I'll burn them all to the ground.' Luckily, he'd learned to control them before he had to carry out his threat. Maybe Cassie had voices screaming in her head, but the necklace should have protected her against them.

I glanced down at her and brushed a tendril of hair away from her face. My attention went to her neckline. She wasn't wearing the necklace. I conjured it around her neck. Her body relaxed and her eyelids fluttered. A moment later she opened her eyes and jumped out of the bed. Her gaze darted across the room until she focused on me. I froze, scared any movement I made would cause her to run.

I tried sending her calming energy, but it didn't work. No surprise there, really. My abilities didn't work on Nick, so why should his daughter be any different? I'd asked Freya about it once – why my mind influence didn't work on Nick. She'd told me something about being descendants and that the fates had made it that way to equal out the battlefield. As usual, I wasn't completely sure what she was talking about.

Cassie bit her lip. 'Jax?' Her brow furrowed. 'Where am I?'

'At my house. You passed out in school, so I brought you here.'

She crossed her arms. 'What the hell? You didn't think to take me to the nurse's office or, better yet, home to my family?'

I shook my head. 'No. You're safer here. They can't

protect you like I can.'

She let out a sigh, her nostrils flaring. 'From where I'm standing, it looks like you're the one I need protection from.' Her eyes moved towards the door and she took a step towards it.

I stepped in the way. 'This isn't the way I wanted to tell you, but I promised your dad I'd keep you safe.'

'My dad's dead. Besides, I can take care of myself,' she snapped back.

'No, you can't. There's a whole world out there that you know nothing about.'

Her face twisted into a scowl. 'Why should I believe anything you say? You're the one that's keeping me hostage.'

Tears burned my eyes, and I clenched my jaw in frustration. 'I'm telling you the truth, Cassie. I would never hurt you. Just give me a chance to explain.'

She let out a sigh. 'Okay. Enlighten me.'

I walked over to the bed, surprised she didn't bolt through the door. Maybe she would actually give me a chance to explain. She glared at me but remained standing as I gestured for her to sit down next to me on the bed.

'Your dad gave you away when you were a baby to keep you safe, but now you're seventeen, your powers are manifesting and you're no longer safe, as they will be able to sense you. I think the reason you passed out was because your new ability overwhelmed you. Your dad had the ability to read minds, and I believe you do too.'

Cassie pursed her lips in a slight grimace. 'So that's what

the voices were? I thought I was losing my mind. Why can't I hear them anymore?'

I pointed at the necklace. 'That helps to control your abilities.'

Her hand moved to touch the necklace. She inspected it with fidgety fingers. 'Who's out to get me?'

I shrugged. 'I don't know. Demons? Your mother died protecting you from them, and your dad's been trying to figure out who's behind it ever since.'

'My dad died in a car crash when I was young. It's how me and Leah ended up in foster care.'

I shook my head. 'It can't have been your dad. He's very much alive. Besides, you're an only child. Maybe it was Leah's dad?'

Cassie went quiet and sat down on the bed. 'I want to believe you. My heart is telling me to believe you, but ...' She took a deep breath. 'I don't know. It's a lot to take in. I need time to process.' She glanced around the bed, her gaze landing on her bag. She grabbed it and pulled her phone out. 'Classes have almost finished. I need to get back home before they start worrying about me. I'm not sure how I got here, but would you mind giving me a ride home?'

The conversation had gone better than I'd expected. I debated whether to just teleport her home but thought better of it. 'Sure. I'll drive you home,' I said as I led her to the garage, where I'd just conjured a car.

A Coffee Shop

An uncomfortable silence arose as I drove Cassie back to her house. My fingers tapped on the steering wheel as I tried to come up with something to say. I glanced over at Cassie. She looked out of the window, absentmindedly fidgeting with the necklace. Maybe I should just let her digest everything I'd told her earlier. It confused me that she hadn't freaked out about anything I'd told her. Did she already know about the supernatural world?

I turned into Cassie's driveway, turned off the engine and got out of the car. Taking a deep breath, I walked around to open the door for Cassie. She glanced up at me, parting her lips as if to say something. When I met her gaze, she looked away and climbed out. I gave her a smile and closed the door behind her, letting my hand rest on the car as I watched her walk up to the porch.

'Cassie,' I called to her. There was so much I still wanted to tell her. She paused and turned around but didn't say anything.

My mind went blank. 'Happy birthday. Don't be a stranger.' She nodded with a small smile before walking inside.

What a stupid thing to say. I dropped my head against the car but quickly straightened my back. Hopefully she hadn't seen that. After wiping my hands on my trousers, I got into the car and drove away.

A few hours later, Cassie sent me a text. I read it with a big grin on my face. She had taken my advice and asked to meet up. Even though she made it clear that she only wanted to talk about earlier, I was already lost in thought. What should I wear? Where should we go? In my excitement I almost forgot to text her back.

Unable to sleep, I headed out to flex my wings and burn away some energy. Flying always calmed me down and helped me clear my mind. With the moonlight on my back, I replayed every moment with Cassie. Why did I have these strong feelings about her? It didn't make sense.

The first rays of the morning sun crept over the trees. Crap! I hadn't meant to be out for this long. I headed home, hoping to at least have a quick nap before seeing Cassie later.

A few hours later, I still hadn't been able to fall asleep. I gave up and went to have a shower. Back in the bedroom, I strolled over to my wardrobe to find something to wear. An hour later, I was still wrapped in my towel, with nearly every piece of clothing I owned, including a few newly conjured ones, strewn across the room. I shook my head. What the hell was wrong with me?

I grabbed a black pair of jeans and a white T-shirt. On the way to the bathroom, I paused to examine my reflection. Maybe this was too casual? Would it help if I did something with my hair? I sighed heavily and rested my forehead on the cold glass of the mirror. Why was I trying to impress Cassie? This meeting wasn't a date; it was Cassie wanting to know more about her parents and herself – nothing more. Despite this, the butterflies in my stomach remained.

I arrived early at the coffee shop where we had arranged to meet, so I could check it out and find a private spot where we could sit and talk without being interrupted. The table in the corner by the window would do.

After ordering a coffee, I sat down. While I waited for Cassie to arrive, I placed a temporary sound barrier around the area to make sure that we could speak freely without worrying about who might overhear us. Taking a sip of my coffee, I tapped my fingers on the table as I waited for Cassie to turn up. Every time the door opened, my heart stopped, hoping it would be Cassie, only to be disappointed. Where was she?

I checked the time. It felt like hours had gone by, but it was only five minutes past the time we had agreed to meet. I'd just started to think about locating her energy when she walked through the door. All my attention went to her, and

I laughed to myself. We almost had matching outfits. She wore a pair of tight blue jeans and a white top. Her hair was up in a ponytail and mascara highlighted her blue eyes. Had she made an effort for me? I'd never seen her wear makeup in school.

Cassie waved and went to order a drink. Heat coursed through my body as she approached my table. Why was I reacting like this to her? I got up and pulled a chair out for her so she could sit down.

She hesitated, looking around the cafe, pressing her lips together before meeting my eyes. 'Should we go somewhere more private to talk?'

'It's okay. I put a sound barrier up. No one should be able to overhear us.'

Cassie's jaw slacked and her eyes narrowed. 'How did you create a sound barrier?'

I shrugged. 'It's simple, really. I just visualise it in my head and push the energy out.'

She leaned in towards the table with a wide smile. 'I should have known you weren't human either. What are you?'

I had no idea how to answer that. I didn't want to mention the D word after telling her demons were the ones that were after her and had killed her mother. I doubted she would have believed me if I'd told her I wasn't like other demons. Clearing my throat, I looked around. 'I'm sort of like you, but slightly different.' I hoped she wouldn't pick up on the fact that I'd avoided the question.

She gazed into my eyes, a smile playing on her lips. 'And what am I exactly?'

I should have seen that coming. I ran my hand through my hair. 'You're a hybrid. A mix of two different beings.'

She nodded. 'Tell me about my parents.'

I scratched my head. 'I didn't really know your mother. I only met her a few times, but she was lovely and caring and she adored your father. Your dad I've known for a long time. We met in school and have been close ever since.'

'Where is he now? Why isn't he here?'

'He's in another realm. I'm sure he would have been here himself if he could, but he can't risk anyone finding out you're his daughter.'

'Why?'

'Because it will put a target on you. So for now, you're stuck with me.'

Cassie stirred her drink for a moment. 'How old are you?'

'It's complicated.'

She gave me a questioning look. 'Try me.'

I let out a sigh. 'Immortal beings age slower than humans, but time also moves differently in other realms, so we don't really keep track of how much time has passed. Our bodies usually portray our mental age.'

'So you're a teenager?'

I nodded. 'I guess you could say that.'

'How long have you been a teenager?'

I shrugged. 'I don't know. Like I said, it's complicated. An hour in the human world can be ten minutes in another realm.'

'You mentioned immortal beings, but you told me my mother died, so she can't have been immortal.'

'Being immortal means you can't die of old age. It doesn't mean you can't be killed. Though there are a few truly immortal beings in the universe, you are unlikely to come across any of them.'

Our eyes met, and I lost myself in hers. It felt like a long time had passed before she pulled me out of my trance.

'Will I get any more abilities?'

I blinked a few times and shook my head to clear it. 'Yes, more than likely. An offspring usually receives some or all of the abilities of their parents.'

A spark appeared in her eyes. 'What abilities will I get?'

'It's hard to say. We won't know about all of your abilities until you turn eighteen. Some abilities will be similar to mine, but others will be completely different. I have a pretty good grasp of your dad's abilities, but I don't know much about your mother's, and it's impossible to know what abilities you have inherited. I think we'll just have to wait and see.'

Cassie hesitated. 'But what if I pass out again or something worse happens?'

I gave her a reassuring smile. 'Hopefully the necklace will help with that. If not, you have me.'

She met my gaze. 'Will you help me with them?'

I nodded. 'But so far we only know about the mind reading.'

'That I can't even control,' she muttered.

'You'll learn. It just takes practice.'

'Can you teach me?'

'I'll try.'

Cassie's phone buzzed in her bag, and she picked it up. 'I can't believe the time. I have so many more questions, but Leah is waiting for me in the car park, so I need to go.'

'Let me walk you.' I got up from my chair and offered Cassie my hand.

An electric shock ran through me as she took it. A feeling of contentment along with the sound of insects and rustling grass entered my senses. I released her hand and apologised.

Cassie met my gaze. 'Actually, I meant to ask about that. Has it happened to you before? Is it part of your abilities?'

I shook my head. 'No, it's never happened to me before, and it only happens with you. I'm not sure why. I asked someone about it when it first happened, but I didn't get a reasonable explanation.'

'Was that why you acted so weird when you came to see me?'

I cocked my head. 'I was acting weird?'

'You were practically stalking me. How did you even know where I lived?'

I stopped in my tracks. How much could I tell her without scaring her away? Moving my hand through my hair, I answered. 'I can sense your energy.'

She let out a nervous laugh. 'Great,' she said in a sarcastic tone. 'So even if I wanted to get away from you, I couldn't?'

My muscles went rigid. I shouldn't have told her.

She pressed her lips together, a smile tugging at them. 'You should see your face. Pale doesn't suit you.'

I let out a breath. 'It doesn't scare you?'

She shrugged and continued walking. 'Not really. For some reason I feel safe around you, but you're definitely weird – borderline stalkerish.'

'I don't spend a lot of time around people.'

'Maybe I can help. You help me with my abilities and I'll try to help you fit in.'

I smiled. 'Deal. Just let me know next time you're free and we'll start practising. It's probably safest to practise at my house ... if you don't mind.'

'You don't randomly ask people to your house.'

I scratched my head. 'But it's not random. The house is protected.'

We continued our walk in silence until we stopped next to a black Mini. 'This is my stop,' she said as she nodded towards it.

She wrapped her arms around me, and as the shock went through me, an image of a field emerged in my mind and filled me with happiness.

Cassie took a step back and smiled. 'I'll see you later.' She got into the passenger seat and Leah drove away.

Frozen in place, I stood there looking after it with wide eyes until it disappeared from view. A big grin appeared on my face. Cassie had said she felt safe around me.

A Walk In The Woods

After I'd returned from seeing Cassie, I walked around the house, still sporting a wide grin. I wanted to tell Nick about the week, but he had told me to be careful and only get in contact if anything important happened. I didn't think Cassie feeling safe around me qualified.

Feeling restless, I turned into a crow. As I soared over the rooftops, I realised I had subconsciously flown over to Cassie's neighbourhood. I threw out my energy to feel for anything supernatural and detected a few magical beings. They seemed to be going about their day and therefore unlikely to be a threat to Cassie, though I made a point of keeping an eye on them. I didn't want to hurt any innocent beings, but if they became a problem, I would do what was necessary.

I spent some more time drifting around. As the moon peeked out from behind the clouds, I made my way home. I checked my phone, happy to see a text from Cassie. She had asked me if I wanted to meet up the next day to start training. I replied with tingling fingers that I would be happy to oblige. I strolled into the living room, my insides vibrating with excitement. Cassie would be in this very spot tomorrow.

I removed the sofa and the table and some other things we wouldn't need. The main part of training includes visualisation within the mind. Having too many things around would only be distracting. I scanned the now empty room and conjured up some yoga mats before calling it a night.

The next day, I offered to pick Cassie up, but she said Leah wanted to drive her. She jokingly explained that Leah wanted to know where I lived in case Cassie didn't come back home. I laughed at the irony. The safest place for Cassie was with me, but Leah didn't know that. She had no idea what I was or what I could do, so it didn't surprise me. It warmed my heart to know that Cassie had people in her life who really cared for her.

While I waited for Cassie and Leah to turn up, paranoia got the better of me and I strengthened the protective spells around the house. Even without them being strengthened, the chances of Cassie overpowering the spells were minimal, but I didn't want to take the chance of someone sensing her.

The black Mini turned in to the driveway. I opened the door to greet them. Cassie got out and said bye to Leah. I took a step towards her but stopped, unsure if I should go in for a hug, but Cassie put her arms around me. The scent of her hair engulfed me in a feeling of peacefulness. The shock hit me harder this time. A feeling of déjà vu overcame me as an image of me sitting in a field with someone entered my mind. The sun warmed my face, and the smell of grass surrounded me. Was it a memory? I tried to recall it, but it stayed below the surface.

Cassie pulled away and bit her lip. 'Are you okay?'

'Yeah, I'm fine.' I shook my head to clear it.

Cassie looked up at me. 'I feel it too, you know. You're not the only one affected.'

I met her gaze and mirrored her smile. We stood there for a while until the sound of Leah's car driving away brought us back to reality.

'Thanks for coming. Let's go inside and get started.' I turned around and made my way towards the living room.

Cassie followed me inside. When we reached the living room, she stopped and looked around. 'It looks different from last time I saw it.'

I had completely forgotten that conjuring things up wasn't a normal thing to do. I guess I had lived away from the human population for too long. I considered coming up with a non-magical explanation but thought better of it. I wanted Cassie to trust me, so I needed to be honest about as much as I could. 'Yeah. I sorted the room out for our training session. I'll change it back when we're done.'

'But where's all the stuff?' Cassie asked me with a frown.

'I can conjure it up or remove it as I wish. It's one of my abilities.'

Cassie scanned the room again with a fresh look of astonishment on her face before turning to me with wide eyes. 'Can you conjure anything?'

I shook my head. 'There are two different ways of conjuring things up. The first way is to conjure something from scratch by manipulating the energy around you to make a specific form. It does have its limitations, and it's hard to do specifics, and some things would be impossible. For example, to be able to conjure up a book, I would have to know the exact contents of the book, or the pages would be blank. But if I already have the book, I can conjure that specific book. Which leads us to the other type of conjuring. I guess you can almost look at it as a form of telekinesis, where you transfer an object from one place to another. And sometimes it's in a non-physical form. Like the sofa is at the moment.'

She took a step towards me and gave me a mischievous smile. 'Can you conjure something for me?'

She observed me and gasped as I made a rose appear in my hands. I handed it to her. 'A beautiful flower for a beautiful lady.' Blushing, she took the rose from my hands and glanced away.

After a moment of silence, I moved over to the yoga mats on the floor and gestured for Cassie to join me. 'Ready to start?'

Cassie nodded and sat down.

'First you need to clear your mind and focus on control.

The necklace should help, but when you can control your ability, you should be able to turn your mind reading on and off without the help of the necklace. The only way to know if you're successful is to remove the necklace. But please only do that when I'm around and can create a protective barrier around us.' I took a deep breath. 'Remember when I said I would try to teach you?'

'Yeah,' she answered, sounding uncertain.

'Well, the reason I said I would try is because I don't have the ability to read minds.'

She pursed her lips. 'So how will you train me?'

I gave her a reassuring smile. 'I have a similar ability – the ability to influence people. I'm hoping it'll work in a similar way.'

Cassie tilted her head. 'How do I know you're not using your ability to influence me?'

'It doesn't work on you.'

Her eyes went wide. 'You tried to use it on me?'

I tensed up. I was meant to be helping Cassie, not scaring her away. Oh well. Might as well be honest with her. 'I tried to get you to calm down when you woke up after you passed out.'

Silence engulfed us as we sat there gazing at each other. I was worried she would storm out and never want to see me again. But she surprised me.

She crossed her arms and broke our eye contact. 'So how do I learn to control this ability?'

I cleared my throat. 'It's all about visualisation. Imagine

the energy running inside you. Pretend you place it in a box and close the lid or that you're turning the energy off, almost like a tap. Either should work, so just choose the one that comes more naturally to you.'

She straightened her back and nodded. 'I'll give it a try.'

'Good. Let's start with some breathing exercises to get in the right state of mind.'

We spent a couple of hours working on Cassie's mind reading ability and trying the different techniques. Eventually she let out a heavy sigh and shook her head. She still hadn't managed to turn her ability off. It didn't surprise me. It had taken me a good amount of time and training to learn my abilities when I'd first discovered them, and I had always known what I was.

Cassie sighed again, bringing me back to reality. Maybe it was time for a break. I got up from the floor and offered my hand to Cassie to help her up. 'How about a break? We can take a walk in the woods. Make the most of the lovely weather.'

Cassie nodded and took my hand. Another shock went through us and she let go. I let out a laugh. 'I keep forgetting.'

She gave me a smile. 'Me too.'

A moment later we were making our way outside. The sun peeked out from the clouds as the cool breeze enlightened us that summer was on its way out. The fresh air entered my lungs.

I watched Cassie in my peripheral vision as we followed the path into the forest. 'I grew up around a forest. It's one of the reasons why I got this house. It reminds me of home.'

'Where did you grow up?'

'In another realm.'

'The same one as my father is in?'

I shook my head. 'No. A different one.'

'How many realms are there?'

I scratched my neck. 'I'm not sure. I've been told the universe is made up of an infinite amount of realms. But I've only been to a few. The one I grew up in consists of a massive forest with giant trees, and lakes and meadows. Everything's bright and colourful, almost like a painting.'

'It sounds beautiful.'

'It is. I was very lucky to have grown up there. How was it like growing up for you?'

'I don't remember my dad much.' She hesitated. 'Leah's dad. He died when I was about four years old. After that, Abigail adopted me and Leah. And shortly after, Mark and Seth. We may not be biologically related, but they are my family. Abigail never spoiled us with presents or money, but she always took family time very seriously. She goes away for work quite a bit now we're older, but she's still very passionate about family dinners.'

The fondness in Cassie's voice made me think that maybe Nick had done the right thing by hiding her and letting her grow up amongst humans. Would her childhood have been as happy if Nick hadn't given her away?

Cassie stopped as the path split into two. 'Can we walk this way?' She pointed to the left.

That path would take us into wolf territory, and who knew what they would do to me if we did? I ran my hand through my hair and looked up at the sky. 'Maybe we should just head home. It looks like it might start to rain.' I started walking towards the house.

She stared at the sky with a frown. 'But there's hardly any clouds in the sky.' She shook her head before quickening her steps to catch me up.

When we got back, I conjured the sofa and sat down. Cassie took a seat next to me and leaned back with a smile. 'Even though I've seen you do it before my eyes, I'm amazed when something appears out of nowhere.'

I chuckled before clearing my throat. 'You'll get used to it. Do you want to continue with the training or should we call it a day?'

She looked away, fidgeting with the armrest.

'We can try some other exercises if you want. Mix it up a bit,' I added quickly, hoping she would decide to stay.

She met my gaze. 'Okay. Let's give it one more go.'

I gave her a reassuring smile. 'How about you try and read my mind?'

'I wouldn't even know where to start.'

'Don't worry, I'll talk you through it.'

I offered her my hand to pull her up from the sofa, but she ignored it. My gaze followed her as she took a seat on the mat again. Not wanting to give any thought to why she hadn't taken my hand, I sat down on the mat to face her. 'I'll think of something, and you can try and figure out what I'm thinking about. Just concentrate on the energy and direct it towards me. Imagine how it connects to my thoughts.'

Cassie nodded and closed her eyes.

I mentally blocked all other thoughts from my mind. I didn't want Cassie to figure out the effect she had on me – at least, not now. I opened up my mind to make it easier for her to connect to it and thought about an apple – how it looked, what colour it had and how it tasted.

Cassie opened her eyes and stared at me. I struggled to keep the mental image of the apple; instead I imagined how it would feel to kiss her. A nervous smile crept over me, and Cassie started laughing.

'Did you pick up on anything?' I asked, worried that she had sensed my inappropriate thoughts.

She shook her head. 'Nothing.'

'Maybe it's time to call it a day.' There was no way I would be of any help with these thoughts about her in my head.

A while later, Leah came to pick Cassie up. Cassie spun the rose around in her hands as I walked her to the car. Joy coursed through me from seeing her cherish the rose I had given her. As we reached the car, a chill went down my spine. Something was different, but I wasn't sure what. Cassie said goodbye and got into the car. I threw my energy out in an attempt to figure out where the feeling came from, and that was when I felt it. Leah had supernatural energy inside her. The type of energy that indicated she was a witch.

Looking For Answers

When Leah's car had disappeared into the distance, I transformed into a crow. Sensing her magic had made me uneasy. Why hadn't I felt this earlier? I had seen Leah several times by now, but I'd never picked up on anything unusual before. What was going on?

I followed them. The clear sky improved visibility, and the black Mini was easy to spot from above. I kept my distance, even though they wouldn't be able to recognise me. The trees gave way to buildings and eventually I was gliding over the rooftops.

I landed in the tree next to the driveway as Leah parked up. Her magical energy was easy to detect until they walked inside. Despite the protective barrier I had put up, I should have been able to detect it. But I couldn't pick up on any supernatural energy – not even the barrier I had put up.

In all my years, I'd never encountered anything like this. Why was it happening? Should I be worried about it? I circled the house a few times, trying to come up with an explanation without any luck. I needed more information, and the only person I knew who might have an idea about it was Freya.

Hoping Cassie would be safe with Leah, I teleported to the forest and made the journey to Freya's house. The door stood open, and when I stepped inside, the whistling sound of a kettle greeted me. I entered the kitchen as Freya poured two cups of tea. She handed me one as I went to give her a kiss on the cheek before she made her way into the living room and sat down on a chair.

'What is troubling you?'

I took a seat next to Freya. 'Something very strange just happened. I realised someone I've been around several times before is a witch. I never sensed her magic before today. I followed them and as they walked through the door to their house, the magical energy disappeared. Almost like it never existed. And the protective barrier I placed on the house is gone too.'

Freya was listening attentively but stayed quiet.

'Do you have any idea why this happened?' I asked her when she still hadn't spoken.

'Ancient magic has the ability to shield; however, such a spell cannot be done by a mere mortal witch. It requires sacrifices and dedication. That begs the question, who would go to those lengths and why?'

That was indeed the question. Had someone figured out who Cassie was? Or did it have something to do with Leah? With the other people in Cassie's house? Were Seth and Mark supernatural too? Abigail? Cassie's calm reaction when I'd told her about the supernatural and her abilities started to make more sense. She must have known about Leah's magic.

'But why haven't I been able to sense her magic before today?'

'The shield may keep them hidden, neutralising the supernatural energy that radiates from them.'

'Wouldn't that mean I wouldn't sense them at all?'

Freya let out a sigh. 'Remember what I taught you. When a being accesses their abilities, their essence or energy is repelled outwards. The residue of this stays, and that's why someone can detect you even when you're not using your abilities.'

'So because she hadn't been back to the house before coming to mine, the residue hadn't been neutralised?'

Freya nodded but remained quiet and picked up her knitting. I finished my tea and said goodbye. I needed to talk to Nick – to let him know about the potential threat. It bothered me that I didn't know why the house had been shielded or who was behind it.

When I entered the area where teleportation was accessible, I teleported to the outside of Nick's house. I changed back into my human form and made my way up the stairs leading to his front door. Knowing the inside of the house was located in another realm, I scanned for any signs that would give it away, but nothing stood out.

Nick opened the door and studied me with a sour expression. 'Why are you here? Did something happen to Cassie?'

I shook my head. 'Cassie's fine. At least for now. There are some other issues I wanted to talk to you about.'

He invited me in and we walked to the living room. I took a seat on the sofa opposite him.

Nick tilted his head towards me. 'Tell me about these issues. They must be quite serious for you to come and see me about it.'

'The house Cassie lives in is shielded.'

He shifted in his seat. 'What d'you mean, it's shielded?'

'The supernatural energy gets neutralised once people enter the house and there's no way of telling if they are supernatural anymore.'

'How did you find this out?'

'Yesterday when Leah, the girl Cassie lives with, came to pick her up, I sensed she was a witch, but her magical energy disappeared as soon as she walked into their house.'

'That's very strange.' Nick rubbed his beard. 'What did Freya say about it?'

'She said an enchantment like that could only be done by ancient magic.'

'What do you know about the other people that live in the house?'

'I thought they were human, but now I'm second

guessing myself. I'll have to ask Cassie about it. They've all lived together from a young age.'

Nick peered into my eyes. 'Make sure she stays safe. I can't break the promise I made to Lily.'

I opened my mouth to tell Nick about the shock between me and Cassie but closed it again. I didn't want to give him anything else to worry about. 'I must be off,' I said as I stood up. 'By the way, Cassie seems to have developed an ability,' I said randomly as Nick walked me to the door. 'I'm trying to teach her, but I can't read other people's minds, so I don't know how much help I can be.'

'She trusts you, then ... that's good. It'll make it easier for you. Just do what you can. The abilities will come to her when she needs them.'

'Like your abilities did?' I said sarcastically, giving him a cheeky grin.

He pretended to be offended and gave me an evil stare. 'They always seemed to work when we needed to get out of trouble.'

'Yeah, trouble that you caused by having them malfunction.'

The side of his lip went up in a small smile. 'You weren't that much better, if I remember correctly.'

We made quite a team back in those days. Through the good and bad times, we always had each other's back, and that's what made us brothers.

I gave Nick a pat on his shoulder and opened the door. 'Anyway, I better get back.'

He nodded. 'Let me know if you discover anything else. But Jax, next time just text me.'

I gave him a confused look. 'Will that work?'

Nick gave me a smile. 'You can turn into a crow and you're questioning why a phone works in another realm?'

I shrugged and stepped through the door. Turning into a crow, I flew back to the college. I needed to know more about the family Cassie lived with and why someone would put a powerful shield on her house. Was it a foe or a friend?

Turning back into my human form, I checked the time. My trip had taken longer than I wanted, though it didn't come as a shock, as time worked differently in other realms. Cassie had sent me a text asking why I wasn't in class. I thought about texting her back, but the last class of the day would finish in less than ten minutes, so there wasn't any point.

I scanned the car park to make sure it was deserted before conjuring my car. I leaned against it as I waited for Cassie. A while later, she walked out of the entrance with Leah. She fidgeted with her necklace as she looked around. When I caught her gaze, her shoulders relaxed, and a smile appeared on her face as she gave me a wave. I waved back, mirroring her smile.

Butterflies fluttered in my stomach as I pushed myself away from the car to go and greet her. Leah's energy appeared neutral again, with no indication of what she was. I gave her a nod. She said bye to Cassie and left. As soon as Cassie and I were alone, I wrapped my arms around her, taking in her scent of spring flowers. A bolt of electricity shot through me, but this time I didn't pull away. Instead I embraced the feeling, allowing the energy to ground me to Cassie. As the electricity faded, an image flicked through my mind. I was sitting beside a girl in the middle of a field. I couldn't make out her face, but I had a gut feeling it was Cassie. The mental image disappeared, and I shook my head before gazing into Cassie's eyes.

'I need to talk to you.' It came out more forcefully than I had intended.

Cassie took a step back. Her smile faded into a thin line.

'Would you mind if we go to my house?' I said in a soft tone.

She nodded and got into the car. She crossed her arms over her chest, her posture rigid. I tapped my thumb against the steering wheel as the tension between us grew. I hadn't meant to sound so harsh.

'I'm sorry about not texting you back earlier,' I said, trying to break the silence.

'It's okay.'

The quietness continued. I darted a glance at her, but nothing looked amiss. I had so many thoughts going on in my mind that I struggled to come up with anything else to say. Should I ask her about her family now? No, it would be better to wait. I wanted to see her reaction.

After I'd parked up, I went around to open the door for Cassie, but she'd already got out. She followed me to the house, and we made our way to the living room. I turned to face Cassie as we sat down on the sofa.

I ran my hand through my hair and gazed into her eyes. 'I'm sorry about worrying you today, but I had some things to take care of. I have a few questions to ask you and I need you to be honest with me.'

Cassie evaded my gaze and looked at her feet. 'I'll try my best.'

'I discovered something strange yesterday. I'm not completely sure what it means, but I need to know about your family.'

She glanced up at me with a frown. 'I thought you and Nick were old friends.'

'We are, but that's not the family I want to know about. Did you know Leah was a witch?'

Cassie's eyes widened before she looked away. 'Um, yeah. She developed her magic when she turned sixteen. I didn't know she was a witch before then, though.'

'And what about the other people you live with – Mark and Seth?'

She crossed her arms and bit her lip. 'What's with all these questions?'

I clenched my jaw and took a deep breath. Why couldn't she just answer the question? 'I need to know so I can keep you safe.'

She let out a sigh. 'You don't need to worry about them. I trust them with my life.'

'That's good to know, but I need to understand the whole picture.'

Her eyebrows drew together. 'Why? Is something wrong?'

'Maybe. I don't know. It might be nothing. I'll tell you about it when I've figured some things out.' Like if she was actually in any real danger. The thought of losing her made me feel sick. I jumped to my feet, pushing the thoughts away.

She took a deep breath and crossed her arms. 'If you must know, Mark's a werewolf and Seth is Mark's biological brother, so I assume he's probably one too, even though he's not able to shift yet.'

Why hadn't I picked up on Mark being a shifter? He sure had the traits of it. I needed to try to get a read of him tomorrow. It shouldn't be too hard, considering he had been bothering me since day one, but him being a shifter could explain that.

'What about Abigail?' I continued to pace the room. Somehow all four of them had supernatural blood. Was that a coincidence?

Cassie shook her head. 'I don't think she's supernatural, but she never seems scared. She always tells Mark and Leah not to use their abilities and that we shouldn't tell anyone about them. According to her, we're being hunted. But I always thought that was to keep us in check.'

Maybe Abigail knew something, but was she just a human or did she pretend to be one to hide who she really was? Was she the one who had put the shield up or did she know who had? I needed to keep an eye on her.

'Have you told Abigail about your abilities?'

Cassie shook her head. 'No, not yet.'

'Good. It's probably safer if she doesn't know. You never know who you can trust.' I stopped pacing the room and gave Cassie a smile. 'Would you like to stay for a bit? How about we watch a film?'

She patted the seat next to her. 'I've told you about my family, so why don't you have a seat and tell me how you met my dad? We can watch a film after.'

I nodded and sat down. 'I met your dad in school. His abilities had just started to manifest. He was bullied, and when he got angry, things got set on fire. I spent a lot of time covering it up until one day I'd had enough. If he didn't learn to control his abilities soon, he would cause damage even I wouldn't be able to fix. So I took him aside and explained what he was. He didn't believe me at first, but eventually he learned to control his abilities and we became friends.'

She looked at me with hopeful eyes. 'He struggled with his abilities too?'

I locked eyes with her. 'Everyone struggles with their abilities when they first get them.'

'Even you?'

I chuckled. 'Yes, even me.'

After a moment of silence, I slapped my hands on my legs. 'How about that film? You can pick whatever you like.'

She opened her mouth like she was going to protest but closed it again, took the remote control from me and flicked through the films. 'How about a comedy?'

I shrugged. 'Sure.' Whatever she wanted to see was fine

with me. I conjured a bowl of popcorn and two cans of Coke to show off.

Cassie laughed quietly before taking the bowl from me. She picked up some popcorn and put it into her mouth. 'That's crazy. It tastes exactly the same as normal popcorn.'

It made me happy to see how at ease she seemed around me. I drummed my fingers on my knees while watching her from the corner of my eye. Ever since I'd talked to Nick, I'd tried to tell myself that my feelings didn't matter. I needed to keep Cassie safe, and that would be easier if we were just friends.

After the film ended, I drove Cassie home. 'Do you want to meet up on Wednesday to practise your abilities some more?' I asked as I opened the car door for her.

'Sure. Will I see you in class tomorrow?' she asked as she stepped out.

I gave her a lopsided grin. 'Yeah. You won't get rid of me that easily.'

She embraced me and the shock went through us. Memories of us in a field flashed through my mind. I could feel the sun warming my face as laughter echoed in my head. This time there was no doubt in my mind it was Cassie. She looked different, with blond hair instead of brown, but her eyes were the same.

Why were my visions about Cassie? Freya had said something about two souls being woken up. I had no idea what she'd meant by that, but somehow me and Cassie were connected. Cassie had said the shocks affected her too, but to what extent? Would it be too intimate to ask her about it?

After Cassie had gone inside, I drove towards my house but stopped after a few miles. I ditched the car, turned into a crow and flew back to Cassie's house.

As I approached the house, I threw my energy out to see if I could pick up on anything. I now knew Cassie's adopted siblings were supernatural, and if it weren't for the enchantment on the house, I would have been able to sense it. However, as expected, I couldn't feel anything that seemed out of place.

I landed in a tree in Cassie's garden. I had a clear view of the driveway, but I could only see Cassie's window from an angle. Hopefully that would be enough – at least if the threats came from the outside. I didn't know whether I would be able to teleport into the house due to the enchantment, but if need be, there was always brute force.

Avoidance

I spent all evening and most of the night sitting in the tree outside Cassie's house. Nick's words about keeping her safe echoed in my mind. Not knowing the purpose of the enchantment or why it had been placed put me on edge. Maybe her biggest threat came from her foster family? I wished there was someone I could ask, but there weren't many beings that I trusted. And if anyone found out about Cassie, it might put her in more danger. It wasn't worth the risk.

When the morning arrived, I followed Leah's car from a distance as she and Cassie left for college. With so many unknowns, I didn't want to let Cassie out of my sight.

Once we reached the campus, I reluctantly left them to change back into my human form so I could attend class. I was heading towards my locker when someone grabbed my arm. An electric current coursed through me, making my arm tingle, engulfing me in a warm feeling. Something inside me tried to push itself to the surface. I whipped my head around and saw Cassie latched on to my arm.

'Sorry.' She grimaced and released me.

I tried to meet her eyes. 'Are you okay?'

She glanced at me briefly. 'Yeah. I just need to talk to you.' Her gaze darted around the crowded corridor while she fidgeted with the necklace I'd given her.

Warning lights went off in my head. Something was up. 'What's wrong? You know you can talk to me.' I scanned the area for supernatural interference but detected none.

'Umm, I don't think we should hang out in between classes anymore.'

I opened my mouth to ask why, but she continued to talk. 'Don't worry about meeting me at the end of the day tomorrow. Leah will give me a lift to your house.'

I moved my arm to touch her but thought better of it. I needed a clear head. There must be a reason for the sudden change. 'Cassie, please talk to me. Whatever's going on, I can help.'

She looked up at me with flushed cheeks. 'You can't.' She took a deep breath, scanning the hallway again. 'I need to go. Just stay away from me.'

She darted away before I could process what she'd said. I stared after her, my mind filled with unanswered questions. What was going on? Had I overstepped?

I exhaled slowly, trying to quell the pain in my heart. It didn't matter. I was only there to help Nick keep Cassie safe. No need to get more involved than that.

Throughout the day Cassie seemed to make a conscious effort to avoid me. My gaze kept wandering to her, but every time our eyes met, she looked away. My heart became heavy. At the final bell, I made my way towards her, but she bolted from the classroom.

I spent the evening sitting in the tree outside Cassie's house, reminding myself not to get too attached. To forget about how she would bite her lip when she got nervous or how she called me out for being weird but still stuck around. How she seemed to accept me for me. Was all of that just a front?

The next day was similar. Even though Cassie didn't completely ignore me, she didn't seek me out.

I was strolling towards my last class of the day, eyeing Cassie from a distance, when Mark slammed me into a locker, balling his hand into my shirt. My nostrils flared as rage consumed me. But lashing out wouldn't accomplish anything. Instead, I clenched my fists to try to control my anger.

'Stay away from Cassie. She doesn't want to see you,' Mark spat in my face.

My eyes widened. Was he right? I recalled the look on her face yesterday. The fear that slipped in and out of her eyes briefly. Was he the reason she was scared? She'd told me she trusted them with her life. Had that been a lie? The demon inside me stirred, probably causing my eyes to turn red.

Mark's breath hitched and he took a step back. A growl escaped him as he marched down the corridor.

I ground my teeth as anger continued to boil inside me. With a heavy sigh I closed my eyes and took a deep breath. I hadn't spent my entire life learning how to keep my demon at bay only for it to surface over something trivial.

My outburst was probably due to lack of sleep. I didn't need sleep to survive, but it made it harder to control the demon inside. I needed to come up with a better system before I outed myself to the whole school as a supernatural being.

I tried to catch up with Cassie at the end of the last lesson to see whether she was still coming over, but she hurried out of the classroom before I had a chance. While I was flying home, I got my answer when I spotted Leah's car heading towards my house. I waited on the porch as she pulled into the driveway.

Cassie got out of the car. My pulse started racing. She smiled and approached me with open arms. Guilt stirred inside me when I pretended not to see it. This hot and cold behaviour confused me. 'What's going on with Mark?' I asked coldly.

She crossed her arms. 'I don't want to talk about it. Let's just go inside and train.' She walked past me into the house.

I glanced over at Leah in the car. She rolled her eyes and shrugged before turning the engine on and driving away.

My chest felt tight as I took a seat opposite Cassie in the

living room. Keeping this professional was going to be murder, but I needed to respect Cassie's wishes. 'Remember what we practised. Imagine a box inside yourself where you contain all your magic. Picture it being closed so no magic can escape.'

Cassie nodded and closed her eyes, slowing her breathing. After a while she moved to undo her necklace, but after she'd unclipped it, she fastened it again with a sigh. 'I still hear mumbles, though not as strongly as before.'

I rubbed the back of my neck. 'Try to imagine putting a lock on the box.'

Cassie closed her eyes again. After an hour, she let out a frustrated sigh and slammed her hands onto the floor next to her. 'It's not working. Every time I take the necklace off, the noises start up again.'

I glanced at her and gave an encouraging smile. 'You need to be patient. You will learn how to do it. It just takes practice.'

'When? I've been at it for ages and I haven't even learned to turn it off. How will I ever be able to actually use it?'

'It takes time. Learning is a process. You don't expect to be able to swim as soon as you get into the water.'

Cassie glared at me, clearly not happy with my answer. 'How long did it take for my dad to learn?'

I thought back to when I'd first met Nick. 'A few months to learn to control his fire. After that, his other abilities developed quicker.'

She pursed her lips and let out a loud breath.

'How about we call it a day and continue another time?' I asked as I got up from the floor.

Cassie nodded and reached for her phone. 'Let me give it one more try before Leah gets here.'

She closed her eyes and took a deep breath. After a few minutes she slowly removed her necklace. A whole minute passed before she put it on again.

I caught her gaze and smiled. 'At least you made some progress.'

She stared at me blankly for a moment before getting up from the floor.

I ran my hand through my hair, mustering up the nerve to ask her why she'd been avoiding me. 'So, about college. Why—'

Cassie cut me off. 'No.' She picked up her phone and started playing with it. She was obviously not in a talkative mood. We didn't say anything else until Leah turned up to collect her. I walked her out to the car, the tension between us still present.

'I really wish you'd tell me what's going on,' I said as we reached the car. She hesitated and turned around, biting her lip and meeting my gaze. Her mouth opened, but she closed it again and got into the car.

'Bye, Jax,' she said and shut the door.

The Bird And The Kiss

After Leah's car disappeared in the distance, I glanced at the door with a sigh. I should watch Cassie, but after the day I'd had, I needed some time to myself. Guilt tugged at my conscience. Just a short nap. I took a deep breath and went inside. I wouldn't be long – just a few hours and then I'd get back to watching her.

When I woke up, the sun was still out. I stretched my muscles and my gaze landed on the light that was shining through the window. I didn't get sunlight in my room in the evening. I jumped out of bed and grabbed the phone to check the time. It was morning, and I'd already missed my first class.

After I got out of the shower, I decided to skip the rest of my classes. I wasn't sure my patience could handle running into Mark. Besides, it wasn't like I needed the grades. I picked up my phone to let Cassie know but put it down again. Why should I care if she didn't?

I flew over to the college and spent the day in various windows watching Cassie from afar before following her home and making myself comfortable in the tree.

Seeing Cassie and Leah laughing and smiling before getting into the car the next morning made my heart heavy. Unwilling to put myself through another day of Cassie avoiding me, I decided to continue to watch her from afar. The day passed uneventfully, and I was back in the tree outside her house before I knew it.

An urge to check my phone emerged. I contemplated whether to ignore it. The only person who had my number was Cassie, but we hadn't spoken for two days. Eventually I left the tree in search of a deserted area where I could transform back into my human form and check. Heat radiated through my body as Cassie's name appeared on the screen. Maybe she didn't hate me after all? I read her text and a chuckle escaped me. She thought she was being followed by an evil black bird. Maybe I hadn't been as inconspicuous as I'd thought?

I texted Cassie back, asking her to meet me at the end of the road. I hoped revealing I was the 'evil black bird' would put her at ease. Hopefully. Either way, she deserved to know.

I turned into a crow and followed Cassie as she left the house. When she had walked a good distance away from the house, I scanned the area to make sure no one was around before landing on the ground in front of her. She jerked to a stop, gasped and took a step back. I transformed back into my human form right before her eyes. While I caught my breath, she slapped my shoulder. The shock vibrated inside me, and for a moment everything felt right.

'Why didn't you tell me you were a shapeshifter?'

I shook my head to get back to reality before tilting it and glancing at her with an ironic smile. Of course she would assume I was a shifter. 'Technically I'm not a shifter.'

She threw her hands up in the air. 'You're unbelievable. You had me thinking I was being stalked by something evil for the last couple of days.' Her scowl knocked me off balance. I pried my eyes from her and rubbed the back of my neck. How could she be angry with me? I'd done nothing wrong. I inhaled slowly.

'I'm sorry I scared you, but you brought it on yourself.'

Her nostrils flared. 'What do you mean by that? How is it my fault?'

I glanced at her quickly before looking away. I didn't want her to see the hurt in my eyes. 'I promised Nick I'd keep you safe, but you made it crystal clear you didn't want to be friends, so I thought I'd give you space and make sure you were okay from afar.'

Her breath hitched. 'That's not what I want.'

I forcefully kicked a stone on the ground and stared at her. 'Then what do you want? Because minus coming to my house the other day to practise, you've been avoiding me.' My voice came out deeper than usual. I backed away, taking a few deep breaths to calm myself. Going demon on Cassie would not help.

'It's complicated,' Cassie said, staring at the ground.

My hands balled into fists inside my pockets. When she looked up, a tear slid down her cheek. My chest tightened and all the anger and frustration disappeared. I hadn't wanted to upset her. I reached out to touch her, but she turned around. 'I need to get home before they wonder where I am.'

'Please tell me what's going on.'

She hesitated. 'Meet me at your house in an hour and we can talk.'

I nodded. 'I'll be there.'

She mustered up a smile and walked back towards her house. I stared after her for a while before turning into a crow. I caught up with her and landed in the tree outside. She looked up at me before going in.

An hour later, Cassie and Leah left the house. I followed the car from above as they made their way to my house. As they approached, I teleported to the porch and transformed into my human form. The second Leah's car pulled up in the driveway, I stepped off the porch, eager to finally get some answers.

I offered Cassie my hand to help her out of the car. The familiar shock went through me, but this time, instead of getting a feeling or a quick glimpse of some potential memory, a whole scene played in my head. I couldn't see the girl, but I knew it was Cassie. We were lying down next to each other in a field, laughing and making up creatures and stories from the clouds passing by.

I blinked my vision clear and smiled at Cassie. Had she experienced something similar? Leah cleared her throat. I let go of Cassie and gave Leah a nod. She said bye to Cassie and me before driving away.

I turned back to Cassie. 'Care to explain what all of this is about?'

She scanned the area and hugged herself. 'Let's go inside first. It's a bit chilly.'

She was right about the chill in the air. Summer seemed to be truly over. I conjured my jacket and placed it over her shoulders even though we weren't far from the door.

When we got inside, Cassie took a seat on the sofa and removed the jacket. I positioned myself so I was facing her. I wanted to give her time and not rush her, so I patiently sat there in silence, watching her play with the zipper on the jacket in her lap.

'Abigail wants you around for dinner and Mark doesn't like you,' she said swiftly, staring at her lap.

It took some time to realise what she had said, but even when I did, I didn't understand why it was important. Was that really why she'd been avoiding me? Human emotions could be so complex. I stayed quiet, not sure how to respond, hoping she would elaborate.

Cassie avoided my gaze and concentrated on the jacket in her lap. 'Mark knows you're not human. He told me if I didn't stop seeing you, he'd tell Abigail or take things into his own hands to make sure I couldn't.'

I bent down in front of her. 'Cassie?'

Tears were streaming down her face as she continued talking. Her words came out rapidly. 'I'm sorry. I should have told you, but it was just easier if Mark didn't see us together while I thought things through. I don't want you to think I'm crazy, and we've only just met, but I like you and I don't want you to ...'

She liked me too. All the feelings towards her that I'd tried to ignore flooded back to me. Before I knew what I was doing, I leaned in and let my lips brush hers.

Her whole body relaxed and went still. The shock that followed made my body tingle. An image pushed through the surface of my mind. The field was back, but this time there was a red blanket on the ground surrounded by candles in the grass. I felt nervous, but in a happy way, kneeling on one knee looking up at Cassie. Only the person I knew as Cassie was called Katie. The realisation had me pulling away.

I shook my head clear of the image. 'I'm sorry. I don't know what came over me.'

Cassie stared blankly into the distance. I waved my hand in front of her face, but she didn't react. My heart got caught in my chest. What had happened to her? I shook her lightly, hoping it would bring her back, without any success. I reached for her hand. 'Cassie, are you okay?'

My throat tightened with fear and tears burned my eyes. 'Please tell me you're okay,' I croaked. Still no response. I shot to my feet and started pacing. I had no clue what had happened, but I'd obviously caused it. She was fine before I kissed her. I rubbed my forehead. What had I done? It was like she wasn't in her body anymore. My vision blurred and I ran my hand through my hair as I desperately tried to steady myself. I slumped to the floor and hid my face in my hands as the walls closed in. *How do I fix this? Do I ask Nick?* I shook my head. He would be furious. *Freya?*

Cassie's voice brought me back to reality. 'You look like you lost someone.'

Relief flooded through me. I crawled over to her and grabbed her hand to make sure it was real. 'I thought I had. You went completely still and non-responsive. I thought I'd broken you.' I couldn't bring myself to take my eyes off her. I was still in shock and worried she would phase out on me again.

A smile appeared on Cassie's lips. 'I'm fine. Stop looking at me like that.'

I reluctantly released my grip and pushed myself to my feet, trying to calm my erratic heart. It was a good thing I couldn't die of a heart attack. I laughed at myself. *Cassie must think I'm crazy.* To calm myself down and stop myself staring at her like she was going to disappear, I conjured two Cokes and handed one to her. I lifted the other to my lips with an unsteady hand. Sugar was supposed to help for shock, so it was definitely warranted for me, and maybe it would be good for Cassie too.

Downing the Coke, I contemplated how to proceed. I had no idea what had happened or whether it would happen again. I peeked over at Cassie. 'I think maybe it's better if I keep my distance. I'd rather stay away from you knowing you're safe than put you in danger.'

Cassie got up from the sofa and approached me. She took my hands in hers and gazed into my eyes. 'I don't want you to leave. I feel safe with you. This connection we have. I can't explain it. I keep seeing visions of us together and I want to figure out why.'

My heart thumped in my chest. She could feel the connection too. I pulled her close, a wide smile plastered on my face. 'I thought it was just me.'

She placed her head on my shoulder before stepping out of my embrace. She looked up at me with narrow eyes. 'The shock is gone.'

The Party

I stared at Cassie. Had I felt the shock when we hugged? I had been so blissfully distracted by the knowledge that she wanted me around that I hadn't paid any attention to anything else.

I reached for her hand to check, and she was right. No shock, no foreign feelings or images. I'd become so used to it happening, it now felt strange to touch her without it.

'Yeah, I guess you're right,' I said. 'I wonder why?'

Cassie shrugged. She didn't seem too concerned by the lack of the shock. I struggled to brush it off. I wanted to know why it had stopped. I couldn't come up with a reasonable explanation, but then again, I didn't know why we had experienced the shock in the first place. Was it worth seeing Freya? She might have some insight. I glanced over at Cassie.

There was no way I would leave her now. Freya would have to wait.

I cleared my throat. 'How do you want to do this? Because I don't think I can handle having you avoiding me anymore.'

Cassie bit her lip. 'I don't know. I want to spend time with you, but I'm scared of what Mark might do.'

I kissed her forehead. 'We'll figure it out. You know I don't mind meeting your family.' I grimaced, regretting the words immediately. 'What I mean is, if I met your family, they might leave you alone. I could even have a chat with Mark.'

Cassie chewed her lip thoughtfully for a while before grinning at me. 'Are you asking me out?'

My heart sped up and I wiped my hands on my trousers, my mind racing. I wasn't sure what to reply. Of course I wanted her as my girlfriend. I hadn't felt anything close to what I was feeling for Cassie about anyone else. But did she want the same thing? 'Only if you want me to.'

Cassie remained quiet for a while before gazing into my eyes. 'I do, but maybe we should take it slow. At least until me and Leah have spoken to Mark.'

A wide smile appeared on my face. 'Take as much time as you need.' I truly meant it. Just being around Cassie and spending time with her was more than enough for me.

Her phone rang. She picked it up and stepped into the kitchen. A moment later she joined me again. 'That was Leah. She needs me. She's at a party.'

I nodded. 'Let me drive you.'

Cassie directed me to a fellow student's house. Music filled the air and cars blocked every available spot. I stopped in the middle of the road and walked around to open the door for Cassie. After she'd got out, I made my way back to the driving seat. She had said she wanted to take things slow, and this was an official party and many of her friends were here. I was reaching for the door handle when Cassie spoke up. 'Aren't you coming?'

I turned towards her. 'I didn't know if you wanted me to.'

'Of course I do.' She tilted her head and looked at the car. 'Maybe we should move the car. You're blocking the road.'

I gave her a lopsided grin. 'There was nowhere to park. Give me a second.' I scanned the area before making the car disappear. 'Sorted.'

Cassie let out a slow breath, her eyes fixed on where the car had been moments before. She shook her head and grabbed my hand. 'Come on. Let's go find Leah.'

The house was full of people standing around talking, dancing and shouting at each other. A massive pink 'Happy 18th Birthday' banner hung across the living room wall. Cassie made her way swiftly through the crowd, greeting people without stopping to chat. I followed closely behind. After we'd walked around for a while, she checked her phone and headed to the back garden.

I took a deep breath of air as we got outside. I much preferred the cool breeze and the muted music. The garden consisted of a large grass area with some trees and bushes scattered around. We walked away from the crowd and through an arch in between a hedge of tall bushes. On the other side was a wooden bench. Leah sat there alone.

'Not a good party?' I asked, confused about why she was sitting outside all by herself.

She wiped her face and turned around. Her eyes seemed red, almost like she had been crying. When she saw us, relief filled her face and she mustered up a smile. 'Cassie. You're here,' she said cheerfully as she got up to give Cassie a hug. She glanced over at me. 'Hi, Jax. I see you guys sorted things out.'

I nodded. 'Yeah, we're on the same page now.'

Cassie gave Leah a look. They had obviously been talking about me earlier, but then again, Leah drove Cassie to my house, so I guess it would have been strange if they hadn't. It made me wonder how much Cassie had told her. Did Leah know Cassie had abilities? Did she know I wasn't human? I mentally shook my head. I should be enjoying my time with Cassie.

'Do you want to leave?' Cassie asked Leah.

She shook her head. 'No. You're here now.' She grabbed our hands and pulled us back inside to the party.

It felt strange being at a human party. When I was at school with Nick, I had been invited to several, but they'd never interested me. Being cramped inside a house with a lot of people made me feel uncomfortable and out of place. I much preferred being outside in nature on my own, but

Cassie wanted me here, so I gladly endured it for her.

We walked around socialising with different people who seemed to know both Leah and Cassie. I struggled to understand the joy of superficial small talk.

My heart stopped as Cassie and Leah let out shrieks while jumping up and down together. 'Beer pong!'

My muscles relaxed, knowing Cassie wasn't in any danger. She pulled me over to a table. 'Have you played beer pong before?'

I shook my head and she explained the rules. 'You play in two teams. If the ball lands in the cup, the opposite team has to drink.'

Leah had set up the table while Cassie was speaking. 'Let's do the first round with soft drinks. Leah's driving, so that way she can join in too.'

Leah and Cassie teamed up against me. Throwing a ball into a cup was as easy as I had imagined it to be. I purposely missed a few so Leah and Cassie could catch up.

'Wow. You're really good at this,' Cassie said with a smile as she downed another cup of soda.

I gave her a wink. 'Maybe you should be on my team next time.'

A crowd gathered around us as we played. When we'd finished, they challenged us to a game. The smell of beer hit my nose as they set it up and I understood why it was called beer pong. The three of us took turns throwing the ball. Every time Leah had to drink, she handed the cup to me. I guess it was a good thing I couldn't get drunk.

After we'd been playing for a while, a guy walked up to us. The opposite team hit the ball into the cup and the guy lifted it and gave it to Leah.

Her smile faded. 'Thank you, but I'm driving.'

He shook his head and got in her face. 'Leah. Always Miss Goody Two Shoes. You shouldn't be playing if you aren't going to follow the rules.'

Leah took a step back. 'Leave me alone, Luke. You're drunk and we both know this isn't about the game.'

The guy she'd called Luke grabbed her arm. A feeling of protectiveness coursed through me and I stepped between them. 'Is there a problem?'

Luke looked me over with a huff. 'Wow. Moved on already? Does this guy even know what a cocktease you are?'

A tic started in my eye, and I clenched my fists. Leah grabbed my hand and pulled me away. 'Thanks, Jax, but he's not worth it. Let's just leave.'

I opened my mouth to disagree.

'Don't,' Cassie whispered as she hooked her arm in mine. A calm feeling entered my body and made my muscles relax, and I allowed her and Leah to usher me away with their arms linked around mine.

When we reached Leah's car, she let go of my arm. 'Thanks, Jax. I'll see you around.' She got into the car, leaving me and Cassie alone.

I pulled Cassie closer to me and wrapped my arms around her before pressing my lips to her forehead. Without the shock accompanying the touch, it didn't feel like enough. I wanted to be closer.

'Cassie?'

She gazed into my eyes. 'Yeah?'

My heart got stuck in my throat. On second thoughts, it would have to be enough. 'Can I see you tomorrow?'

'Yeah. I'll text you,' she said as she got into the car.

'I'll see you at home in a bit.' I put my hand over my mouth. Why did I say these stupid things?

She shook her head, a goofy grin appearing on her face. 'Goodnight, Jax.'

I watched as the car drove away before I walked a bit further away from the party and turned into a crow to fly after them.

Voices In My Head

I landed in the tree and made myself comfortable. Leah and Cassie got out of the car and Cassie looked up at me and smiled. I jumped around on the branch in contentment.

They walked inside, leaving me with my thoughts. The sound of a window opening brought me back to reality. Cassie leaned out of the window and faced me. 'Goodnight, Jax. I'll see you in the morning.'

Her thoughtfulness warmed my heart. I cawed back, unable to physically talk to her in my crow form. Her laughter echoed through the open window until she closed it and turned the light off.

I was studying the stars in the sky, deep in thought, when I almost fell off the branch as Cassie's voice echoed inside my head. *I'm scared.*

The heat drained from me. I flew over to the window. The street light reflected off it, making it impossible to see anything inside. I tapped my beak against the glass. I needed to make sure she was okay.

I tried talking to her through my mind, but I didn't hear her voice in my head again, so I had no way of knowing if she hadn't heard me or if she was missing. I continued to tap my beak against the window. If she didn't answer me soon, I'd fly straight into the glass and break it. It was easy to fix a broken window, but that would be the least of my problems if something had happened to Cassie.

After what felt like hours, Cassie opened the window. She gave me a sleepy smile. 'What's wrong?'

I scanned her closely. *Are you okay?* I asked to her mind. She didn't give any indication she had heard me. Maybe I'd imagined her voice in my head?

I let out a caw. Cassie studied me for a while. 'I'm fine. Just a bad dream.'

I longed to take human form and hold her in my arms until she fell asleep again, but I was scared my transformation would alarm whoever had placed the enchantment on the house. Instead, I stayed on the internal windowsill in my crow form.

Cassie crawled back into bed. Her breathing became slower, lulling me to sleep. I allowed myself to drift off. Being near her made me relaxed, knowing I would easily wake up if anything were to happen.

The warm rays of early sunlight woke me up, and I spent

the next few hours observing Cassie in her sleep. She looked so peaceful, her breathing slow and steady. Her brown hair was messy and covered part of her face, but she seemed blissfully unaware. It pleased me that she had managed to go back to sleep, and she wasn't awake and aware of me staring at her. It'd freaked me out hearing her voice in my head the previous night. I hadn't expected it. But to be honest, it was a common ability amongst demons and higher beings. Even the shifters had the ability to communicate with their pack through their minds.

Maybe Nick was right and her abilities would materialise when she needed them. But why now? Did the bad dream have something to do with it?

After a few hours, Cassie woke up. She got out of bed and her eyes landed on me. I forgot to breathe, as I wasn't sure how she would react to me being inside her room.

She gave me a smile. 'Good morning, Jax.'

I flew up to her shoulder and placed my head by her cheek. It made her laugh.

'I'm fine, really. You don't need to worry.' She brought her hand to her shoulder, and I jumped onto it. She kissed the top of my head and walked towards the window.

'Go home. I'll see you in a few hours.'

I cawed, and she gave me a push out of the window.

The Park

I got home and went for a shower. Turning the water off, I got out and stepped up to the mirror, wiping the steam away. Based on how I felt, I should look severely sleep deprived, but my hazel eyes stared back at me brightly. I smiled. Sometimes being an immortal had its benefits. Cassie texted me as I got dressed, asking me to meet her by the large fountain in town.

The fountain was located at the corner of the park, with the high street a road away. Transforming or teleporting into a crowded area wasn't ideal, though between people's logical thinking and my ability to influence people to believe they hadn't seen anything, I could get away with it. Since I wasn't constrained by traffic, and knowing Cassie would more than likely be late, I took my time drifting through the sky and landed in a sheltered area in the park before making my way over. Taking a seat on one of the benches surrounding the fountain, I recalled the previous night's events as I waited for Cassie to arrive.

Cassie's laugh made me look up. She was approaching with a guy I'd never seen before. I sent my energies out and my body jerked to life. The person she was talking to was a shifter. I stood up and marched over to them. I glanced at Cassie's neck; she still wore the necklace. Between that and the enchantment on the house, no one should be able to tell she wasn't human.

'Hi,' I said as I hugged her, glaring at the guy next to her. He stared back at me.

Cassie stepped out of the embrace and turned her attention to the shifter. 'It's just around the corner. You can't miss it.'

The shifter smiled at her. 'Thanks. I'll see you around.'

As soon as he'd walked away, I grabbed Cassie's arm and ushered her in the opposite direction. Several people turned their heads, but I ignored them.

Cassie dug her heels into the ground. 'Jax, stop. What are you doing?'

'Who was that? You can't just talk to strangers. You never know what they may be after.'

She sighed. 'You sound just like Abigail.'

'Maybe Abigail has the right idea.'

Cassie took a step back, arms folded.

I closed the distance. 'I'm sorry. I didn't mean for it to sound so harsh. I'm trying to keep you safe.'

'Maybe you can do it in a nicer way. And for your information, that was Mark's friend.'

I let out a deep breath. 'I'm sorry. The thought of anything happening to you scares me, and I overreacted. Can you forgive me?'

She stared at me, a smile tugging at her lips. 'If you stop acting like a jealous boyfriend.'

I wrapped my arms around her and kissed her head. 'I'll try.'

She hooked her arm in mine. 'How about we go to the park? It's likely to be less crowded.'

I nodded and followed her. The pavement gave way to a gritted path surrounded by grass and trees. We strolled along it in silence until Cassie pulled me between some bushes at the side.

She stopped underneath a large oak that overlooked a river. 'I come here to draw sometimes or to clear my head. Because it's away from the main path, there's usually less people around.'

I glanced around and conjured a blanket for us to sit on. Even though no one else was about, I still closed my eyes to place a sound barrier around us. The shifter had put me on edge, so I added a protective layer just in case. I didn't want to take any chances.

When I opened my eyes, Cassie was studying me with a tilted head. 'What are you doing?'

'I'm making sure no one can hear us talk.'

Cassie gave me a bright smile. 'Like you did in the coffee

shop?'

I nodded. 'Yeah, exactly like that.'

'How do you know it's working?'

I leaned back. 'Remember how I asked you to picture the energy inside yourself?' Cassie nodded. 'It's similar to that. You build up the energy from the inside and visualise what you want it to do, then you push it out. I know it's working because I can feel the energy around us.'

She leaned towards me with raised eyebrows, a smile playing on her lips. 'Would I be able to feel it?'

I shrugged. 'I don't know. Why don't you give it a try?'

She nodded and closed her eyes. She pressed her lips into a grimace. 'I can't feel anything.'

I removed some hair from her face. 'Don't worry. This is all still very new to you.' I met her gaze. 'That brings me back to last night. What happened?'

She rested her head on my shoulder. 'I don't know. I had a nightmare.' Her attention shifted to her hands as she placed them in mine and intertwined our fingers. I hadn't wanted to remind her about her nightmares, but I needed to know what had happened and how she'd managed to talk to me.

'Did you know you were talking to me?' I asked carefully, observing her face.

She looked up at me with a shy smile. 'I thought it was strange you came to the window, but I thought maybe it was a coincidence.'

'I heard you loud and clear. I tried talking back to you.'

Cassie's eyes widened. 'So it's a normal thing to do?'

'In a way, yes. Well, for beings like us it is; however, there needs to be a connection. I wouldn't be able to talk to anyone who didn't have the ability of telepathy, and it won't work over long distances.'

She frowned. 'How come I didn't hear you?'

I rubbed my forehead. 'I thought maybe you had.'

Cassie shook her head. 'I could tell you were worried about me, but I didn't hear your voice in my head.'

'Maybe it's something you need to practise, like your mind ability?'

Cassie's face lit up. Her voice filled with excitement. 'Speaking of which, I want to show you something.'

I was intrigued, but when she removed the necklace, my breath caught in my throat. It was a good thing I'd put up a protective barrier. I studied her closely, waiting for her to pass out or show any sign of discomfort, but it didn't happen. I couldn't get over how relaxed she seemed without the protection of the necklace to redirect her ability. She had obviously been practising without me. Would she be able to read people's minds now as well? Could she read mine?

Just to be on the safe side, I mentally blocked my thoughts from her. 'I'm impressed.' I gave her a smile. 'You got any further with reading people's minds?'

She stared at her hands while chewing on her lip. 'I haven't managed to hear anything yet, but I only tried at home.'

'There's an enchantment on your house which may affect your ability. I'm really proud of you, though, for learning to control it.' I mashed my lips together in a grimace. I hadn't meant to bring up the enchantment. I watched Cassie closely for any reaction, but she seemed oblivious to what I had just said about the house. Had she not picked up on it or did she know about the spell on the house already? I felt doubt creeping in, but surely she would have told me about it the other day if she'd known?

I took her hand in mine. 'Maybe you can try to read some people's minds while we're here. But put the necklace back on. It'll help to focus your ability.' It would also help hide the energy radiating out of her every time she used it.

Cassie looked at me for a while, her eyes distant. I was almost certain she was trying to read my mind. I relaxed, knowing I had blocked my thoughts. No need for her to read what was on my mind; it would only worry her.

'How about you try to send me another telepathic message?' I said with a smile.

I took her hands again, hoping our physical connection would help. I cleared my head and waited, but unfortunately, I couldn't hear anything. I attempted to talk to her through my mind, but she didn't seem to pick up on anything. Eventually she opened her eyes and pulled her hands from mine with a big sigh. 'It's not working.'

'How about some lunch?' I asked, getting up from the blanket.

Cassie agreed, and we walked into town to find a place to eat.

We took a seat on the outdoor terrace of one of the

restaurants. With it being too late for lunch and too early for dinner, the restaurant was fairly empty, with only a few tables occupied.

A waitress in her early twenties came over almost as soon as we sat down. She gave us a warm smile. 'Are you ready to order?'

'I'll have a bacon burger and a Coke,' I told her.

'That's a great choice. We do have the best burgers in town.' She scribbled on a piece of paper and glanced at Cassie.

'I'll have the same,' Cassie said with a smile.

The waitress turned back to me. 'Anything else?'

I shook my head. 'We're good, thanks.'

Her gaze lingered on us as she walked away. I sent my energy out, but she was just human.

There was a moment of silence, and I took the opportunity to come up with an idea for Cassie to use her abilities. I turned to her with an encouraging smile. 'When the waitress comes out with our food, try to read her mind.' It was usually easier for me to influence the mind of a human, so maybe Cassie would have an easier time picking up the thoughts of humans too.

Cassie closed her eyes as the waitress walked towards our table with two plates, which she put down in front of us. The food smelled delicious. Cassie still had her eyes closed, and even though I was dying to know whether she had managed, I didn't want to rush her. I took a bite of my burger to keep myself occupied.

Cassie opened her eyes and caught my gaze. She let out a

squeal. 'I think I may have done it.'

I swallowed the food in my mouth and gave her a smile. 'That's great. What was she thinking?'

'She thought you were hot and that I'm a lucky girl,' she said with a wink before she picked up her burger and started eating.

A mischievous smile appeared on my face. 'You sure that isn't your thoughts?'

Cassie slapped my arm jokingly. 'Of course not. My thoughts would have been much dirtier.' She gave me a cheeky grin and stole one of my chips.

My heart stopped, and I almost choked on my burger. I discreetly let out a cough. She was joking, but a picture of what it would be like to make love to Cassie entered my mind and I struggled to keep eye contact with her. Instead, I concentrated on the people walking past. I didn't want to do something stupid, like sending her into another coma by kissing her again.

I tilted my head towards the passers-by. 'How about you try reading someone else's mind?' I hoped her confidence would have grown from being able to read the waitress's mind.

Cassie nodded without closing her eyes and pointed at the people walking past. 'That guy is thinking about work. The girl over there is checking out some guy. The elderly woman that just passed us is missing her husband.'

My mouth fell open as I stared at her in awe. I could hardly tell she was concentrating. Was she pulling my leg?

'How do I know you aren't making this up?'

Cassie looked at me with raised eyebrows. 'You think I'm lying?'

She wouldn't have led me on about her ability, but maybe she was trying too hard and everything was just in her head. How could I audit her mind reading ability?

'Maybe I can plant some thoughts into some people's minds that are walking past, and you can tell me what thought I planted?'

Cassie surprised me by getting most of the thoughts correct. She struggled with one person, even though she read his mind. It wasn't the thought I had planted, but the person may just have been so strong-minded that my suggestion hadn't taken hold. It happened sometimes.

When we'd finished eating, Cassie looked at her phone and asked if I'd mind if Leah met up with us. I didn't mind at all.

'How much have you told Leah?'

Considering how close they were, I was curious to know how much Cassie had told Leah about everything that had been going on. Did she know about Cassie and her abilities? Did she know I wasn't human?

Cassie pursed her lips. 'I told her about us, but I left out all the supernatural things.'

I rubbed my forehead. 'Do you trust her?'

As soon as I asked, Cassie looked offended. 'Of course I do.'

'Then why haven't you told her?'

'I don't know,' she answered thoughtfully, stirring the ice in her glass. 'It's just … it's a lot to take in. What if it changes things between us?'

'Why would it?' Cassie shrugged but remained thoughtful.

After I'd paid for the food, we walked back to the park where we had decided to meet Leah. We didn't have to wait long before she turned up. She gave Cassie a hug and said hi to me. I could sense her magic. Without even thinking about it, I opened my big mouth. 'You've been practising magic again?'

Leah cocked her head at me with a raised eyebrow. She crossed her arms and turned to Cassie. 'You told him?'

Cassie's posture slumped and she gave me an evil look.

I took a deep breath. 'Actually, I felt it the other day, when you picked Cassie up at my house.'

Leah frowned. 'How could you sense it?'

Crap. Why did I say anything? I couldn't answer honestly without revealing I wasn't human. I regretted even mentioning it in the first place, but this could be an opportunity to find out whether Leah knew anything about the spell on the house. Besides, Cassie had just said she trusted Leah, so maybe I could get away with a half truth.

I shrugged. 'I grew up around magic.' Leah's eyes got big.

Cassie rolled her eyes. 'I've been hanging out with Jax to see if I have any magic abilities.'

Leah's smile disappeared and she looked at the ground. 'You could have asked me.'

Cassie touched Leah's shoulder. 'I didn't want to get your hopes up. I know how disappointed you were when nothing happened to me when I turned sixteen.'

Leah shook her head. 'It's fine. I understand.'

After a moment of silence, Leah glanced at me with a sigh. 'Yes, I've been practising, but it hasn't been going great. It's been two years and I can only manage basic stuff. I don't even know what I should be able to do. I'm really struggling, and it doesn't help that Abigail won't let us practise in the house and I don't know anyone else that could help me.'

I gave her a sad smile. 'Unfortunately I don't have the same type of magic. Do you know why Abigail is so anti-magic?'

Cassie discreetly kicked my leg, but I ignored it.

Leah sneered. 'According to her, everyone is out to get us. And the less we use our abilities, the quicker we can go back to being "normal" people. She won't even let Mark shift.'

It was strange. From what I knew about shifters, they needed to shift to stay healthy. Was it possible that the enchantment on the house was strong enough to override that need? And why would Abigail think they would go back to being normal? Something didn't feel right. I needed to know if the enchantment was a threat – if there was a possibility that it would strip them of their supernatural abilities like Abigail thought.

I ran my hand through my hair. 'Cassie, I'm really sorry, but I need to go.'

She pinched her lips together. 'Do you really need to

leave right now? Leah just got here.'

I gave her a pained expression. 'I'm sorry. I'll make it up to you.'

Cassie stared at me with raised eyebrows. 'You better.'

Stop Talking In Riddles

Walking away from Cassie and Leah left knots in my stomach. Cassie saw Leah as a sister and wanted us to get along. This would have been a perfect opportunity to get to know her better, but everything that was going on weighed heavily on my shoulders. Something didn't feel right about the enchantment.

While I made my way over to Freya's house, I contemplated my day with Cassie. Her control over her ability impressed me, and she was already showing signs of telepathy. I remembered how clearly I heard her voice in my head last night. It was strange she hadn't heard me when I'd tried to answer but somehow picked up on my emotions. Maybe she just needed practice; after all, her abilities wouldn't develop properly until she was eighteen years old, so the fact that she had already exhibited two abilities was quite amazing.

Freya's house came into view and I descended, transforming into my human form when Freya came out of the front door. She carried a tray with a teapot and two cups over to the two chairs in the corner of her veranda and put the tray down on the table between them. She gestured for me to come and join her.

After I'd taken a seat, she poured the tea into the cups and handed me one. 'I take it you found out some more information you want to discuss?' She looked at me and again I was amazed how she always seemed to know what was going on.

I nodded. 'Yeah. The teenagers that live in the house are all supernatural – a witch, two shapeshifters and a demon.'

It felt a bit wrong calling Cassie a demon, as she was really a hybrid between light and dark, but I didn't want to give away the fact that she was Nick's daughter, even though Freya in all likelihood already knew.

She gave me a smile. 'That's an interesting mix. Do they get on well?'

I shrugged. 'I guess so.'

'What about the caretaker? Is she a supernatural being too?'

I shook my head. 'They seem to think Abigail's completely human, but she knows about the supernatural and apparently she tries to stop them from using their abilities. She told them the less they use their abilities, the quicker they can become normal. She even told the shifters not to shift.'

'I see,' Freya said tentatively before she went quiet, a distant look on her face.

Was Abigail tied to the enchantment?

'This is much bigger than the caretaker. The house will speak, but only to those who are observant. Listen to your heart. Trust is a delicate thing, but no one can help if they do not know what is going on.'

I let out a sigh. Typical Freya, never a straight answer.

I glanced at her. I often forgot how tiny she was, given her powerful presence. By the time I was twelve years old, I had already grown taller than her, but only a fool would underestimate her. 'What do you think I should do?' I pleaded, hoping she would actually tell me.

Freya laughed. 'Silly boy, you know I cannot tell you that. You need to make your own decisions.'

She got out of the chair and returned the tray to the house before re-emerging – a clear sign she'd finished talking and wouldn't tell me anything else regarding the matter. I got up from the chair, ready to say goodbye when she placed an arm around my waist and tilted her head to meet my gaze. 'Tell me, does the spark still happen?'

The spark? For a moment I had no idea what she was talking about. Then I realised she was referring to the shock me and Cassie shared every time we touched.

I shook my head. 'Not since I kissed her, but she went into shock after that, so I'm too afraid to do it again.'

Her eyes reflected an understanding of my worries. 'Love is never evil, but fear will hide the truth.'

I sighed. Why did she have to say things that didn't make any sense?

I gave her a kiss on the cheek and left. I hoped Cassie was safe. It felt like we had a special connection and if something were to happen to her, I would somehow sense it, but maybe it was just wishful thinking.

When I got back to Cassie's house, it was past midnight. I flew over to her window to make sure she was safe and sound. The window was open. I wasn't sure if she had opened it for me, but there was a red blanket underneath. I hopped inside and looked over to the bed. My body relaxed and my heart slowed. Cassie's deep breathing reassured me that she was safe and peacefully asleep.

When I woke up the next morning, Cassie was no longer in her bed. How had I not woken up? I was usually a light sleeper.

My heart sped up, and I flew over to the bed to investigate. Had someone taken her while I was asleep? Her bed was still warm. Would it be safe to send my energies out inside the house? Before I got carried away, her voice sounded from downstairs. I let out a breath of relief. Why hadn't she woken me up? Was she mad at me for leaving?

I paced back and forth for what seemed like forever until Cassie finally entered the room.

'You're still here?' she said with annoyance.

I tilted my head. Why had she left the window open if

she didn't want me around?

She placed her hand on her hip. 'You really threw me under the bus yesterday and then you just disappeared. I have no idea where you go, and you don't tell me what's going on. It's not right. I deserve to know. I know you worry about me, but I worry about you too.' She fidgeted with her necklace, her lips pursed. 'I think you should go. Don't worry about me. I'll be safe with Mark and Leah.'

I looked up at her, surprised at her outburst. I hadn't told her about any of it because I didn't want to worry her, but I probably wasn't giving her enough credit. She had dealt with a fair number of supernatural things without freaking out. She didn't even seem scared by my abilities. A normal person would run a mile if they saw anyone transform from a bird to a human, but not Cassie. She had seemed relieved when she'd realised it was me. I didn't want to push her away, but if I told her what was going on and something happened to her because she was helping me, I didn't know what I would do with myself.

Cassie walked over to the window. 'I'm serious, Jax. Come back when you're ready to tell me what's going on.'

Realising she wouldn't budge, I left to patrol the area. Her mannerisms reminded me of Nick. When I'd first met him, I hadn't intended to get involved. Freya had sent me to evaluate a powerful interference in the human world. I only went to observe but ended up getting involved.

Nick had had no idea what he was or that his emotions caused his powers to manifest, setting things on fire. In the beginning, I easily cleaned up his messes without anyone noticing, but when he accidentally set one of his bullies on fire, I knew I had to step in and teach him how to control it. Even then, it had been hard to convince him that he'd caused the fires. As we became friends, I asked him why he even bothered to attend school. He told me his father had been a lieutenant in the army but had lost his life during deployment, so it was only him and his mom now and he wanted to make her proud.

Nick's stubbornness and determination not to let anything or anyone control him, even after he found out he was a demon, was truly impressive. It reminded me that we all have a choice and gave me the strength to continue to fight my nature and show people that I wasn't just a typical demon that didn't care about anyone but himself. Maybe that was why Freya had sent me there.

A Place Of Knowledge

In an attempt to distract myself from Cassie, I decided to try to help Leah. Cassie had told me she trusted her, so it couldn't hurt to help her out. But first I needed to know more about her magic and what type of witch she was.

I went to get my laptop and tried to search for Leah's parents. At least one of them had to have been a witch, as magic passes down from generation to generation. I didn't get very far.

Most supernatural beings in the human realm keep to themselves and try to make as little noise as possible so as not to frighten humans. Human history is full of stories that have proved humans can be very cruel toward anything they don't understand. Witches were once valued by humans for their magic, but somewhere along the line, things went wrong, and many witches lost their lives. The witch trials are a prime example of humans' inability to show kindness to people who are different. They even burned their own kind during those times just because they stood out from the norm.

It truly disgusted me. Everyone was always making out how evil demons were and how they couldn't be trusted, and I guess it was true for some of them, but humans were just as bad. They acted just as evil sometimes. Which is why it's important to judge the individual instead of the species.

I shook my head. I was getting off topic. The internet hadn't been helpful. How else could I get information about Leah?

I sat down on the floor in the living room and recalled the energy I'd felt coming off her. Analysing the energy in more depth, I realised it was made up of elemental magic, which meant Leah's magic was connected to the four elements, just like that of the witches I used to live with. But there used to be a lot of covens about, so it was probably just a coincidence. I considered going back to Freya to see if she had any insight but reached out to an old acquaintance instead – Baqer, a collector of magic and knowledge. He owned a warehouse full of magical artefacts and books. If anyone would have anything that could help Leah with her magic, it would be him.

I teleported over to Baqer's warehouse, which was located on an industrial estate. When I walked inside, he appeared from a door at the back of the room, wearing a traditional long white tunic called a dishdasha, with a dark keffiyeh and agal. He looked like he should be in his thirties. Unfortunately, looks were deceptive in supernatural society. It was impossible to tell how old someone was based on their appearance, and different beings aged at different speeds. I knew he was older than me, but I had never asked how much older.

'Ahh, Jax. Long time no see. How are you? What can I do you for?' he said as he walked towards me to kiss my cheeks. I wasn't comfortable with this type of intimacy from an acquaintance, but I knew it would offend him if I refused, and considering I was asking him for a favour, it was better not to get on his bad side.

'I'm looking for a book on elemental magic.'

Baqer frowned. 'Why? You can't wield that power.'

'It's for a friend.'

His face lit up. 'Ahh ... trying to impress a lady, are we? She must be really special.'

When I didn't answer, Baqer ushered me to the back. We walked through the door he had entered from and into a massive room with a high ceiling. Even though I had been there before, I couldn't help but be amazed by the collections of things he had on display. There were several lines of display cabinets; the one closest to me contained swords and daggers in various shapes and designs, each completed by a note of information. I would have loved to have a look around, but Baqer passed them without a second glance.

We stopped in front of a massive bookcase, several metres wide and stretching all the way up to the ceiling. It must have contained thousands of books. Baqer retrieved a ladder and climbed up it. He pulled out a book from one of the higher shelves. When he reached solid ground again, he handed it to me to inspect.

'This book should be sufficient, unless you are looking for something more specific.'

It was a heavy, leather-bound book that smelled of musk and dust. The cover seemed very old with cracks in it. The words 'Elemental Magic' had been burned into the leather on the front. I skimmed through some pages. There were smudges on some, but they all seemed to be intact and the writing still readable. It contained a mix of information and spells. 'This is great. Thank you,' I said, still scanning the pages. Hopefully this book could help Leah with her magic.

I exchanged payment for the book and bid Baqer goodbye before heading home.

After I had arrived home, I checked my phone, but there was still no text from Cassie. I sighed. Maybe it was time to tell her about everything that was going on with the house.

Coming Clean

I teleported to Cassie's neighbourhood and wiped my hands on my trousers as I approached her house.

Cassie opened the door, and I gave her a big smile. 'I'm sorry.'

Leah's voice echoed from inside the house. 'Hi, Jax. Where did you disappear to the other day? You left a bit abruptly.'

I tried to locate where the voice was coming from. Maybe I should have brought the book. I could easily conjure it, but I was wary of using my abilities near the house.

'Hi, Leah. Yeah, I'm sorry about that. I just remembered I needed to take care of something.' I gave Cassie a quick look. 'Speaking of which, can we talk?'

She put her hands in the pockets of her hoody. 'Sure.

Abigail won't be home for another hour. Do you want to come in?'

I shook my head. 'I think it's better if we go somewhere else.'

'Let me just get my coat.' She closed the door in my face but opened it a few minutes later wearing a brown leather jacket.

We started walking away from the house. I gave her a nudge. 'You're being very quiet.' She shrugged. I grabbed her hand and pulled her towards me. 'I've already said I'm sorry. Tell me how I can make it up to you.'

She removed her hand from mine. 'You can tell me why you left yesterday.'

I looked behind me to see how far away we had got from the house.

'Are you going to tell me?' Cassie asked.

'I will, but we need to get further away from the house first.'

She glanced around with a grimace. 'Why?'

'I'll tell you, but not here.' I continued walking.

She caught up with me. 'Where do you want to go?'

I grabbed her hand as an idea struck me. She wanted me to let her in. What better way to do it than to show her what I could do? 'Do you trust me?'

She remained quiet, setting my nerves on edge. Maybe I didn't want to know the answer. After what felt like an eternity, she nodded. 'Yes, I do.'

I gave her a smile and scanned the area to make sure we

were alone. 'Okay. Hold on to me and close your eyes.' Teleportation could be a bit confusing, and I wasn't sure how Cassie would react. The last time I'd teleported her, she had been unconscious.

When we appeared in the woods by my house, Cassie released her grip on me and looked around with her mouth open. 'How did you do that?'

I gave her a lopsided grin. 'Magic.' She frowned. 'I teleported us here.'

Her eyes widened. 'That's awesome. Will I be able to do that?'

I smiled. 'Probably. Most immortals are able to teleport, conjure and use telepathy in one capacity or another, but let's talk about what I found out yesterday.'

She turned her head and looked at me with big eyes. 'What did you find out?'

'Remember I told you that the house was enchanted?'

'You didn't tell me,' she snapped. 'You mentioned it and quickly changed the subject like you didn't want me to know about it.'

I let out a sigh. 'There's an enchantment on your house that neutralises your supernatural energy.'

'What does that mean?'

'It means once you've been inside the house, your energy signature reads like a human's.'

She frowned. 'Isn't that a good thing?'

'Maybe. I don't know. I was told an enchantment like that could only be placed by a powerful witch.'

'Who do you think placed it?'

'That's what's worrying me. I have no idea who placed it or why. But whoever did it knows about the four of you. That's why I didn't want to talk in the house – in case someone is listening or observing you.'

'You think Abigail has something to do with it?'

'I don't know. You told me she's human. But my gut feeling says she knows something. Her ending up with the four of you doesn't feel like a coincidence.'

Lines formed between Cassie's eyes. She pushed her hair behind her ear and looked into the distance while biting her lower lip before gazing up at me. 'How can I help?'

It was a relief to hear her say that. Now I just needed to explain my plan. 'Remember how you told me that Abigail wanted to invite me around for dinner?'

She gave me another look and our eyes met. I thought back to the day we kissed, when she had explained her reasoning for ignoring me.

'Yeah. She wanted to get to know you better because she thought I was seeing you.'

'How about you invite me to meet Abigail? Maybe if I'm close, I can get a read on her.'

She took a step back. 'You know Mark will be there, right?'

'I can handle Mark. It's more important to figure out what's going on and if you guys are in danger.'

'But didn't you say the house neutralises supernatural energy?'

I nodded. 'Yeah. I haven't thought it through completely yet. But that's all I got. Maybe she'll slip up.'

She was quiet for a while, probably thinking things over. She took a deep breath and met my gaze. 'Fine. You can pick me up from my house on Tuesday.'

I grabbed hold of her. 'I would be delighted, but wouldn't it make more sense to invite me to the house?'

A smirk tugged at her lips. 'Abigail will ambush you and invite you herself when you come to pick me up.'

'Really?'

Cassie gazed into my eyes, a grin on her face. 'I guess you'll find out.' She took a few steps away but turned around and walked back to me. 'There's something I wanted to discuss with you, but it can wait. I need to get back before Abigail gets home.'

'Are you sure?'

She nodded. 'It's nothing to worry about. I can tell you about it later tonight.'

'I think it's safer not to talk about anything supernatural in the house. We don't know if anyone is listening. How about we meet up tomorrow?'

She shook her head. 'Abigail wants us to have a family weekend. I won't be able to properly see you until Monday.'

I let out a sigh. 'Okay. But I'm here if you need me.'

She smiled. 'I know. Now would you mind getting me back to the house?'

I bowed my head in a playful gesture. 'Your wish is my command.'

A New Ability

I arrived at Cassie's house and entered the open window after patrolling the neighbourhood. Without Cassie around, the weekend had gone slowly. I watched her sleep peacefully for a few hours but struggled to stay still. I couldn't wait for the morning to arrive so she could tell me what was on her mind.

The wind from the window ruffled my feathers. I looked at the night sky. The moon and stars shone brightly. Maybe it was time to patrol the neighbourhood again. Enjoying the chill breeze, I circled the area. The streets were empty and there was nothing out of the ordinary to detect. I landed in the tree and tried to sense the other people in Cassie's house, with no luck. How did the enchantment inhibit the energy? Was there a way around it? I sent out my energy again. After a lot of tries, it bounced back, carrying with it a weird type of energy. I couldn't place where it was coming from or what type of energy it was. I spent the rest of the night trying to locate it.

I managed to narrow it down to somewhere around or inside Cassie's house. Maybe it was the enchantment I could feel, but I had never felt it before, so why now?

The sound of a car startled me. When had it become morning? Leah's car was driving away from the house. I followed it and landed by the car park on the campus.

It felt a bit strange going back. I hadn't been there for a long time. I caught up with Cassie as she was walking to our first class. 'What did you want to talk about?' I asked her.

'Hi to you too.' She gave me a smile. 'Something happened when I was out with Leah. I think maybe it was related to an ability, but I'm not sure.'

'What happened?'

She looked around the hallway, where several groups of teenagers were making their way to their classrooms. 'I'll tell you about it later, after class, when there's less people about.'

I was about to tell her I could create a sound barrier when she hooked her arm in mine and walked towards our first class.

I sighed internally. *I guess I'll have to wait a bit longer.*

Cassie and I spent most of the day together; however, it couldn't have gone more slowly. As we were walking out of the entrance, Leah caught up with us. It reminded me that I had got her a book. I conjured it into my backpack.

'Leah, I have something for you,' I said as I handed her

the book.

She frowned at me before she realised what it was.

'I know I said I couldn't help you, but maybe the book can.'

'Thank you.' She flung her arms around me. My breath caught in my throat. She had never hugged me before.

I smiled at her. 'I'm glad you like it.'

She turned to Cassie. 'I'll pick you up at Jax's in about an hour or so. It should give you enough time to talk.'

We got into my car and drove out of the car park. 'We're alone now. Care to tell me what happened?' I asked as I navigated towards my house.

She looked over at me, and I quickly caught her gaze before turning back to the road. 'Leah tried to teach me magic.'

I rolled my eyes. Cassie wasn't a witch, so she would never be able to control elemental energies. 'You still haven't told her?'

Cassie hesitated. 'No. I'm waiting for the right time.'

'There may never be a right time. I think you should just tell her. What've you got to lose? Besides, you're immortal and she's not, so she'll find out eventually.'

Cassie remained quiet, looking out of the window. I didn't want to push it, so I let her be.

After we arrived at the house, I turned off the engine and turned to Cassie. 'What happened when she tried to teach you? Is that what you wanted to talk about?'

She nodded. 'Something strange happened.'

'Talk me through it.' I sat back and listened to Cassie telling the story.

'She told me to concentrate on the water, to see if I could make it move like she can. I tried, but nothing happened at first. Eventually an image appeared on the surface and I could see a field, and you and I were sitting in it. Something else was going on, but when I tried to get a closer look, Leah pulled me back. She said my face was so close to the surface, it looked like I would drown myself. I wanted to try again, but Leah didn't like it. She thought I'd better talk to you first to see if you knew what had happened.'

'It sounds like scrying. Your dad has that ability, so you probably do too. Only he scries in fire.'

Cassie tilted her head and pursed her lips. 'What's scrying?'

'It's a way of seeing past, present or future events.'

'So do you think I saw the past or the future?'

That was a very good question. It sounded like the flashes I'd got when we touched, back when the shocks went through us. But it had been several days now and there was still no shock. I kind of missed it. The last time it had happened was when I kissed her and somehow put her in a trance or something. Had that changed things? We'd never actually talked about what had happened.

I was about to ask her about it when I heard another car pull up. I looked out of the window. Leah had come to pick Cassie up. Had we really been sitting in the car that long?

Cassie glanced over at me, and I shrugged. 'I wish I knew.'

She stayed quiet for a while before getting out of the car. I joined her a second later.

Leah spoke up as I approached her. 'Thank you for the book. It's very interesting. I didn't know just how many things I would be able to do.'

I gave her a smile. 'I'm glad you like it.'

'Cassie, we should probably head home before Abigail wonders where we are.'

Cassie gave me a hug. 'When are you planning on picking me up tomorrow?'

Leah's eyes bulged. 'You guys are actually doing this?'

I wasn't sure what to say, as I didn't want to ruin things with Cassie by saying the wrong thing. I looked at Cassie, my heart beating slightly faster than usual.

She gave me a reassuring smile. 'That's the plan.'

'You're going to tell Abigail you're going out on a date? You know she's going to want him over for dinner to check him out?'

Cassie crossed her arms and released a sigh. 'We've already talked about it.'

I smiled. 'Yeah. I'm looking forward to meeting the rest of your family.'

Leah cocked her head and raised an eyebrow. 'Even Mark? You know he doesn't like you, right?'

Like I could forget after everything he had put me through. I chuckled and gave her a nod. 'Yes, even Mark.'

Her eyes lit up, a big smile plastered on her lips. 'So this is really happening?' She put her arms around us and pulled us together for a group hug. 'I'm so happy for you guys.' She let go and turned to Cassie with a grin. 'I'll be in the car when you're ready.'

Cassie squeezed my shoulder before getting into Leah's car.

I was happy Leah had found the book useful, and part of me was curious about what she would be able to do. Maybe I could ask her to show me at some point.

After sorting out some stuff in the house, I flew over to Cassie's and landed in the tree. The way I saw it, the only strange thing that had been happening was related to the house. Maybe I was overreacting, but something didn't feel right, especially not after I had been able to detect the weird energy.

I thought about everything that had happened and what Cassie had told me. Out of nowhere, chills went down my spine. My chest tightened and it became harder to breathe. I didn't know what it meant or what I should do about it. Was Cassie in danger?

I flew up to her window but couldn't detect anyone in the room. I flew around the house to see if any of the other windows were open so I could get inside, without any luck. My heart rate quickened. What was I going to do?

I transformed into my human form and ran to the front door. Cassie stormed out, slamming the door after her. She marched right past me. I caught up with her. 'What's going on?'

She glared at me before walking in another direction.

Something was obviously wrong. I placed myself in front of her again.

She evaded my gaze. 'Jax, just get out of my way. I need to be alone.'

As she tried to get away, I grabbed hold of her. She was shaking, her eyes tearful. She tried to break away from my grasp.

'Calm down. Please tell me what's going on so I can help.'

She continued to struggle until her body went limp and she started crying. I held her tightly, letting her cry on my shoulder. I felt completely helpless. I didn't know what was going on or how to help her.

Eventually her crying quieted. I lifted her away from my body and brushed some hair out of her face so I could look into her eyes. 'Do you want to talk about it?'

She nodded, but every time she looked as though she was about to say something, she started crying again.

'Just take your time. I'm not going anywhere,' I said in a soothing voice as I stroked her back. I was anxious to find out what was wrong, but I knew there was no point in rushing her. After I'd held her for a while, she gazed up at me.

'I don't know what happened. This isn't me. Mark was telling me off for dating you and all of a sudden, anger exploded in my chest and I had to get away.'

I swallowed to try to ease the pain in my throat. 'We don't have to go on a date tomorrow. We can take it as slow as you want.'

She tugged on her bottom lip. 'But what about Abigail

and the house?'

I took her hands in mine and looked into her piercing blue eyes. 'You are important to me. If you aren't ready for me to meet your family, that's okay. I don't want you to do anything you aren't comfortable with. There are other ways I can try to figure out what's going on.'

I could feel her body relax against mine as I caressed her.

She gazed into my eyes. 'Are you sure?'

I nodded. 'Since I met you, you're all I can think about. It's not just about the promise I made to your dad anymore. You are my priority. I care about you – about your feelings. I want to make you happy. To see you smile, hear you laugh. I ...' My voice died down. I took a deep breath and ran my hand through my hair. 'I've never felt this way before. I would never forgive myself if I lost you.'

Cassie closed her eyes. 'I care about you too.' She stepped out of my embrace. My body felt cold, like she had taken all the warmth with her. 'I'd better get back.'

'Let me know if you need me. I'll always be here for you.'

She nodded and turned towards the house. I changed back into a crow and flew onto her shoulder. It was my little way of showing her I was with her. As she reached the house, I flew up to the tree.

I wasn't sure what her outburst was about. Nick had always been hot headed, but I had never got that vibe from Cassie, so it didn't seem like she had inherited it from him.

What other things could cause an outburst of strong emotions? I narrowed it down to two possibilities. She was either very stressed or it was a new ability – maybe empathy? She wouldn't have got it from Nick, but maybe her mum had had the ability for empathy. It was common among beings of light.

My thought process was interrupted by Cassie opening her window to say goodnight.

Goodnight, I replied with my mind, not knowing whether she would hear me, but it was worth a shot. A moment later Cassie leaned out of the window with a smile on her face. 'I heard it.'

Excitement coursed through me and I smiled back at her. Not that anyone could tell; crows don't really show emotions.

ELEMENTAL MAGIC

The next morning I watched as Cassie and Leah left the house. Where were they going? It was too early for them to be going to college. Cassie waved at me and pointed to her phone before getting into the car. I thought about following them but decided to teleport home and check my phone instead. Cassie had texted me, explaining that they were picking up some supplies, and she asked if I could meet them in a clearing in the woods in a couple of hours.

I was intrigued by the situation. Cassie didn't seem like someone who skipped classes, but I wasn't as sure when it came to Leah, who seemed to do as she pleased.

I passed the time until I had to meet them by having a shower and getting something to eat. I twirled my phone in my hand as I ate. Should I text Nick? I didn't want to worry him over nothing, but I needed to know whether Cassie had the potential to develop empathy. In the end, I sent him a message and left the house to patrol the area before heading over to the clearing in the woods. The wind ruffled my feathers as I flew between the trees. I landed in a tree overlooking a lake. Was this where Cassie and Leah had been a few days ago?

I caught Cassie's eye as they arrived, and I flew into the woods to take my human form. Leah gave me a blank look as I emerged on the opposite side of the clearing.

'Jax?' She glanced around. 'Where did you come from?'

'I was in the neighbourhood,' I said coyly, giving Cassie a wink. Cassie shook her head as I went to give her a hug.

Leah walked up to a rock and put down the bag she was holding. 'I'm glad you could make it. I found this spell in the book which is supposed to reveal which elements I have an affinity for. I'm so excited. Me and Cassie spent the morning gathering all the supplies we needed. Do you think it'll work?'

I shrugged. 'This book was written by someone with your kind of magic, so I don't see why it shouldn't.'

Leah gave me a nod. She opened the book and placed her finger over the writing. 'It says to make a circle and call the elements one by one, asking them to connect with my soul. An outsider will be able to tell if there's a connection.' She shook her head. 'I don't understand why it mentions an outsider. Wouldn't I be able to feel it too?'

I scratched my face. 'I don't know. I guess we have to wait

and see what happens. Don't forget you need to cleanse yourself before you do the spell.'

She placed a hand on my shoulder. 'Thanks. I almost forgot.' She went over to get a white robe from her bag and glanced around the area. Her cheeks turned pink as she opened her mouth.

I cut her off. 'Don't worry. Cassie and I can go for a little wander to give you some privacy. Just text Cassie when you're done and we'll come back.'

Leah thanked me. I went over to Cassie and guided her into the trees. When I was sure we were far enough away for Leah to have her privacy, I pulled Cassie towards me and gave her a kiss on the forehead. This had ended up being my go-to place when I wanted to kiss her.

'I can't believe you actually heard me last night. I guess your abilities are starting to finally work,' I said with a big grin on my face.

She wrapped her hair around her fingers and looked up at me with sparkles in her eyes. 'Maybe we should skip the actual date and just do some more practising tonight.'

I rubbed my neck. 'If that's what you want, then that's what we'll do.' I bowed my head and faked a smile. 'Your wish is my command.' I couldn't help feeling disappointed. It had taken me hours to figure out where I wanted to take her.

Cassie gave me a nudge. 'It can still be a date and you can still pick me up. I'm just excited about learning how to finally talk to you when you're a bird.'

'If you don't mind, then maybe we can fit both in.' I squeezed her shoulder in an attempt to tell her the ball was in her court but I very much wanted to take her out. Before she had a chance to reply, her phone went off.

'Leah's ready for us to come back,' she said after she checked the phone. I nodded and took her hand in mine as we walked back to the clearing.

Leah approached us in a white robe. 'That water was freezing, but I'm all set. Don't forget to look out for each element.'

We stood back and watched. Leah walked around in a circle, pouring salt as she went. When the circle was complete, she took a seat inside and faced north. She lit a green candle and picked up some soil from the ground. 'I call upon Earth, the force of nurturing and strength. Without you, life would not exist. Please hear my call as I lay myself bare, offering you into my soul.'

At first nothing happened, but slowly vines grew up from the ground, travelling up Leah's legs and arms. They turned into small lilac blossoms. She turned to face east and lit a yellow candle. She picked up a white feather. 'I call upon Air, the force of wisdom and mind. Without you, life would not exist. Please hear my call as I lay myself bare, offering you into my soul.'

The blossoms blew off her and circled around her in a breeze. It grew in strength, causing leaves to twirl around her. The wind outside the circle remained still. Before long, a powerful tornado had engulfed her.

This meant Leah had an affinity for Earth and Air. From what I remembered, it was common for an elemental witch to have an affinity for two elements.

Leah turned to the south and called on Fire. The wind died down and the leaves drifted to the ground, glowing amber at their edges. The earth caught on fire, immersing Leah in flames.

Cassie gasped beside me. I squeezed her hand, hoping to reassure her. Even though the flames were raging, Leah seemed oblivious and unaffected by them. She turned to the west and called on water. The flames died out, replaced by water. Leah became blurry, her shape more and more transparent until there was only mist.

Cassie took a step towards the circle. I held her hand steadily, stopping her from interfering. 'She's fine,' I said as I put my arm around her.

I stared at Leah in awe. This confirmed she had an affinity for all four elements.

After she had finished, she walked over to us. 'That was amazing. It felt so unreal. Like I was part of the elements – part of the universe. Did you guys see anything?'

'You seem to have a strong connection with all the elements. It's truly amazing. I've only seen that a few times. You must have some powerful ancestors,' I said with a smile.

'I wouldn't have been able to find out without your help, so thank you, Jax.'

Cassie stood frozen beside me as Leah placed her arms around her. 'It's okay.'

Tears fell down Cassie's face. 'Please don't do that again. I was so scared when you turned into mist. I thought I'd lose you.'

Leah wiped away Cassie's tears and gave her a heartwarming smile. 'I'm still here, and I'm not going anywhere.'

The rest of the afternoon consisted of us having a picnic and chatting about random stuff. Leah tilted her head towards me. 'What was it like growing up around magic?'

I hesitated, unsure how much to share. 'It wasn't anything special. I lived with a farmer at first, then moved into the village when the witches needed my help.' I tried to think back to something specific, but my memories were hazy.

'What did they need help with? Wait. You told me you didn't know much about *my* kind of magic. Does this mean you know about other types of magic? What abilities do you have?'

I debated what to tell her. Cassie had said she trusted Leah, and after what had happened today, I wouldn't want to get on the wrong side of her. Besides, she had trusted me with a personal part of her. It would make sense if I did too.

'I can turn into a crow.'

Leah's mouth fell open. 'Shut the front door. Really?'

I chuckled. 'Yeah, and I'm deadly with a sword.'

Leah stared at her hand, which became engulfed in flames. A smirk appeared on her face. 'I bet I could take you.'

I raised an eyebrow. 'You sure about that?'

I was about to get up from the ground when Cassie placed her hand on me. 'Please don't. I've had enough excitement for today. Besides, I think we need to head home soon.'

Leah extinguished the flame and checked her phone. 'You're right. We need to leave so we can get you ready in time for your date.'

I thought Cassie looked perfect the way she was, but I'd learned a long time ago not to question the logic of women.

Leah stood up. 'Jax, I'll have her ready for you around six. Are you happy to come around and pick her up then?'

I found it a bit ironic that Leah was taking over. I gave Cassie a quick smile before jokingly answering Leah in a deep voice, 'Yes, ma'am.'

Leah gave me a playful punch on my arm. 'And don't be late.'

THE OFFICIAL DATE

I spent some time trying to find the right outfit. Eventually I settled for a pair of grey trousers and a black shirt. I stepped up to the mirror and took a deep breath. Bright hazel eyes stared back at me. It was really happening. I picked up my car keys with clammy fingers and fidgeted with them as I made my way to the garage.

I had booked a table at a restaurant by a river. It looked nice and cosy with an outdoor terrace overlooking the scenery. My first thought had been to go somewhere fancy, mainly to show off, but I figured it wasn't Cassie's style, and she would probably appreciate this place more.

As I neared the house, I checked I had the rose I'd bought. I knew it was outdated, but I liked the gesture.

I rang the doorbell. Mark opened the door looking less

than impressed. 'Oh, it's you. Would you believe me if I told you that she didn't want to see you?'

A woman with dark hair and high cheekbones walked into the hallway 'Mark, I told you to behave.'

'If you hurt Cassie or let anything happen to her, I will tear you to shreds,' Mark said in a low growl before he walked away.

I had no doubt in my mind he would be able to do that to a human. Me, not so much. However, if anything did happen to Cassie, I wouldn't forgive myself, and I might even volunteer for the beating.

The woman gave me a smile. 'You must be Jax. It's nice to finally meet you. I'm Abigail.' She held her hand out and I shook it.

'Hey, Abigail, it's nice to meet you too.'

Leah shouted from upstairs that Cassie would be down in a moment.

'How are you settling in?' Abigail asked. 'Cassie told me you're new in town.'

'Yeah. It's going well. I'm grateful to have met Cassie.'

'Yes, I understand that you two are dating. I'd love to invite you over for dinner on Sunday to get to know you better, as you're such an important part of Cassie's life.'

I smiled. 'I'd be honoured.'

Everything was going to plan. I had tried to get a feel for both Mark and Abigail as I stepped inside the house, but I couldn't feel any supernatural energy radiating from either of them.

'How about six o'clock?'

I started to answer, but I lost my train of thought as Cassie walked down the stairs. She looked more beautiful than I had ever seen her. She was wearing a black dress with some flowers on it. The colour of her eyes had been enhanced with makeup, and her long straight brown hair now had some soft curls in it. She looked absolutely stunning.

'Hi, Jax,' she said as she walked up to me. She took the rose from my hand before giving me a hug.

I was gobsmacked and struggled to get any words to come out of my mouth. Eventually I managed to say 'Wow'. Cassie laughed at me.

Leah chose that moment to walk down the stairs. 'Did the cat get your tongue?' she said playfully.

'Hi, Leah. I guess you had something to do with this.' I gestured towards Cassie. 'I've never seen you look more beautiful,' I whispered as I caught her gaze. I was completely mesmerised.

Abigail cleared her throat. 'I expect you to have her home safely by ten-thirty – it's a school night, after all.'

Cassie and I said our goodbyes and got into the car. I knew she wanted to practise her abilities, but I desperately wanted to take her out on a proper date, and considering how amazing she looked, I also wanted to show her off. Besides, all the time she spent getting ready would be wasted if we just went over to my house to practise.

'How about we go out and eat first, and if there's time, we'll go back to mine to practise?'

She smiled. 'Sounds like a plan.'

I grinned. I couldn't wait to show her the restaurant I had picked out. I was sure she was going to love it.

When we arrived, I got out of the car and raced around to open the door for Cassie. I took her hand, hoping she wouldn't be able to feel my erratic pulse, and led her to the entrance. When we got inside, the waitress was ready for us and led us out to the terrace, giving us a perfect view of the river. The background noise from the restaurant was replaced by the soft melody of running water and nature. It worried me that it might be a bit too cold to sit outside and eat, but luckily there were heat lamps by the tables.

While we waited to order, Cassie looked around. Her eyes grew wide, and her mouth was open slightly. 'It's amazing.'

I gave her a warm smile. 'I'm glad you like it. I didn't know if you'd been here before.'

She shook her head. 'We don't really go out and eat.'

After the waitress had taken our orders, we talked about the day and how crazy it had been, and I felt myself relax.

Cassie looked at me with bright eyes. 'I'm surprised you told Leah you could shift into a bird. I thought for sure that you'd deny having any abilities.'

'You trust her. Besides I wouldn't want to get on the wrong side of Leah. Who knows what she may do to me?' I said with a wink.

Cassie laughed. 'Leah wouldn't hurt a fly.' She became a bit thoughtful. 'Do you think I should tell her about me?'

I nodded. 'You know I do, but it's up to you. What's holding you back?'

'She's my sister. If I tell her, that proves she's not actually my sister.'

'But you already know that.'

Cassie opened her mouth to say something but closed it again as the waitress approached. She leaned back and crossed her arms over her chest. The waitress placed a steak in front of me and my mouth started to water. Cassie's chicken looked tasty too. We stopped talking for a while and just enjoyed the food.

'The view is so beautiful. I'm glad we decided to go out,' Cassie said with a smile.

The sun had started to set, painting the sky and the river in shades of purple and pink. It was beautiful. The river mirrored the colourful sky, while insects chirped in the distance.

When we'd finished our food, I looked up at Cassie. 'We can either have dessert or go back and practise. What would you like to do?'

She leaned forward, taking my hands in hers. 'It feels like a waste of time if we leave now. I know I said I wanted to practise, but maybe we can leave it for another day. I'd rather just enjoy spending time with you without having to think about magic and abilities.'

I smiled. 'Sounds good to me. We have the rest of eternity to practise.'

Cassie snorted. 'I'd like to think I'd have mastered my

abilities before then.'

When we'd finished our chocolate pudding, I checked my phone. 'How strict is Abigail with curfews?'

'I'm not sure, but she's likely to wait up for me.'

I nodded. 'I know you said no magic, but I'm not going to be able to get you home in time unless we teleport. Don't want Abigail to think I'm irresponsible and not respecting the curfew.'

We left the restaurant and walked to an empty area. Cassie pointed to the sky. 'Look – there's a shooting star. Make a wish.'

I raised an eyebrow. 'How would something entering the atmosphere be able to make a wish come true?'

Cassie hit my shoulder. 'You're ruining it. I know it doesn't make sense, but neither does magic.'

I opened my mouth to argue but thought better of it. I held out my hand as I scanned the area. 'Ready? Don't forget to close your eyes.'

She stepped into my arms and leaned her head against my chest. Warmth spread through me. I teleported us a fair distance away from the house and we walked back to it hand in hand.

Cassie stepped up to the front door and turned around. 'I had a great time tonight.'

'Me too,' I said with a smile. I shifted my stance. I wanted to kiss her. She leaned forward until our lips were almost touching. The memories of her becoming motionless entered my mind. I pulled back, catching sight of the curtains moving in the window.

I cleared my throat. 'We're being watched.'

Cassie sighed. I reached over and gave her a kiss on the forehead. 'I'll see you later.' She nodded and went inside.

I walked away from the house. When I was a good distance away, I turned into a crow and flew back.

Cassie had left the window open. She smiled at me as I entered and made myself comfortable on the blanket she had laid down for me.

Leah walked into the room. 'Hi, Cassie. How was the date?' Her gaze landed on me and she frowned. 'Is that Jax?' Cassie nodded. Leah gave me a wave. 'Hi, Jax.' She turned back to Cassie. 'You'll have to tell me about the date later.'

I let out a caw and flew out of the window. I didn't want to come between them; besides, the neighbourhood could do with being patrolled.

A Magical Tree

I threw out my energy without a thought as I patrolled the neighbourhood. It had become second nature. I picked up on the strange energy surrounding the house without a problem. How was this possible? A week ago, I hadn't even known it existed.

Maybe Freya would know? I didn't like to depend on her, but this was beyond me. I needed to talk to her about the energy and ask her whether she knew anything about Leah. As far as I was aware, an affinity for all elements was only transferred through generations. Which meant one of her parents must have had some powerful ancestors, but why had they abandoned her? Cassie had told me her father had died in a car crash, but what about her next of kin?

If I left now, I would still be able to meet up with Cassie

after college. I sent her a text so she wouldn't worry before teleporting to Freya's realm.

Freya was sitting in a rocking chair on the porch with a cup of tea in her hands when I arrived. The stars shone brightly, welcoming the new dawn that was awakening on the horizon. I was sure Freya would have been asleep had she not known I was coming.

'Would you like some tea?' she asked. I shook my head.

She took a sip of her tea. 'Tell me what is on your mind, my child.'

I took the seat next to her. 'I don't really know where to start. The witch that lives in the house has an affinity for all four elements.'

'That is wonderful.'

'Yeah, but I'm trying to figure out why. The only way I can think of is that she must have some powerful ancestors. But who are they and why would they have given her up?'

'Life carries many questions.' She squeezed my hand. 'Your past will show you the answers you seek.'

'I've tried thinking back to my time at the witch village, but I can't recall anything specific. The more I focus, the hazier it becomes.'

'It's all connected. Let your heart guide you.'

I sighed. Helpful as usual.

We sat in silence, watching the sun rise over the treetops in the east. It brought me back to simpler days. 'I'd forgotten how beautiful the sunrises are here. So much more colourful.'

Freya let out a soft laugh. 'Beauty is all around us. You

just need to know where to look.'

I cleared my throat. 'Speaking about looking, I've been detecting an energy around Cassie's house that I never felt before. Do you think it's the enchantment?'

Freya nodded. 'It's running low on magic and is no longer able to conceal itself. Its purpose has almost reached its end. Keep your eyes open and you will understand. Everything is connected.' Freya got up from her chair. 'I cannot help you the next time, so save yourself the journey.'

I had no idea what she was talking about, but I guessed I would find out soon enough. Before I transformed into a crow again to make my way back home, Freya embraced me. 'Your love will not be lost for long. Listen to your heart and you will find it. Strong is the connection that shares a soul.'

I said goodbye and began my journey back. Knowing I still had time before classes finished, I drifted through the forest, appreciating its beauty and the creatures that lived in it.

After I got home, I drove my car over to the campus and waited for classes to finish for the day. A wide smile appeared on my lips as Cassie approached me.

She gave me a hug. 'I missed you. How was your day?'

'It was fine. I went to see Freya.'

We got into the car and Cassie closed the door behind her. 'Who's Freya?'

'She's the woman who raised me.'

'That must have been nice. Do you see her often?'

I shrugged. 'I've been seeing her a bit more than usual

lately.' I turned the engine on and drove away from the car park. 'Anyway, how was your day?'

Cassie played with her necklace. 'It's been okay, though something strange happened this morning.'

I sucked in a breath. Maybe I shouldn't have left. 'Strange how?'

'Somehow I kept feeling what Leah was feeling.'

'That's interesting. It sounds like you may have the ability of empathy. It could explain what happened the other night as well. How did you figure out it was Leah's feelings?'

'A random feeling entered my mind. I wasn't sure where it came from, but I knew it wasn't mine. We were talking, and in the end, I just asked her about it.'

Talking about her potential ability reminded me I had sent Nick a text earlier. Maybe he had finally texted back?

I checked my phone after I parked up. I was right – there was a text from Nick: 'Yes, Lily did have that ability.' It still didn't confirm Cassie truly had the ability for empathy, but between that and what she had told me, it seemed to be the most reasonable explanation.

We went inside and got comfortable on the living room floor next to each other. 'Clear your mind and listen out for anything. I'll try and talk to you in your mind.'

After a few moments of silence, Cassie spoke up. 'Have you started yet? Because I haven't heard anything.'

I adjusted my position. 'Let me try something else.' Instead of talking to her, I recalled the memories of our date and how much I had enjoyed it.

'You're happy over something,' she said, giving me a smile.

'What am I happy about?'

'The view.' She squealed. 'You're trying to tell me about our date.'

'Can you hear me or are you just guessing?'

'I can't hear your voice, but I can sense your feelings and see pictures.'

It was a bit strange, but I couldn't recall how it had been for me when I'd first learned how to use telepathy. Maybe this was how it started?

We continued training until Leah turned up. We went out to the driveway to greet her and she got out of the car and skipped over to us with a smile. Magic energy radiated from her, a stark contrast from the neutral energy that normally surrounded her due to the enchantment on the house.

'How's the magic coming along?' I asked.

'Great.' Leah's smile became wider. She gave Cassie a hug. 'I have something to show you. It's really cool.' She glanced around the house. 'Do you have a garden?'

'Of course. Follow me.' I walked through the house, Leah and Cassie following behind.

Leah's eyes grew wide when we entered the back garden. She gestured to the forest at the back. 'Can you change into other animals too, or is this just for show?'

I gave her a look. A regular shifter could only change into one type of animal, and surely she would know this because of Mark being one. But maybe her subconscious had picked up on the fact that I wasn't a shifter.

'Just a crow, but the forest makes me calm.'

Leah placed a hand on her hip and studied me.

There was a moment of silence before Cassie spoke up. 'What did you want to show us?'

Leah didn't answer but gave Cassie a smile and walked further into the garden, past the paving slabs and flower beds. She didn't stop until she was at the edge, where the grass ended and the trees took over. Cassie and I hung back, as we weren't sure how much space Leah needed for what she was about to show us.

Leah bent down and placed her hands on the ground. She closed her eyes and her breathing became slow. Her lips were moving like she was saying something, but it was too quiet for us to hear, which made me think it was probably some sort of chanting.

I didn't know what we were supposed to be looking out for, but out of nowhere, greenery appeared from the ground in front of Leah. It grew and slowly turned into a small tree. When the tree reached about a metre in height, it stopped growing. Instead, more leaves appeared and small white flowers started to bloom. A sound of amazement escaped Cassie's lips.

After a while, Leah stood up. A frown appeared on her face as she studied the tree. 'That's never happened before.'

'What's never happened before?' I asked.

'The flowers. In all my previous attempts, I only managed to make the tree appear. It never had any flowers.'

She shrugged. 'Maybe there's something magical in these woods.'

Leah's gaze moved to the edge of the forest. It looked like she was trying to figure out where the magic could be coming from.

I studied her for a while. Where could the extra magic have come from? I put my palm to my face. It wasn't elemental magic, but it was the most reasonable explanation. 'Your magic probably got a boost from the protective layers of magic surrounding this house.'

Leah cocked her head and raised an eyebrow. 'Why do you need protection?'

'The protective layers are here to stop any magical or supernatural energy from being picked up by other supernatural beings and to stop certain types of entities from entering the house.'

'Did you place them?'

'Yeah, I put them up.'

Leah gave me a tentative smile. 'So you're not actually a shifter?'

I shook my head. 'No. Far from it.' I walked back towards the house, hoping this would make Leah understand that I'd rather not talk about it any further.

She seemed to get the point. 'Come on, Cassie. We'd better get back before Mark and Seth eat all the food without us.' She grabbed Cassie's arm and marched past me back to the front of the house. I followed behind.

Before Cassie got into the car, she came up to me and gave

me a hug. I hugged her back and was reminded of the fact that the shock between us was gone. It made me feel less close to her.

When the car had disappeared around the bend, I went back to inspect the tree Leah had created. It looked completely natural, with no indication it hadn't been there an hour ago. It stood out slightly from the other trees, mainly because of the blossoms. Most of the other trees had started to prepare themselves for winter, and their leaves painted a lovely picture of green, yellow and red.

FEELING OF ENERGY

I caught up with Cassie the next day. She gave me a smile which faded as I got closer. Knots appeared in my stomach. I grabbed her hand and pulled her to one side. 'Are you okay? Did anything happen?'

She bit her lip and met my gaze. 'I can't see you today after class. I promised Leah I'd spend time with her.'

My body relaxed and I gave her a reassuring smile. 'You don't need to feel bad or worried about wanting to hang out with your other friends.' I put my arm around her. 'You are allowed to have a life outside of us. I don't expect you to spend all your time with me.'

She leaned against me and let out a loud breath. 'Thank you. I was worried …'

I stroked her face, gazing into her eyes. 'I never want you

to be worried about talking to me or asking me things.' Our foreheads touched and we stood there in silence until the bell rang.

She had made it feel like she had to ask my permission to not spend time with me. I hated it. The last thing I wanted was to make her feel like she couldn't have a life without me. I needed to give her more space – maybe even keep more of a distance while looking over her, so she wouldn't know I was there. Hopefully it would help her realise she didn't need my permission and didn't need to apologise whenever she had plans that didn't involve me.

We made our way to class and the rest of the day went smoothly. Mark seemed to have backed off a bit, or maybe he just didn't want to shove me into a locker when Cassie was around. Either way, it was heaven sent. Leah met up with Cassie and me during lunchtime, and they talked about their plans for the evening, which consisted of spa treatments, takeaway and a film. I could tell they were excited about it.

When the day came to an end, I gave Cassie a hug and told her to enjoy herself. Knowing she was with Leah made me relax. Leah's powers had grown, and it gave me confidence she would be able to handle anything that may be thrown at them.

I spent the rest of the day drifting around in nature, but when night descended, I found myself outside Cassie's house. Her bedroom window was closed. Hopefully she was having a good time with Leah.

I made myself comfortable in the tree and felt for the

energy surrounding the house. Freya had said the reason I could sense the enchantment was because it was running low on magic; however, the energy felt exactly the same to me as the first time I'd noticed it, so it couldn't be running out of magic too quickly.

I was lost in thought regarding the enchantment on the house – why it was there and whether it would cause a risk to Cassie's safety – when I heard Cassie's voice in my head telling me goodnight. Joy spread through my heart, knowing she had been thinking about me. It also proved her telepathic ability was becoming stronger.

Cassie opened the window. I was tempted to fly inside but remembered that I had promised myself I would give her more space. I ignored the urge to be close to her and stayed in the tree.

The sun woke me as it appeared on the horizon. I watched the colourful display of pink and orange in the sky for a while before flying over to Cassie's window. Her deep breathing told me she was still asleep, but she moved around in the bed like she was restless. Hopefully she wasn't having another nightmare. I stayed until she calmed down before stretching my wings to have a look over the neighbourhood. Nick's words about keeping her safe echoed in my head, but where were all these threats Nick had been so worried about? I had expected there to be some signs of demons or other creatures trying to kill or kidnap Cassie, but so far the main worry seemed to be the enchantment on the house.

I settled back in the tree. Cassie moved around in her

room. The window remained open, tempting me to go and see her, but I forced myself to stay put.

When Leah and Cassie left the house, Cassie gazed up towards me with narrow eyes, her lips pressed together, before getting into the car. I wasn't sure what it meant, but no doubt I would find out about it later.

Once there, on my way to my first class, Cassie pulled me into an empty classroom. Her nostrils flared. 'Why didn't you say good morning to me?'

Was that why she was upset? I tilted my head and looked into her eyes. 'Did you want me to?'

She avoided eye contact and gritted her teeth. 'Of course I did.'

I guessed I had read the signals all wrong. I scratched my neck. 'I thought I'd give you some space. I don't want you to feel like I'm always around.'

She took a deep breath and gave me a kiss on my cheek. 'I like having you around.'

My chest swelled with happiness. I opened my mouth to say something sweet back to her, but the bell rang, ruining the moment.

During lunchtime, Leah came over to eat with us. She told Cassie she may have found a spell that could help us with our shock problem. I didn't even know she knew about it, but I started to get a bad feeling.

'When did you tell her about the shocks?' I looked at Cassie and then at Leah, wondering whether they were going to confirm my suspicion.

'We got talking last night and it came up,' Cassie said in a low voice, picking at her food.

I straightened my posture and let out a breath. 'Let me get this right. Last night, while you were in the house, you told Leah about it? Even though I specifically told you not to talk about anything supernatural in the house?' I clenched my fists under the table to keep my anger under control.

Cassie opened her mouth to say something but closed it again when Leah spoke up. 'Why can't we talk about it in the house?'

I shifted my gaze to Leah. 'I'll tell you about it later.'

What could I do? Would they be safer away from the house? Had anyone actually heard them talking about it? There was no way of knowing. I just knew that I would have to step up my game to keep them safe.

My shoulders slumped. 'What's done is done, but maybe you two should come around mine today. You obviously can't be trusted on your own. Besides, I want to talk to Leah about the house.'

Leah rolled her eyes but agreed.

After the last class, me and Cassie made our way over to Leah's car. I told Cassie to go with Leah, as it made more sense to have her drive to mine. After they drove away, I went to find a less crowded area, where I turned into a crow and flew home.

After they arrived, we walked through the house and out to the garden. I double checked that the protection spells were still in place before I spoke up.

'I don't know if Cassie told you, but there's a strange energy surrounding your house. Which is why I lost my cool when I realised you had been talking about magic in the house. I don't know who put it up or why it's there. What's weird about it is that it neutralises supernatural energies.'

Leah raised an eyebrow. 'How do you know this?'

'Remember how I told you I could feel that you'd been practising magic?' Leah nodded. 'That magical energy I could feel on you disappears as soon as you walk into the house. Even when you walk back out, it's still gone. It proves the energy around the house isn't just a protective barrier.'

Leah frowned. 'Why are you telling us this?'

'I'll get to that.' Having seen what Leah was able to do the other day had boosted my confidence she would be able to pull off what I wanted her to do. 'I know magic is fairly new to you. But have you felt any energy radiating from people yet?'

Leah shook her head.

'Okay, let me go back to basics. Everyone has their own special energy, even normal humans. The energy of supernatural beings is usually stronger, and that's how we can tell when someone isn't human. Or how I could tell you had been practising magic. As a witch, you should be able to pick up on these various energies.' I looked over at Cassie, who had remained quiet since they'd arrived. 'You should be able to detect these energies too at some point,' I said with a smile.

'How would I pick it up?' Leah asked me.

'I'll talk you through it, but after a while it'll become

second nature and you won't even realise you're doing it.' Leah and Cassie nodded. 'First step is to clear your mind and connect with the energy within you. After that, visualise yourself throwing out your energy to pick up other energies surrounding us. When it bounces back to you, analyse the energy.'

'Sort of like echolocation that bats use but with energy instead of sound?' Leah asked.

I nodded. 'But each type of being has a specific energy.'

'How will we know what the different energies mean?' Cassie asked.

'It'll come with time. Now how about you try and sense my energy?'

Leah nodded at me and closed her eyes. Her forehead creased from concentrating. Cassie had her eyes closed too, but every so often she would give a big sigh.

'Can you feel anything?' I asked.

'No,' they said in unison.

'Okay. Try one more time.' I enhanced my own energy output to make it easier for them to detect it. I should have done that for their first try.

'I think I can feel something,' Leah said as she opened her eyes again.

'What are you feeling?'

She shrugged. 'I'm not really sure.'

'Did you feel anything?' I asked Cassie. She shook her head. I turned to Leah. 'How about you try and feel Cassie's energy?'

It would be easier for Leah to feel Cassie's energy. I'd had centuries of practice at minimising my energy output, making it harder for others to detect me; however, Cassie hadn't learned how to do that yet.

Leah turned towards Cassie and closed her eyes. Her forehead creased again. 'I can't feel her energy as strongly as yours.' She moved her hands out, her palms towards Cassie. 'Hers is slightly different – light, less dense somehow – but there's something similar to yours as well.'

As Leah was describing Cassie's energy, I realised Cassie was still wearing the necklace I'd given her, so in reality it should have been almost impossible to sense her energy, but maybe their close relationship helped.

'That's amazing, Leah. I hadn't expected you to learn how to do it on your first try,' I said with a smile. Her cheeks turned red, and she looked away from me.

'Let's try something else. Follow me.' I started walking to the front of the house. When we got there, I stopped. 'This time I want you to try and feel the protective layer surrounding the house.'

She nodded and closed her eyes. 'I can feel something.'

'Good. Can you tell me where it starts?'

She moved towards the house while holding her hands up. She stopped right in front of where the protective barrier started. Her hands were moving almost like she was touching a solid wall. 'Is this where the protection spell starts?'

I was impressed. I had expected it to take a few tries, but not only could she tell where it started, but it looked like she could feel it too. 'Yes. You're a natural.'

We got back into the house, and Leah and Cassie sat down on the sofa.

'I'm grateful for the lesson, but I feel like you have an ulterior motive,' Leah said as she turned to stare at me.

I gave her a shy smile. 'You're correct. A few weeks ago I felt a weird energy surrounding your house. I spent hours trying to pinpoint exactly where it came from without any success, but I think it has to do with the enchantment.'

Leah interrupted me. 'Is that why you didn't want us to talk in the house?'

I nodded. 'A friend of mine told me that it was created by witch magic. I thought maybe because you're a witch and it's built on your type of magic, you'd have an easier time feeling the energy and retrieving some more information.'

Leah raised her eyebrows. 'You think I'd be able to feel something you didn't?'

I shrugged. 'You don't know until you try.' I turned to Cassie. She had been very quiet ever since they'd arrived. 'Are you okay?'

She gave me a small smile. 'Yeah. I'm just digesting it all.'

I wasn't sure I believed her. Something was definitely up.

An awkward silence followed before Leah spoke up. 'Abigail's away, so we might as well give it a try today, but I could do with some food first. Anyone for takeaway?'

'What would you like? I'll go and get it,' I said, hoping Cassie would at least open up to Leah about what was going on with her.

A Pentagram

When I got back from collecting the food, I was met by laughter. It made me happy to see that Cassie seemed to be back to her old self again.

After we'd finished eating, Leah and Cassie got into the car. I flew up and perched on the bonnet to tell them I was ready to go. I could have caught a ride with them, but I much preferred flying.

I soared over the town and landed a bit further down the road before transforming back into my human form. Leah caught up with me and I joined them on the driveway.

'I'm not sure where the best place would be to sense the energy. I'm usually in the air. Maybe you can walk around the house after you get a feel for it,' I said to Leah.

Leah nodded. She closed her eyes and put her hands out

in front of her as she made her way around the house. Cassie and I followed her at a distance. Every now and again Leah would stop and feel around on the ground, telling us the energy was denser in those areas. I marked them with some stones I found lying around. I started to get the feeling we weren't dealing with a circle at all.

After Leah had finished, she turned to face us. 'There's a circle around the house, with five places that contain more concentrated energy.'

'Let me check something,' I said, walking away from the house to turn into a crow. I landed briefly on Cassie's shoulder before taking to the sky.

'He's going to have a look from the air,' Cassie told Leah as I ascended.

From the air I could see the areas we had mapped out. They were at an equal distance from each other. I was about to tell Cassie what I was seeing but remembered that she struggled to pick up my words. Instead, I sent her a mental picture of what I could see. I wasn't sure it was going to work, but it was worth a try.

When I got back to Leah and Cassie in human form, Cassie was beaming.

'Did you see the image I sent you?'

Cassie nodded. 'Yeah, it was really cool. How did you do that?'

'When we practised the other day, you seemed to have an easier time picking up pictures, so I thought I'd try to send you what I saw.'

Leah looked between us, confusion written all over her face. 'What are you guys talking about?'

Cassie gave me a glance. 'Me and Jax have a mental connection, and while he was a bird, he sent me a mental picture of the house from above.'

Leah raised her eyebrows. 'You can talk to each other in your minds?'

'Well, it doesn't always work,' Cassie said.

I could hear that she wanted to explain more to Leah, but this wasn't the time and place for it. 'We're getting sidetracked. You guys can talk more about it later, when we're not around the house,' I said in a firm voice.

I pulled out a map that I'd conjured up earlier, on which I had marked all the dense energy spots. Cassie and Leah looked over my shoulder as I drew the lines that formed the pentagram. 'It's not a circle, it's a pentagram.'

Leah took the map from my hand and studied it. 'That's interesting. I read that pentagrams are used as protection.'

I grimaced. 'It still doesn't tell us exactly what it's protecting. Besides, pentagrams have other uses too.'

Was it protecting Cassie and the others from the outside world, or was something else hiding beneath the surface? It was witch magic, so maybe there was something about it in the book I'd given Leah. 'Does your book mention anything about protection spells?'

Leah frowned. 'Did you not read it before you gave it to me?'

Was that a normal thing to do, to look through books

before you gave them away? I shook my head. 'It's not my kind of magic.'

Leah gave me an understanding look. 'Okay, I'll have a look at it.'

'Thanks,' I said with a smile.

An awkward silence formed before Cassie cleared her throat. 'Should we go back to Jax's house or just hang out here?'

I gave her a kiss on the forehead. 'It's up to you. I don't mind.'

Leah hugged herself. 'How about we go inside and watch a film or something? It's starting to get a bit chilly out here. And we can have a look in the book. Unless it's too dangerous to look at it in the house?' she added with a smirk.

I let out a sigh. 'I'm sorry for being cautious.'

'It's fine.' She rolled her eyes, her voice dripping with sarcasm. 'But don't you think they would have picked up on the fact that there's a crow in Cassie's room most nights? Not to mention when Mark turned into a werewolf inside the house or when I made all the lights explode. So if anyone is actually watching, I'm pretty sure they already know we're not normal teenagers.'

I put my hands up in defence. 'Okay, you have a point. I just think it's better to be safe than sorry. We don't know why this enchantment is here or who put it up.'

Leah nodded. 'I'll be careful. I don't practise magic in the house anymore anyway.' She turned and walked inside.

I glanced over at Cassie. She shrugged and hooked her

arm in mine as we followed Leah into the house.

Cassie wandered into the kitchen to sort out some popcorn and drinks the human way. I would have helped, but I didn't feel comfortable using my abilities in the house, despite what Leah had told me.

'Where's Mark and Seth?' I asked.

'They're out camping with some friends. Well, that's what they told Abigail. I think they're with the other werewolves by the nature reserve.'

'Would you mind if I have a look around?'

She shook her head. 'Not at all, but please stay out of their room. It's the furthest one from the stairs. I don't want Mark to have another reason to hate you.'

I nodded and strolled up the stairs, sending my energy out as I went. I couldn't detect anything out of the ordinary. My eyes swept over the landing. Two of the rooms had their doors ajar. I knew one of them belonged to Cassie, and from the sound of pages being turned, I assumed the other belonged to Leah. There was a closed door to my left and another at the end.

I opened the door to my left and stepped inside. It appeared to be Abigail's room. It contained a massive wardrobe and a double bed. It was extremely tidy, and no personal items were on display, but there was no indication that anything but a human lived there.

'What you doing?'

I jumped and turned around to face Leah. 'Sorry. I was just looking.'

She raised an eyebrow. 'Did you find anything?'

I shook my head. 'No. Everything appears normal.'

Leah grabbed my arm. 'Come on. Let's join Cassie downstairs. Abigail won't be happy if you touch anything. She doesn't like us being in her room. She freaked out when Mark used her bed once. Anyway, I had a quick look in the book, but I couldn't find anything that seemed useful.'

We walked into the living room, and as I sat down next to Cassie, she snuggled up to me, so I put my arm around her.

Leah grinned at us. 'You look cute together.'

A warm feeling came over me and I squeezed Cassie a bit tighter, which made her giggle.

Cassie and Leah tried to come up with what to watch. They continuously asked me what I thought, but I was too caught up with having Cassie in my arms to care.

A Spell to Recall Memories

The fire scorched my face. I tried to move away from Surtr, tried to escape the torture, but I couldn't move. I bolted upright and opened my eyes, ready to summon my weapon and defend myself. I wasn't going to go down without a fight. My eyes wandered about the place. This wasn't Surtr's realm. Where was I? The room seemed familiar. My gaze settled on Cassie and my body relaxed.

She stared at me with bulging eyes, her hand over her mouth. 'What happened?'

I let out a nervous laugh and scratched my forehead. My memories from the day before came back to my mind. We must have fallen asleep. 'Sorry. I'm a bit jumpy in the mornings.' It was an understatement. I wasn't used to waking up next to someone else.

Leah gave her body a stretch. 'Good morning.' She looked from me to Cassie. 'Did I miss something?'

I glanced over at Cassie, wondering if she would mention anything to Leah, but she stayed quiet.

Leah stood up. 'Anyone for breakfast?'

I rubbed my neck, feeling embarrassed and uncomfortable. 'I think I'm just going to head home.'

'Suit yourself. I, for one, am starving,' she said as she walked into the kitchen.

Cassie gave me a questioning look, but I wasn't ready to answer any questions. I gave her a kiss on the forehead. 'I'll see you later.' She nodded in response.

'Bye, Leah,' I shouted, hoping she would hear me from the kitchen. I made my way to the door and let myself out.

At a fair distance away, I turned into a crow and spent the next few hours drifting, feeling the air under my wings.

When I arrived home, I checked my phone and saw that Cassie had texted me. She was in the woods with Leah and I could come and meet them if I wanted to, but she was happy to come here afterwards if I wasn't up for it.

Determined not to let my startled response from the morning stop me from seeing Cassie, I flew over to meet them. When I landed on Cassie's shoulder, I overheard them mentioning the house. I jumped to the ground and transformed back into my human form.

Leah took a step back. 'I knew it was you, but it's still a shock.'

'What were you saying about the house?' I asked, giving

Cassie a hug.

'So we're eavesdropping now too,' Leah said with a wink.

Cassie shot her a look. 'We were just trying to figure out who had placed the spell around the house.'

'Did you figure anything out?'

Cassie shook her head. 'Not really. It doesn't make any sense.'

I agreed with her. I had been trying to figure out what was going on from the moment I'd learned about the enchantment. I shrugged. 'I don't know what to make of it either.'

After a moment of silence, Leah spoke up. 'How about we get to the reason why Cassie asked you to meet us here?'

I cocked my head. I hadn't realised there was a specific reason. 'And what reason was that?'

'There's a spell in the book to recover lost memories. Cassie told me that when you guys touched before and got a shock, it was like an old memory was trying to surface. Did you feel that way too?'

There had definitely been something trying to push its way through to the surface. I wasn't sure if it was a memory, though, but it couldn't hurt to try the spell. I turned to face Leah. 'I'm in. What do we need to do?'

Leah opened the book she was holding. 'The book says you need to hold each other's hands and focus on the energy and what you want to remember. The energy will take physical form, which you have to consume.'

It sounded simple enough. Cassie fidgeted with her

necklace, so I put my arms around her to reassure her. 'Don't worry about it. I'm sure it'll be fine.'

Leah gave us a smile. 'You guys ready?' Cassie and I nodded in response.

Leah positioned us so we were facing each other. Cassie held her hands out, palms up, and I placed my hands on top of hers. Leah placed one of her hands under Cassie's and the other on top of mine. 'Now close your eyes and concentrate on what you want to remember.'

It was easier said than done. I tried to focus on Cassie, but my thoughts kept turning towards the witch village. What was the name of the High Priestess Freya seemed to believe Leah was related to?

After a while, Leah let out an excited gasp. 'It's working.'

Inside our hands was some sort of fruit. It almost looked like a heart-shaped apple but smaller, with the skin of a plum. Leah picked up the fruit and cut it in half. The inside was dark purple. She handed one piece to me and the other to Cassie.

I gazed into Cassie's eyes. 'Ready?' She nodded. 'Here goes nothing,' I said as I lifted my half towards her mouth. She mimicked my gesture and put the fruit into my mouth as I fed her the other half.

The consistency was almost like that of a plum, but it tasted more like an orange. I swallowed it and glanced over at Leah. 'What's next?'

'I'm not really sure.' She scanned the pages. 'The book doesn't specify anything. I thought maybe you'd just start remembering.'

That was typical. I guessed we would have to figure it out on our own. I tried to see whether I could recall anything, but I had no luck.

Cassie placed a hand on Leah's shoulder. 'It's okay. At least we tried.'

We spent the rest of the day hanging out. After a few hours, Cassie and Leah decided to head home, as Abigail would be back from her work trip. I walked them to their car. Cassie gave me a hug and reminded me about the dinner the next day. Not that I needed reminding. She apologised that we hadn't spent any alone time together, but I didn't mind. I enjoyed spending time with both of them. Leah had grown on me, and I was happy Cassie had her as a best friend.

When they drove away, I resumed my crow form and followed them home.

Leah and Cassie walked into their house, and a moment later Cassie opened the window for me. I flew inside. Cassie tilted her head and stared at me.

She let out a sigh. 'You can't hear me, can you?'

I shook my head. She slumped down on the bed. I sent an image to her mind.

A smile appeared on her face, and she told me what she saw out loud. I bounced up and down on the spot, happy she'd got it right. My heart sped up as I sent her an image of us kissing. I'd been too scared to act on it.

Cassie's cheeks became pink. She opened her mouth to say something when Abigail shouted from downstairs.

'Dinner's ready.'

Cassie blew me a kiss. 'I'll talk to you later.' She walked out of the room, and I made myself comfortable on the blanket by the window.

I woke up hearing Cassie's voice in my head. I must have fallen asleep. Cassie was sitting on the bed. I sent an image showing her how proud I was that she had finally managed to get her message through to me before asking if we could talk outside.

'It'll have to be quick. I'll tell Abigail I'm going to the shops.'

I lifted my beak in a nod and flew out of the window. A moment later Cassie joined me outside. When we were some distance from the house, I changed into my human form.

Cassie hooked her arm in mine and leaned her head against my shoulder. 'What did you want to talk about?'

'I never asked you what you saw after I kissed you.'

She smiled. 'I'll tell you what I saw if you tell me what happened this morning.'

I shrugged. 'I had a nightmare and forgot where I was.'

She raised her eyebrow and gave me a stare. 'That's it?'

I nodded and took her hand. 'Your turn. What did you see?'

She let out a sigh. 'I was somewhere else. Like memories, but I can't recall what was happening. Almost like what used to happen when we touched, but stronger and more intense. That was why I wanted us to do the memory spell with Leah. Shame it didn't work, though.' Cassie checked her phone. 'I have to get back.' She took a step towards the house but stopped and turned around. 'Can you conjure something for me so it looks like I actually went to the shop?'

I made a bar of chocolate appear in my hands. 'Thanks.' She took it from me and gave me a hug.

I turned back into a crow and followed her home before making my round of the neighbourhood to make sure that there weren't any threats around.

FAMILY DINNER

Cassie had mentioned she liked waking up and seeing me, so when the sun peeked over the horizon, I flew over to her room and made myself comfortable on the blanket by the window. Her slow regular breathing told me she was still asleep.

After a while, her voice sounded in my head. *Good morning.* She stretched her arms and got out of the bed.

Good morning, beautiful, I answered. We exchanged some pleasantries until Cassie excused herself to have some breakfast and get ready for the day.

I stayed in her room, not ready to go home just yet. When she came back, she told me she was going to spend the day with Abigail and Leah. Them spending time with Abigail worried me. Even though everything pointed towards the fact that she was just a human, I didn't trust her. Something was going on, and my gut told me Abigail was in the middle of it.

I should be coming up with a way to determine if she was human or not, but my paranoia had me following them for most of the day. Nothing happened. I reluctantly headed home a couple of hours before I had to be at Cassie's to get myself ready for the family dinner. Even though Cassie didn't seem to mind my ragged look, I wanted to make a good impression on the rest of the family.

While I was getting ready, I considered what the custom was nowadays. I couldn't turn up for dinner empty-handed, but what should I bring? Getting my laptop out, I searched for appropriate things to bring and found that flowers and wine were most common. I didn't want to conjure anything in case someone picked up on it. Besides, it was seen as lazy – at least that's what Freya had told me. Never conjure a gift.

Instead, I stopped at the corner shop before heading over to Cassie's house. I picked out some flowers and asked the person behind the counter to get me some nice wine, appropriate for a family dinner. He asked for my ID and handed over a bottle of Pinot Grigio.

I walked up to the front door of Cassie's house with a racing heart. It was silly – on the battlefield I was fearless; however, a dinner with the family of the girl I loved and I was partly crippled with fear. I wanted everything to be perfect. Part of the reason why I was doing this was to get a feel for Abigail and see whether she was a threat to Cassie, but I would be lying to myself if I believed it was the only reason. I wanted to be part of Cassie's life, but more importantly, I wanted to be the one she could always count on.

Cassie opened the door with a smile. She had made an effort, or maybe Leah had had a hand in it. She wore a pair of fitted dark jeans with a lovely loose flowery top. She had on a minimal amount of makeup, just enough to highlight her blue eyes. Her hair remained straight and loose. Cassie never failed to make an impression on me. She looked stunning; however, seeing her in pyjamas had been quite a turn-on too, so I guessed I was biased.

'Hi, Jax. Please come in.' She gave me a hug and ushered me inside.

'Welcome to our house,' Abigail said as she walked towards us.

'Thank you for having me.' I gave her the wine and flowers I had bought.

'That's very thoughtful of you.' She inspected the wine as she walked back into the kitchen, probably to sort out the food. Hopefully the wine would be good enough.

Leah came downstairs. 'Hi, Jax. I'm happy you could make it.' She hugged me and whispered in my ear. 'I've threatened Mark to be on his best behaviour.'

I chuckled as I pictured the conversation between them. We walked into the living room and sat down on the sofa. Seth nodded with a smile, while Mark gave me a grunt as an acknowledgement. Leah gave him an evil stare and he shrugged.

Both Mark and Seth had made an effort to dress up. No doubt to make Cassie happy, or maybe Abigail had forced them. Either way, it was obvious they couldn't care less about what I thought.

Mark had made it clear from the start that he didn't like me or the fact that I was hanging around with Cassie. I hadn't met Seth before, but it was easy to see the resemblance between him and Mark, so I assumed he would have a similar view of me. After all, shifters weren't supposed to like demons.

An awkward silence developed.

'Well, isn't this fun?' Mark said sarcastically.

Leah glared at him. 'Don't push it.'

Abigail walked into the room with a smile. 'Dinner's ready.'

All of us got up and made our way over to the dining table. It smelled delicious. Abigail had made a roast. As I put the first piece of food in my mouth, Abigail spoke up. 'I understand you're new in town. How come you moved here?'

I swallowed my food. 'My family moves around a lot because of my dad's job.'

'What does your father do?'

'He's an engineer.'

'And what about your mother?'

'She works from home.'

Abigail nodded. 'How do you find it here?'

'I like it. I enjoy the nature around these parts.'

'Yeah, there are quite a lot of trees around.'

Cassie let out a sigh. 'It's supposed to be a family dinner, not an interrogation.'

Abigail turned to her. 'I'm just being friendly.' She went back to asking me more questions. I had no problem answering any of them, as I had prepared myself. Abigail seemed pleased with the answers, and I was sure she hadn't realised everything I'd told her was a lie.

While everyone was busy eating, I tried to get another feel of each person's energy. I found it interesting but at the same time disturbing, as I couldn't tell that any of the people around me were supernatural beings, even though I knew they were.

I let out a breath and looked at Abigail. Maybe if I got her to talk, she might slip up? 'Cassie tells me you're away a lot for work.'

Abigail smiled at me. 'Yes. Unfortunately it's a requirement.'

'What is it that you do?'

'I work for an organisation that helps children in need.'

'Is that how you ended up with this family?'

Her smile wavered, but she quickly recovered. 'Yes. It's a blessing in disguise really. Now if you'll excuse me, I need to sort out the dessert.' She got up and started collecting everyone's plates. Cassie got up to help.

I glanced around the table, Mark glared at me like he had throughout the dinner. It was obvious he didn't want me around. Maybe it would be better if I left promptly after dessert so as not to overstay my welcome.

Abigail brought out some sticky pudding. We ate in silence, and when everyone had finished, I excused myself and thanked her for the lovely dinner.

Cassie walked me to the door. 'Anything?'

I shook my head and gave her a kiss on the forehead. 'I'll see you later.'

The door closed behind me. I walked to my car and started driving away from the house. When I was a good distance away, I abandoned it, transformed into a crow and flew back.

Cassie's window was closed when I returned. Maybe she was still downstairs with the others, talking about how the dinner had gone. I made myself comfortable in the tree and waited.

After a while, Cassie called me mentally, telling me she needed to talk. I didn't know what it was about, as I thought the dinner had gone fine, but she sounded upset. I let her know I was outside and ready to talk when she was.

She walked out of the house and down the road. I followed her until we were far enough from the house that I felt comfortable transforming back into my human form. I walked up to Cassie to give her a hug, but she stepped out of my reach.

I studied her and my eyes stopped at her face. She looked away, avoiding my gaze. Her lips trembled and her eyes appeared damp. She hugged herself, rocking back and forth, like she was trying to hide the fact she was shaking.

Something must have happened to make her feel and act the way she was.

'What happened? Is everything okay?' I reached out to touch her, but she jerked back, so I shoved my hands into my pockets. 'What's going on?'

Cassie played with the zipper of her jacket. 'Mark told me something, and I need to know if it's true.' Her eyes pierced mine. 'Are you really a demon?'

My brain shattered. How had Mark figured it out? The energy around the house neutralised everyone's energy. If he could sense my energy, it must have been from our altercations between classes. But why wouldn't he have said something before now?

With a defeated and apologetic look, I answered her. 'I wanted to tell you, but I didn't know how, and I didn't want to scare you away.'

'I trusted you, Jax.' I could hear Cassie's voice break. I hated myself for upsetting her. If only I'd taken the time to explain it to her earlier, maybe she would have understood. All I had wanted to do was to keep her safe.

'I'm still the same person. I still care about you. Nothing has changed, Cassie.'

Cassie threw her hands in the air. 'How can you say that? You told me demons killed my mother and that demons were out to get me. I looked it up. Demons are known to be evil and manipulate people to do their bidding. But you're a demon, so how can I believe anything you say?' She turned and started to walk back towards the house.

This was it – I was going to lose her. I could feel my heart breaking. I needed to do something. I followed her and grabbed hold of her shoulder to stop her from walking any further. 'Cassie, wait. Let me explain.'

Cassie turned around and looked me straight in the eyes. No love remained, only coldness. 'You had a million chances to explain, but instead you lied to me. Our connection, was any of it even real?' I opened my mouth to respond, but before I had a chance, she continued. 'I don't want you in my life anymore. Just leave me alone, Jax.' She gave me a death stare before she turned around and ran back to the house.

I just stood there. I didn't know what to do with myself. I had allowed myself to fall in love with her, and I'd thought she loved me back, but when it came down to it, no one could actually love someone like me.

After what felt like forever, cold drops of rain hit me and pulled me out of my despair. I returned to my crow form. Even though Cassie didn't want to see me, the urge to make sure she was okay, that she was safe, made me go back to the house.

Her crying broke my heart all over again. I couldn't stand seeing her like this, but there was nothing I could do to fix it. It wasn't like I could change what I was. If that were an option, I would have done it ages ago.

I didn't want to leave Cassie alone in the state she was in, but knowing I was the cause of it, I made sure to keep my distance. It wasn't until Leah came into Cassie's room that I decided to leave. I had a lot of faith in Leah. I wasn't sure why, but knowing she was with Cassie made me relax. I needed to get home and lick my own wounds and come up with a plan of action. Cassie hated me now, but she was still everything to me, and I'd still made a promise to Nick that I intended to keep.

With a hollowness in my chest and silent tears escaping my eyes, I placed my head on the pillow. What was I going to do? I must have been completely drained, because before I knew it, I was asleep.

THE PROMISE

I'm making my way over to the horses' field with a head collar in my hand. Edmond, the farmer I work for, has asked me to take one of the horses back to the stable. But as I'm walking, the sound of crying reaches me. I search for the source. It's a girl. I'm sure she lives in the village, but I'm not supposed to talk to anyone there. Edmond has warned me about going into the village. They will banish me if they find out what I am.

The girl's beauty is captivating, and against my better judgement, I talk to her. I can't stand seeing her upset. I ask her whether she wants to come with me to try to catch a horse. While we're strolling around the fields, trying to locate the horse I'm looking for, I keep telling her silly stories in an attempt to make her laugh. It seems to be working.

Eventually, we find the horse and I head back to the farm. As we get closer, the girl excuses herself and leaves. I'm happy because she's in a much better mood than when I found her. But my heart yearns to see her again.

I woke up, but the dream lingered in my mind. It surprised me how much the girl in my dream reminded me of Cassie. The place looked exactly the same as when I used to live in the witch village, but no matter how hard I tried, I couldn't remember ever meeting a girl there.

I checked the time. Our first class would start soon. I teleported to the campus and searched for Cassie, but there was no sign of her. However, I did have a run-in with Mark. Him, being his normal charming self, slammed me into the lockers. 'You better stay away from Cassie or I will rip you to shreds.'

I gritted my teeth and spun around, glaring at him. I was done playing nice. 'Maybe you should watch your temper. If you know what I am, then surely you know what I can do, even to someone like you, wolf,' I whispered back, knowing he could still hear me while no one else could.

A growl escaped him before he hurried down the corridor.

By the second class, the realisation that Cassie wasn't around had sunk in. I searched for Leah. Maybe she would let me explain, but when I couldn't find her, I gave up for the day. There was no point in me being there.

I flew over to Cassie's house. Her window was closed, but the lights were on. Cassie and Leah sat on her bed together.

Knowing they were safe, I made myself comfortable in the tree. How had it come to this? Everything had been going so well. Would Cassie have reacted differently if I'd told her what I was – what we were – or would I just have lost her that much sooner?

I caught Cassie's gaze as she left the house the next day. *Leave me alone, Jax,* she told me in my mind before getting into Leah's car. Her voice was filled with hatred. It hurt. I needed to talk to her, to explain, but Leah or Mark escorted her to all her classes, making it impossible for me to get near her. I tried talking to her mentally, but she didn't look my way, so I had no idea whether she'd even heard me.

By the time classes had finished, I was completely depleted. I didn't know what to do. Even though I couldn't see Cassie, I still flew to her house to sit in the tree to observe and make sure she was safe.

A few days went by in the same fashion, and I debated whether to visit Nick and tell him what was going on. To tell him I'd screwed up. Though I wasn't sure how he would react, especially if I told him about me and Cassie. I shook my head. There was still time to fix this. Besides, I was still making sure she remained safe. Even if it was from a distance.

When I flew over to Cassie's on Friday afternoon, I couldn't get close to the house. It felt like I'd flown into a wall. Why couldn't I get to the tree? I flew above it, around it, but I couldn't get through. I threw my energy out in an attempt to figure out what was going on. There was a force field of energy. I tried to break it down, but it didn't work. I slammed into it, hoping brute force would work. I even tried teleporting to the other side without any luck.

Cassie wouldn't talk to me and now I wasn't even able to watch over her. I had completely failed Nick, not to mention my heart. I slumped down next to the wall, defeated.

After a lot of thinking, I considered whether it would be worth going to see the werewolves and Mark to find out what was going on. Luckily my common sense kicked in. It would be more beneficial – and safer – to try and talk to Leah. She'd seemed to like me before. If I caught her alone, there was a chance she would hear me out. I could go to the clearing in the woods and wait for her to turn up. It wasn't ideal, but it was my best bet. I looked up at the darkening sky. She wasn't going to be there at night. Better to wait until the morning.

When morning arrived, I did a quick sweep of the neighbourhood before flying over to the clearing where Leah normally practised her magic.

I landed in a tree overlooking the lake. It was a beautiful morning. The sun sparkled on the water. I contemplated how it would go. After a few hours, doubt settled in. Would Leah even turn up? I convinced myself to stay for a bit longer.

Eventually she walked through the trees. I didn't want to scare her; however, I was desperate to make sure Cassie was okay. When Leah walked past the tree I was sitting in, I jumped off and transformed into my human form.

Leah jumped back, eyes wide. 'What the— Oh, it's you.' She glanced at me, her eyes narrow. 'What do you want, Jax?' She folded her arms over her chest.

'Someone put up a force field around your house. I can't get through to make sure Cassie's safe.'

Leah sighed. 'I put it up. Cassie doesn't want you to stalk her anymore.'

I took a breath and the tension in my muscles disappeared. I hadn't even considered the possibility of her putting it up. 'Is she okay? Are you keeping her safe?'

She studied me. 'You really do care about her, don't you?'

'Of course I do. I would sacrifice myself if it meant Cassie would be safe and happy.'

Leah gave me a nod, like she actually believed me. At least I hoped she did.

She looked out over the lake. A sigh escaped her. 'To answer your question, Cassie isn't okay. She just found out her boyfriend is a demon.'

'I should have told her, and you too,' I said sincerely with sorrow in my voice before I continued. 'But it doesn't change anything. I'm still me and I still love Cassie and I would still do anything for her.'

Leah turned and looked at me with a frown. 'If you truly mean that, then you'll stay away from Cassie, because that's what she needs right now. Time.'

Would I really be able to stay away from Cassie without knowing whether she was safe? It would be one of the hardest things I would have to do, but maybe Cassie would be better off without me in her life. 'I'll do it, but you need to promise me you'll keep her safe, and if you can't, you need to call me.'

Leah rolled her eyes at me. 'Sure. I'll text you if I need

you.'

I clenched my fists. Why wasn't she taking me seriously? I grabbed her shoulder and stared into her eyes. 'You don't get it. Cassie's special. At some point someone might discover who she is, who her father is, and come after her, and when they do, it may be more than you can handle. And we still don't know if whoever placed the enchantment is a threat.'

Leah took a step back and rubbed her shoulder. She met my gaze. 'Okay. Fine. I'll keep you updated if I see anything suspicious.'

'You need to promise me,' I said forcefully to make her understand that it wasn't a joke.

'I promise. Now leave so I can be alone.'

Leah walked away from me, but I lingered. This would be the last chance I had to get a message to Cassie, to tell her she was part demon. It wasn't ideal. I would have liked Cassie to have had the choice of whether or not to tell Leah about it, but she needed to know what she was, and I couldn't see any way around it.

I ran my hand through my hair and marched after her. 'Leah, wait up.'

She stopped in her tracks and sighed. 'What?'

'Before I go, would you mind telling Cassie that everything I've told her is true? Her dad is truly alive, but he's a demon like me, which means Cassie is part demon.'

She turned to face me. 'You can't be serious?'

'I know you don't trust me, but it's the truth, and if she ever wants to talk to me again, tell her I'll be there in a heartbeat for her.'

'Fine. She's not going to like it, but I'll tell her. Now leave me alone,' Leah said in an aggravated tone.

I lifted my arms to hug her but lowered them again. Considering the circumstances, she probably wouldn't appreciate it. I turned into my crow form and flew home. I would keep my promise and stay away; I just hoped Leah would be able to keep Cassie safe and that she would truly let me know if anything was too much for her to handle.

Missing Cassie

Weeks went by. Leaves fell to the ground, making the trees emptier by the day, just like my heart. I didn't even go to class anymore. I had promised Leah I would stay away from Cassie and give her time. Not seeing her made it easier. I still patrolled the area, though, making sure there were no threats around.

I thought about letting Nick know what had happened, but Leah had promised to keep Cassie safe. Besides, I didn't want to tell Nick I had failed him. I could still fix this.

My dreams were filled with more memories from the witch village I used to live in, but all the dreams somehow included Cassie. It confused me. I had no real memories of any girl when I lived in the witch village, let alone someone who looked like Cassie. But I cherished them like they were long-lost memories. My heart stung as I thought of Cassie and the possibility that I may have lost her forever.

In an attempt to think about Cassie less, I kept myself busy by sorting out the house and the garden while looking after the tree Leah had grown from nothing. The flowers had been replaced by what looked like apples. They were currently tiny, but I had faith they would grow bigger with time, just like a normal apple tree. With fondness in my heart, I thought back to the day when Leah had come over to show me and Cassie what she could do.

I was watering the tree when I heard a car approaching. I marched round to the front of the house, curious to see who it may be. I wasn't expecting anyone, and only a few people knew where I lived.

As I reached the driveway, Leah's black Mini pulled into the drive. My heart stopped. Had Cassie come to see me? I let out a breath of disappointment. Cassie wasn't with her.

Leah got out of the car. For the first time since I'd met her, she wasn't wearing makeup. Her eyes were puffy, with dark circles under them.

Her gaze darted away from me. 'Cassie's missing.'

As soon as she said that, I froze. What did she mean, Cassie was missing?

'Hello?' Leah waved her hand in front of my face. 'Anyone in there?'

I slowly recovered. 'What do you mean, she's missing? You were supposed to look after her.' Anger built up inside me, and I clenched my fists to try to keep it under control.

'Whoa, calm down. No need to shoot the messenger. I didn't have to come here, you know, but I did because I promised you I would.'

I reeled in my emotions. 'Sorry. Tell me what happened.'

'I was with Cassie last night, but when I went to her room this morning, she was gone. I asked if Mark or Seth knew where she could be, but they didn't. It's not like her to leave without letting me know something's up. I even tried to locate her with magic, but it's like she's fallen off the face of the earth.' Leah gave me a stern look. 'I'm taking a risk by trusting you, so you better not let me down.'

My feelings were in turmoil. I was thankful Leah had trusted me enough to tell me what was going on. It showed me she'd believed me when I'd told her I still cared for Cassie. Maybe there was an actual chance of rebuilding my relationship with her and Cassie again. We just needed to find Cassie first.

I let out a hard sigh and closed my eyes so I could concentrate on locating Cassie's energy. But I couldn't find any trace of her anywhere. It was like Leah had said – Cassie had disappeared from the face of the earth. It could only mean one of two things. Either she was dead, which I felt in my heart wasn't true, or she was hidden. I prayed it was the latter.

I opened my eyes. 'I can't feel her anywhere. If she was somewhere in the human realm, I should have been able to sense her.'

Tears fell down Leah's face. 'Do you think she's dead?'

I swallowed and gazed into her eyes. 'Let's not think about it. There are other reasons why I wouldn't be able to sense her.'

She wiped her tears away. 'So you don't think she's dead?'

'I think I would feel it.'

She frowned. 'Why?'

'I've felt it before, like a chill going down my spine. When she fainted on her birthday and again when her empathy overwhelmed her.'

'But you don't know for certain.'

I shook my head. My chest tightened with fear. What if I was wrong?

Leah took a deep breath. 'I'll remove the force field around the house and leave Cassie's window open so you can have a look around. She can't just disappear. Something must have happened to her.'

I watched as Leah drove away. I had no idea what to do. Would Freya have any advice? Last time I'd seen her, she'd told me she wouldn't be able to help me next time. Was this the time she meant? I tried to think back to our conversation. It felt like years ago. She had said something before I'd left – what was it? I spent a few moments trying to recall exactly what she had said, then I remembered: 'Your love will not be lost for long. Listen to your heart and you will find it. Strong is the connection that shares a soul.' Had she been talking about Cassie?

I held my breath as I flew over to Cassie's house. It felt

strange being back. All my suppressed feelings started to surface, but I pushed them aside. I didn't have time to think about Cassie and remember everything we had shared and done together. Cassie was missing and I had to find her, for her sake and my sanity. No doubt Nick would have my head on a platter if he found out what was going on.

I got into Cassie's room. Everything looked completely normal. I sent out my energy to see if I could pick up on anything. Something felt off, but I couldn't place it.

After a while, Leah walked into the room. 'Meet me outside the house. Something else has come up that may be related.' She proceeded to walk back out and down the stairs.

The front door opened. I followed her as she continued to walk away from the house. After a while, I turned back into human form so I could talk to her. 'What's up?'

She took a deep breath. 'Mark can't shift.'

I didn't really follow. 'What do you mean, Mark can't shift?'

'We were all really worried about Cassie, so as I went to see you, Mark decided he was going to shift into his wolf and see if he could pick up on Cassie's scent around the house, but he can't.'

'Maybe the enchantment is blocking it. Has he tried away from the house?'

Leah rolled her eyes. 'Of course he has. He's been trying for over an hour and he's freaking out.'

That was a new development. Maybe it had something to do with Cassie or maybe it was completely separate;

however, I couldn't afford to take any chances.

'There's something off in the house. Let me go back and examine it a bit more closely. I can't believe I'm even considering this, but can you and Mark – Seth too, if you want – meet me at my house in a couple of hours?'

Leah grimaced. 'I'll try, but I can't promise Mark will come, but maybe he'll do it for Cassie.'

I left Leah on the street and transformed back into my crow form to investigate the house further.

HISTORY OF THE SHIFTERS

I went through the whole upper floor of Cassie's house and picked up on something. There was an energy that didn't belong. The enchantment around the house also felt different, but was that because it had changed or had I just not felt it in a long time?

When I got home, I found a bundle of leather books lying on the kitchen table. I approached them to examine them more closely. On top of the bundle was a note in Freya's handwriting. 'Listen to your heart, for it will guide you.' I picked up the books and was going through them in the hope of finding any information or connection between Cassie's disappearance and Mark's lack of abilities when the doorbell rang.

'It's open. Just step inside,' I yelled. I didn't have time to go and open the door for them. With my head still in the books, I saw Leah in my peripheral vision walking into the living room followed by Mark and Seth. I was both grateful and surprised Mark was with her.

'I don't trust you, demon, but I'm willing to set our differences aside until we can figure out what's going on,' Mark said in disdain.

I looked up from the book I was reading, feeling a new kind of respect towards Mark. 'It is in your DNA, so I wouldn't expect anything else.'

Mark's head flinched, and he looked at me with a slack expression.

'How much have the other wolves told you about the history and legacy of the shifters? Do you know where you come from? Why you were originally created?' I asked.

Mark continued to stare at me as Seth answered. 'We were created to protect the humans from vampires.'

I glanced over at Seth and nodded, impressed he had spoken up. He'd always seemed shy and mainly stayed quiet in the background. 'That is partly true. Shifters were originally created to protect humanity from being used by demons.'

Seth took a sharp breath, and from the corner of my eye, I saw Leah wrinkle her brow and put her hand to the throat. I guess she hadn't expected me to be quite as honest; however, I did have a point to make with my story, so I continued. 'In ancient times, a treaty was made: the shifters would leave our kind alone as long as we let the humans be. Some demons moved to other dimensions, where they could wreak havoc without being policed; some demons stayed and blended in with society; however, a certain type of demon had become addicted to human blood. This is the type of demon you call vampires.'

Mark held my gaze and Seth leaned closer, intrigued by the story of their origin.

'Nowadays, shifters mainly deal with vampires, but you still have the ability to detect any demon that's nearby, which is why Mark has had a problem with me from day one. He may not have realised what I was, but the wolf in him did. I just didn't put it together at first, as I couldn't sense his shifter side.'

Mark nodded his head in realisation, and for once he wasn't being a pain.

I gave them a moment to digest what I had just told them before I continued. 'The reason why I wanted you and Seth here is because, for obvious reasons, I can't go into the wolves' territory and ask for help, as they are likely to tear me to pieces before asking any questions.'

Mark let out a grunting laugh.

I shook my head. 'Anyway, I was wondering if you guys wouldn't mind asking them for help – to have them check the house and see if they can detect anything out of the ordinary that we may have missed.' I gave Mark a look. 'And while you're at it, tell them to have a good sniff at you. Maybe they can detect something that explains why you can't shift.'

Mark gave me a nod and gestured to Seth to come with

him. He walked towards the door and Leah threw her keys to him, but before he opened it, he hesitated and gazed back at her.

'It's okay, Mark. Jax won't hurt me,' Leah told him with a reassuring smile.

It made me happy to hear Leah say that. It meant that she trusted me enough to be alone with me again, and maybe eventually she would forgive me for not telling them what I was.

While we waited to hear back from Mark and Seth, we spent some time flipping through books, hoping to find any explanation of what could have happened or why.

I glanced over at Leah. 'When you tried to find Cassie, what spell did you use? Map and pendulum?'

'Yeah, why?' she replied with a frown.

'Well, just because you couldn't find her doesn't mean she isn't nearby.'

'I'm really not following.'

'There are several dimensions linked to this one, or someone may have put a blocking spell on her. Maybe we can try to find a more powerful spell to use.'

Leah nodded at me but continued to skim through the book she was holding. After a few moments she slammed the book down on the table. 'This is useless. We don't even know what we're looking for.'

She needed a break. I could probably do with one too. Not knowing whether Cassie was alive or not had us all stressed. 'Leah, there's something I want to show you. Why don't we go outside?'

She peered through the window with a frown, probably questioning my sanity. Dark clouds covered the sky and it looked like it could start raining at any moment, but she grabbed her coat and followed me out.

Before I even had a chance to say anything, she saw her tree. 'I can't believe it's still growing, and it looks like there are apples on it. That's amazing.' Leah walked up to the tree and touched the fruit. After a while, she spoke up. 'It's infused with your magic as well. I can tell you've been nurturing it.'

'I didn't have much else to concentrate on.'

Her smile turned into a straight line, and she crossed her arms.

Why did I say that? I stared at the ground, desperate to come up with something to say to fill the awkward silence.

A few drops of water fell from the sky. Leah cleared her throat. 'Maybe we should head inside before we get soaked.'

I followed her back into the house. After she'd taken her coat off, she turned towards me and opened her mouth to say something. At that moment Mark walked through the front door.

'Witch magic,' he said as he sat down on the sofa and looked defeated.

Leah spoke up. 'What do you mean, witch magic?'

'The wolves said they could smell witch magic all over me.'

My bad feelings started to multiply. 'Have they been able

to smell it on you before?' It could be because of the enchantment, but something was telling me it wasn't.

He gave me a grunt. 'No. Before, I smelled normal; this time they could smell it on me before I even had a chance to ask them.'

Leah glanced around 'Where's Seth?'

'He went with the other wolves to check out our house.'

I was lost in thought for a moment, then I had an idea. 'Leah, remember when I asked you to feel mine and Cassie's energies and then the energy of the house?'

She nodded. 'Yeah.'

'Maybe you can try to do the same with Mark. If he smells of witch magic, maybe you can pick something up and compare it to the energy of the house. That way we'll know for sure whether they're related.'

'Okay. It's worth a shot.'

She walked up to Mark, who gave her a nod and let his arms fall to his sides. She closed her eyes and placed her hands in front of her. Mark followed them with his gaze but remained still. After a few minutes Leah started talking. 'It feels like something's blocked. I can't get a proper read. It feels like there's a wall of power I can't get through.' She closed her eyes again and moved her hands around Mark. 'The wall has a familiar feel to it, but I can't place it.'

I'd just opened my mouth to ask some more questions when both Mark and Leah's phones went off.

Leah went to check her phone. 'It's Seth. The wolves had a sniff around; they could smell some witch magic around the house but couldn't find anything else that seemed out of place and no trace of Cassie. Also Abigail is back home wondering where we are. I guess we'd better head home.'

Mark gave me a grunt and walked out of the door. Leah lingered.

'I'm sorry. I'm sure we'll find her. I'll come by tomorrow with an update.' She gave me a hug, which caught me by surprise. 'I'm sorry I doubted you.' She looked up at me with watery eyes. 'We should have heard you out. It's just … this is all new to us and it's hard to know what to believe, but I trust you now.'

A warm feeling in my chest erupted and worked its way through my body. I blinked a few times, trying to keep my eyes from tearing up. It was the most heartfelt apology I had ever heard.

I nodded and gave her a smile. 'It's okay. I'm sorry too.'

Connecting With Cassie

For the rest of the day, I didn't know what to do. I walked around the house, then went back to the books. Failing to find anything useful, I got up and walked around again. I felt so powerless. This was so much worse than when I'd had to stay away from Cassie. At least then I knew she was alright. Now I didn't know anything.

I turned into a crow and flew around for a while. It usually helped to calm me down and to sort out my thoughts and feelings. Should I go and see Freya? No – she'd told me that she couldn't help. Should I tell Nick what was going on? I decided against it. I told myself it was because I didn't want to waste time, but in reality, I didn't want to admit to Nick that I had failed. Besides, it was my mess to clean up.

I headed back home when the sun came up. Knowing I

wouldn't be able to sleep, I slumped down on the sofa. Where could Cassie be? Leah hadn't been able to locate her, and I couldn't feel her energy. The wolves hadn't found any traces of her leaving the house, so she was either still in the house somewhere concealed in a cloaking spell or someone had transported her to another dimension. But who was powerful enough to do that and why? Was it the same being that had placed the enchantment?

The doorbell interrupted my thoughts. I checked the time. It was only 9 a.m. Before I had a chance to open the door, Leah busted in. 'Abigail knows something.'

I wasn't following. Leah must have seen my confused look, as she started to elaborate. 'At dinner, Abigail said Cassie had decided to go away to a health retreat for a few days, but we both know Cassie would have told me about it if she was considering it.'

Leah walked into the living room and slammed her book down on the table. 'She said Cassie had told her she'd been feeling suicidal over the whole break-up with you but didn't want to bother us about it, so she talked to Abigail instead. It's bollocks. Why would Abigail say something like that unless she's involved?'

Even though I knew it wasn't true, my heart ached for Cassie and for the pain I'd caused her. I followed Leah into the living room, but I wasn't able to get a word in before she continued talking.

'I had another feel of the energies around the house. They've shifted. It felt like there's some new energy mixed with it now, similar to the energy I felt yesterday around Mark. I think Abigail did something to Mark. Maybe Cassie found out and that's why she's missing.' Leah gave me an annoyed stare. 'Why aren't you more freaked out?'

I shrugged. 'We may not know exactly what we're up against or where Cassie is, but at least we have a person of interest that probably knows what's going on. Maybe with a bit of persuasion she'll talk.'

Leah took a step back. 'Your eyes just changed colour.'

I collected myself. 'Sorry, I was just thinking—'

Leah interrupted me. 'I don't think I want to know what you were thinking.'

She was probably right; it had become quite graphic. If I had Abigail in my grasp, I would inflict more and more pain on her until she told us where Cassie was. I shook away the image and took a deep breath to get the demon inside me under control. 'So, what's the plan of action?'

Leah flipped through the pages of her book. 'I've been thinking, you and Cassie have a special connection. I may be able to use that.'

She reached the page she was looking for and showed it to me. It wasn't quite a location spell, which I'd thought it would be, but a spell about strengthening connections and connecting to each other's minds. How would that help us rescue Cassie?

'What do you think?' Leah looked at me with raised eyebrows.

I hesitated. 'I don't know. But I'll try anything to get

Cassie back.'

She gave me a smile. 'I thought you'd say that. I've brought the ingredients.'

Leah spent some time preparing the spell – or rather, potion. When she was done, she handed me a small vial with a dark green liquid in it and told me to drink it, close my eyes and concentrate on Cassie.

At first, nothing happened. A ringing started in my head, and I opened my eyes. There was nothing but darkness. I closed my eyes again and sent out my energies. They bounced back at me like a massive echo. A moment later, a thin thread of light appeared in the darkness. I picked it up and sensed Cassie's energy. I followed the thread and entered a white room. As I did so, the ringing stopped and everything became quiet. Cassie's energy engulfed me. She had to be here somewhere. The room looked strange. It didn't have any walls but reminded me of a huge white cloud. I continued to walk, but it didn't feel like I was getting anywhere. I started to doubt myself, and that's when I saw her. Cassie was sitting on a bench in the middle of the white room.

I ran towards her. When she saw me, a smile appeared on her face, but it faded as I got closer. She pulled herself up into a tense position. I refrained from giving her a hug and let my arms fall to my sides. 'I can't believe it worked.'

Cassie raised her eyebrows. 'What worked?'

'Leah did a spell. We were trying to find you, but it's like you've vanished. What happened?'

Cassie's body relaxed at the mention of Leah. 'The night

I got taken, I heard voices in the house I didn't recognise. They were chanting something. I followed the voices into Mark and Seth's room. I couldn't understand why they hadn't woken up. The voices were so loud. A moment later, everything went black.'

That was probably the reason why Mark couldn't shift. Someone had cast a spell on him. I shook my head and pushed my thoughts aside. It didn't matter right now; all that did was getting Cassie back. 'Do you know where you are?'

'No. Everything around me is dark. I think I'm in a room, but there's no windows or doors.' She took a deep breath. 'I'm scared, Jax.'

I took her in my arms and held her, relieved to finally be able to feel her and talk to her again. 'Don't worry. Leah and I will find a way to get you back. I won't stop looking until I find you.'

Cassie shook her head. 'I'm sorry, Jax.' It sounded like she was about to say something else, but I put a finger over her lips.

'We'll talk about it later, when you're safe. Let's concentrate on getting you home first.' Cassie nodded. 'Neither me nor Leah can sense you. Do you know if you've left the house?'

Cassie bit her lip. 'You think I'm still in the house? How is that possible?'

'That's what we're trying to figure out. We think you're either in a different dimension or someone put a cloaking spell on you. Do you remember anything?'

Cassie became thoughtful.

I grabbed hold of her shoulders as something pulled at me. It felt like I was attached to a rope that was being hauled back. I fought it, but in the end, I lost and fell backwards into darkness.

HIDDEN DOORWAYS

'Dammit, Jax, Wake up. Don't do this to me.'

I opened my eyes but struggled to see. A dark haze lingered in my vision. After blinking a few times, I realised I was lying on the floor with Leah sitting on top of me, her hands over my chest. What was going on?

'Thank god, you're awake.' Leah looked at me, relief written all over her face. 'Your heart stopped. What happened? Did you talk to Cassie?'

I collected myself and explained everything that had happened. Leah listened attentively, but when I got to the end, she seemed disappointed. She let out a sigh. 'So we still don't know where she is?'

I gave her a small smile. 'But at least we know she's alive.'

A moment of silence followed. I guessed we were trying

to come up with a plan of action.

My head jerked up. 'Leah, does your house have a basement? Or an attic? Or is there a door that's always been locked that you were never allowed into?'

Leah looked at me with a frown. 'What are you saying?'

'Well, the wolves couldn't find any trace of foul play around the house, so Cassie is unlikely to have been dragged away, as I'm pretty sure they would have picked up on that. It almost makes sense if she's still somewhere inside the house.'

Leah sent a message to Mark. A moment later, her phone vibrated. 'Abigail has gone out. Mark doesn't know when she'll be back, but maybe we can go to the house and have a look.'

Leah offered to drive us back, but I was too impatient. 'Would you mind if I teleport us over?'

She cocked her head. 'You can do that?'

I smirked. 'Yeah. Just grab my hand and close your eyes.'

She did what I said and within a second, we were outside the house. I hadn't even bothered hiding my ability this time. Someone had Cassie, so I may as well show them what they were dealing with.

Leah stared at the house. 'This is so cool.' She turned back to face me. 'But if you can teleport, why can't you just teleport to Cassie?'

I took a deep breath, hopelessness filling my heart. 'If only it was that simple, but I can't teleport if I don't know where I'm going.'

Leah gave me a sad look. 'I'm sorry.'

We walked into the house and were greeted by Mark. 'That was fast.' He seemed surprised but didn't elaborate. 'I don't know how long Abigail will be out for. I think she went to the shops, so we'd better make this quick. What's the plan?'

He looked at me, but Leah answered before I had a chance to even say a word. 'Jax thinks Cassie may still be somewhere in the house, or at least that she didn't leave the house the normal way.'

Mark agreed. 'Yeah. I think the other wolves would have picked up on her scent if she had. But where could she be?'

This time I answered. 'We know there's strong witch magic at play, so maybe there's a clue somewhere in this house as to where she may be. How about we split up? Mark, maybe use your senses and see if you can smell anything that's out of place.'

Mark gave me a stare and opened his mouth. I cut him off. 'That isn't me,' I added with a grin.

He grunted and smiled. It surprised me that he hadn't slammed my head into something yet. I started to gain respect for him. Maybe he felt the same about me.

'Leah, see if you can feel any energies that seem out of the ordinary. I'll do the same, but you'll probably have more luck than me, as I'm not as in tune with witch magic as you are.'

When I'd finished giving instructions, both Leah and Mark walked off. I closed my eyes and concentrated. The weird energy I had felt around the bedrooms yesterday had almost disappeared. But some sort of energy was still lingering. I walked around trying to locate it and stopped outside Abigail's bedroom. The energy originated from inside her room. I was sure of it. I felt the handle, but the door was locked. I was thinking about trying to unlock it when Leah shouted from downstairs. I ran towards the sound and almost ran into Mark by the stairs leading down to the basement.

'What is it?' I asked with my heart in my throat.

Leah was standing by a brick wall in the basement. She moved her hands back and forth in front of it. 'There's something here.'

I moved over to where she was standing, trying to get a better feel of the energies. Now that she'd pointed it out, I could detect a small amount of foreign energy. It wasn't the type of energy used in a spell, but it was similar to what I felt when I went through a portal to another dimension.

'I think there's a portal here,' I said, pointing at the wall.

Mark and Leah shot me a look. 'A portal? Like a doorway to somewhere else?'

I nodded. 'I have no clue where this portal leads, though, and I don't know how to activate it.'

Leah shook her head. 'You're saying that there's a doorway to somewhere else in our house that we haven't noticed while growing up here?'

'Yeah, but how often did you go down to the basement actually looking for something out of the ordinary?'

'He's got a point,' Mark said.

Leah crossed her arms. 'What's the plan? I guess we're assuming Cassie will be on the other side of this door?'

'Maybe. I don't know. There's something going on in Abigail's room too. But her door is locked, so I couldn't make out what it was.'

The front door closed. We froze and stared at each other in silence.

'Seth's still with the wolves,' Mark said.

'What do we do now?' I whispered. 'I doubt Abigail would be pleased to see me here or that you guys are snooping around.'

Leah met my gaze. 'Jax, can you teleport me and you out of here? Mark, just pretend you're looking for a light bulb or something.'

Both me and Mark nodded before I grabbed Leah and teleported us back to my house. I had been so caught up in the moment that I hadn't even considered whether it would work or not. I guess the enchantment didn't interfere with my abilities after all.

Leah let go of my hand and smiled widely. 'I could get used to this. Does Cassie know you can do this?'

I thought back to the few times I had teleported with her. 'Yeah, she does.'

Leah let out a sigh. 'I guess I better go. I'll keep you updated.'

She headed to the door. I called after her. 'Leah?'

She turned around. 'Yeah?'

'Let me know if you manage to check out Abigail's room

or the basement a bit more.'

Leah nodded. 'Okay, I'll try, but it may be hard with Abigail around.'

After she had gone, I went back to the books. Freya had told me to listen to my heart. Leah's comment about teleporting to Cassie had got me thinking. Maybe it would be possible to teleport to Cassie with the help of magic. A plan formed in my head. I wasn't sure it would work, but it was worth a try. I spent some time locating all the summoning and connecting spells I could find. I was worried it would be too much to ask of Leah, but having seen her magic grow, I felt confident she could pull it off.

'We'll get you back,' I whispered under my breath and wished with all my being that I was right.

I went to stretch my wings and think over the idea and how best to present it to Leah.

Guided By My Heart

Leah came to the house the next day. I was eager to share my plan, so before she even had a chance to say anything but good morning, I started talking. 'I think I know how we can get to Cassie.'

'Really? How?' Leah sounded hopeful, but at the same time she looked a bit sceptical.

I gestured for her to follow me into the living room and approached the table where I had left all the books I had picked out the day before. I showed her several pages from different books. 'Maybe you can try to send me to Cassie, almost like a reverse summoning spell.'

Leah glanced at all the books and notes with raised eyebrows. 'None of these spells seems to show you how to do that. And there's nothing in my book either.' Her shoulders sagged in defeat.

I put my hand on her shoulder. 'You can make one up. All these spells were once created by someone. Maybe if we use the base from a lost and found spell, mix it with the potion you did to connect me with Cassie yesterday and add the summoning part of this spell.' I pointed towards a book so she could check out which spell I was talking about.

Leah shook her head. 'I don't know. I've never created my own spell before.'

I gave her an encouraging smile. 'I feel in my heart that this will work, and Freya told me to listen to my heart.'

Leah raised an eyebrow. 'Who's Freya?'

'She's an old friend of mine. She's never been wrong.' I didn't tell Leah that Freya never completely made sense either, but it wasn't important. We needed to get Cassie back, and this was the best way of figuring out how. I had faith. It even surprised me how confident I was that this was going to work.

I conjured a notepad and handed it to Leah. 'Here, just give it a go, for Cassie's sake.'

Leah looked at the notepad and then up at me before she took it from me. 'You never fail to amaze me.' She hesitated. 'What if I can't do it? What if it backfires like last time?'

'It didn't backfire last time. You got me to Cassie.'

'But it almost killed you.'

'But it didn't.' And even if it had, it would have been worth it, though I didn't tell Leah that. Instead I gave her an encouraging nod and peered into her eyes. 'I believe in you.'

She nodded and studied the books more closely, filling her notepad with notes. I wanted to stand over her shoulder to hurry her up, but I knew it would be a bad idea and probably stress her out. No one likes to have people watching their every move.

To keep myself busy, I walked into the kitchen and started cooking a massive breakfast; eggs, bacon, sausages, hash browns, baked beans. When I was done, I brought food over to the dining table and asked Leah to join me.

She laughed when she saw the food. 'Did you expect to feed an army?' I gave her a look that said she was being silly and told her to dig in as I did the same.

After we had eaten, I asked Leah how the spell was coming along. 'I think I've almost figured it out, but we need something to draw energy from.'

'What about the apples from your tree?'

She smiled. 'That's a great idea. Apples stand for love and protection, which is what we need.' She added some notes to the notepad. 'Okay, I think I have it. It may not work, but I guess it's worth a try. I need to make a potion. You need to join me in the circle and think of Cassie the whole time. Fingers crossed it will get you to her. There's only a small problem. I have no idea how to get you back.'

A lightness appeared in my chest at the thought of finally getting Cassie back. It was the only thing that mattered. 'I don't care. Besides, I can probably just teleport back. As long as I can get to Cassie, I'm willing to try.'

Leah gave me a nod. 'I need to go and get some

ingredients, unless you already have them in the house or can conjure them up?'

I shook my head. 'It has to be natural. Conjuring them wouldn't work.'

Leah walked out of the door and left me alone with my thoughts. A while later she returned and dropped the bag of ingredients on the kitchen counter.

I paced the room, trying my best not to disturb her as she sorted out the potion.

She looked up from what she was doing. 'How about you sit down? You're stressing me out.'

'Sorry.' I slumped down on the sofa and played with the arm rest. It felt like an eternity before Leah finished.

'I'm ready when you are,' I said as I jumped up from the sofa.

Leah rolled her eyes but remained quiet. She grabbed some candles and salt. 'Where do you want me to place the circle?'

In my excited state I had forgotten all about that. I made some furniture disappear to make space. Leah watched me with big eyes.

'It has to be nice to be you.' I knew she was referring to my abilities, and I had to agree that they were rather handy; however, my life hadn't really been a bed of roses.

Leah placed everything in the middle of the room. 'Come and sit next to me so I can make the circle.'

I joined her. She picked up the salt and poured it as she walked in a circle around us. She called the elements one by one. They responded immediately. It smelled of wet ground. My skin warmed like the sun was shining on it, and the wind blew in my hair. It was magical. I had never been inside a circle before.

She picked up the potion. It had the same dark green colour as the one I had drunk before. Leah handed it to me. 'I've altered it slightly. Hopefully this time it won't stop your heart.'

'You've done all you can. I trust you. Besides, it's worth the risk,' I said before downing the liquid in one gulp.

She picked up the apple and cut it in half. 'Now close your eyes and think of Cassie.' She started chanting. Her words became background noise as I thought of Cassie and all the moments we'd shared together.

I wasn't sure whether it had worked, but a gasp made me open my eyes. It was pitch black, but I could sense Cassie's energy. I conjured a ball of light and ran towards her. Within a minute, I had her in my arms, our bodies pressed against each other. I promised myself I was never going to let her go again. I had missed her so much, and I couldn't believe I was finally holding her again.

Before I could stop myself, I pressed my lips against hers. She placed her hand on the back of my head and deepened the kiss. My heart pounded loudly in my chest, yearning to be closer to her. The next moment, the dark room ceased to exist, and Cassie was no longer in my arms. I looked around. I was in a field. The same field I had been dreaming about – the same field where I'd lived and worked during my time at the witch village.

I tried to walk, but my legs wouldn't move. I opened my mouth, but no words came out. I had no control over my own body. It was like I was watching a memory through my own eyes, unable to do anything to change it.

A Trip To The Past

I was back in my past body watching through the eyes of a younger me. I worked for a farmer, Edmond. Freya had sent me there to get acquainted with the human world. His wife had died a few years ago and his children had moved away, so it was mutually beneficial. He knew what I was but treated me like a son. I had been warned about using my abilities and discouraged from going into the village, as it was full of witches that didn't take well to outsiders. There was also the chance someone would discover what I was.

While I was on my way to pick up a horse from a field, I ran into the most beautiful woman I had ever met. She looked like Cassie but slightly different. She had the same piercing blue eyes, but her hair was blond. She looked up at me with watery eyes and apologised for trespassing. I shrugged and asked whether she wanted to come with me to collect a horse. On the way, I told her stories, hoping it would cheer her up. It seemed to be working, and by the time we got to the horse, she was smiling. When we got back to where I had first seen her, she excused herself and walked towards the village.

The time flashed forward. It was now the next day, and I hadn't been able to stop thinking about the girl. I hadn't even asked for her name. I walked to the field where I'd first met her, doubting I would have any luck in seeing her again. However, the fates obviously had plans for me. I sprinted over to her in excitement. We sat down in the field and talked about everything. I finally learned that her name was Katie and she was a High Priestess in training. The reason she'd been in the fields the previous day was due to an argument with her parents. She had needed to get away.

Several scenes passed by of us sitting in the field talking, kissing or displaying our abilities to each other. We seemed to become closer and closer with each passing day. It amazed me how much I loved this woman. It was like she understood me and was made especially for me.

The scene changed again. The sun was setting and the field where I normally met up with Katie had been decorated with candles, giving out a warm, romantic glow. I stood in the middle of it all, watching as Katie strolled towards me. She wore a smile on her face. When she got to where I was standing, she walked over to try to give me a kiss, but I held my hand up to stop her. She took a step back, confusion displayed on her face.

I went down on one knee. 'You are the most beautiful and astonishing woman I have ever met. I would love nothing more than to have the chance to show you every day just how much I love you. You are everything to me. Without you, life doesn't seem worth living. A lifetime with you will not be enough, and I promise wherever you are, I will find you in the next life and love you again no matter what. Our love has no boundaries. You are truly the missing part of my soul. So, Katie Leah Whitelake, will you marry me and make me the happiest being in existence?'

Tears ran down Katie's face. I hoped they were happy tears. She gazed at me lovingly and nodded her head. 'Yes.'

I put the ring on her finger and when I was done, she embraced me. We had the most passionate and incredible night together and fell asleep naked in each other's arms.

The next morning, I woke up as the sun rose in the sky. I gave Katie a kiss. 'Good morning, beautiful.'

She opened her eyes and scanned the sky. 'It's morning?'

I nodded. 'Yeah. We must have fallen asleep.'

She jumped up and gathered her clothes. 'My parents will worry and wonder where I am. I'm not supposed to be out past curfew.'

I gave her a kiss and pushed her towards the village. 'Then go. Maybe they're still asleep and haven't realised you're missing.'

'I'll see you soon.' She gave me a smile and ran towards the village. That was the last time I saw her for quite some time. I spent every day waiting for her in the fields for an hour or two, but she never turned up.

One day I noticed a letter underneath a stone. It was addressed to me, so I opened it and read it.

'Dearest Jax, not a day goes by that I do not think about us and the beautiful night we shared together. However, my parents were deeply appalled when I didn't come home and again when they saw the ring on my finger. I have been forbidden to see you and promised to a respectable witch. They will not listen to reason. I fear this may be goodbye. Do not come up to the village to see me. The others will not understand. They will torture you for what you are, and I cannot stand for you to be punished for something you cannot help. I will always love you, in this life and in the next. Our love has no boundaries. Never forget that. Love Katie.'

My heart shattered. A couple of weeks ago, I was the happiest being in the world, but now my world was crumbling, and I didn't know what to do. All because of what I was. I cursed myself for ever having been born. Why did I have to be a demon? Why couldn't I have been a normal human? Or someone who was worthy of Katie's love?

When I returned to the farm that night, Edmond walked up to me. 'What happened?' I shook my head. My heart wasn't ready to talk about it. He placed his hand on my shoulder. 'I'm here for you. Let me know if there's anything I can do.'

A tear slipped down my cheek. 'Why does everyone hate me?'

He looked at me sympathetically. 'People do not hate you, but they fear what they do not know – what you are capable of. They look at you and see a demon, but they are too afraid to look into your heart.'

I gave him a hug. 'Thank you for seeing me.'

When the embrace had finished, he looked back up at me. 'Why don't you take a few days off? I can manage the farm by myself for a while.'

I agreed and went to visit Freya. I hadn't seen her for a few years, and I could do with seeing a familiar face.

When I got to Freya's, she was expecting me, which didn't surprise me. She always seemed to know when I was coming round. After I'd transformed back into my human form, she came over and embraced me. 'Do not let hate fill you with anger. Anger comes easily to your kind, and if you let it, it will destroy you. Instead, fill your heart with love and the fates will guide you.'

My initial plan was to stay with Freya for a couple of days, but it quickly turned into a week. I liked Freya's place; I had grown up there and I could be myself. No one was judging me because of what I was. Freya kept a room for me, but I hardly used it. I spent most of my time in the forest, flying around and watching as the world went by.

The forest around Freya's house was filled with supernatural beings – pixies, fairies, nymphs and other creatures that had sought refuge here. Everyone lived in peace, and the ones that didn't were banished from Freya's land.

One day when I got back to the house after one of my flying trips, Freya was sitting in her rocking chair on the porch. As I transformed into my human form, she got up and walked towards me. 'You've been avoiding life long enough. It is time for you to go back to the farm.'

'Can't I stay a bit longer?'

She shook her head. 'Fate is in motion.'

I let out a sigh. Freya took my hand and placed a necklace in it. 'This is a talisman. It will dim your energy, making it harder for anyone to sense what you are, and it will help you to control the energies inside yourself as long as you do not give in to hatred.' She gave me a hug. 'Please be safe.'

I wasn't completely sure what she meant, but it was rare that I did. Besides, I didn't want to outstay my welcome, so I gave her a kiss on the cheek and made my way back to the farm.

The sun had started to set when I arrived. I knocked on the door to Edmond's house. Usually, I would just come and go as I pleased, but because I had been away for a long time, I didn't want to startle him.

Edmond opened the door with a wide smile. 'Please come in. Dinner is waiting in the kitchen.'

I tilted my head. 'How did you know I'd be back?'

'A little bird told me. I've been looking forward to having you home all day.'

While we were having dinner, he told me what had been happening and mentioned that one of the horses had fallen ill, but he wasn't sure what was wrong with her. He asked me if I wouldn't mind going to see her after dinner.

I walked into the stable and over to the horse that was lying down. She was beautiful, mainly brown with a few white spots on her forehead and a dark brown mane. I spent some time talking to her. She seemed weak. I sent her some of my energy, visualising it healing her. I wasn't sure whether it would work, but after a couple of hours, she perked up and was able to stand.

FIGHTING FOR KATIE

The next day, even though I knew I wouldn't see Katie, I went to the place where we used to meet up. Memories of us together flooded my mind and made me miss her all the more. I blinked away some tears. Would I ever see her again? My eyes fell on the spot where I'd proposed to her. I spotted another letter underneath a stone. I bent down and picked it up. It looked a bit battered, but it was still readable. It was addressed to me. I opened the envelope to read it, and my heart stopped. The letter was from Katie. She was writing to tell me she was expecting and I was the father.

All common sense left me, and I made my way to the village. I needed to see Katie. I didn't care who I would have to fight to get to her. I knew her mother was the High Priestess and they lived in the middle of the village, so that's where I headed.

When I got to the edge, I stopped and looked around. I had never been into the village before. Edmond had told me it wasn't safe, but at the moment I couldn't care less. There were small white stone houses scattered around a gritted road. I followed the road with my eyes. It led to a grand building that seemed to be located in the middle of the village. It looked like some sort of temple. I was certain I would find Katie there.

I marched towards the temple. Several people stopped what they were doing and stared at me, whispering to each other. Did they know what I was? I touched the necklace Freya had given me. I trusted her. Maybe they weren't used to seeing strangers in their village. I took a deep breath and continued walking. I was here to find Katie; nothing else mattered.

The temple drew nearer. It had large stone pillars that supported the roof. There were several small stairs on either side of a waterfall that led up to the entrance. It was beautiful, and I could easily see myself and Katie getting married there. I walked up the steps and entered the building. The inside didn't disappoint; it was spacious and decorated sparingly, with an altar at the end of the room. Fresh flowers hung on the stone walls, which helped to brighten it up with some colour.

While I was looking around, taking it all in and daydreaming about my and Katie's wedding, I heard a low whisper. 'Jax, what are you doing here?'

I turned around and my heart sped up. Before I could collect myself, I ran towards Katie. I picked her up in a warm embrace and spun her around in my arms. 'I've missed you so much. I'll never let you go again.'

The embrace was cut short as someone cleared their throat. I looked up and saw a young man with blond hair and intelligent green eyes. He held his hand out. 'I'm Henry, Katie's fiancé.'

I stared at him and the hand he was holding out for me, then I looked back at Katie. How could she betray me like this? I'd thought what we had was special. I'd thought she would always love me – she'd even said so herself. I could feel my anger building up.

Katie excused herself and pulled me to the side so Henry couldn't hear us. 'Jax, calm down. I love you. Henry is the man my parents want me to marry. I have no feelings towards him and I don't want to marry him.'

My body relaxed. She always seemed to know what to say to me. I glanced over her shoulder and gave Henry another look. What made him so special? I turned back to Katie. 'How about we just run away?' I said hopefully. I knew she would never agree to it.

She shook her head. 'Jax, you know I can't. I have a duty of care to my people. I can't leave them.'

I gave her a smile. 'I wish you would reconsider, but I guess I'll just have to fight Henry for your hand and persuade your parents that I'm the only man for you.' I placed my hand on her stomach. 'We three belong together, and I'm not going to let anyone keep us apart.'

She glanced towards the entrance. 'I guess you can start now.'

I followed her gaze and saw two middle-aged people walk into the building. By the attire they wore, it was easy to tell they were the High Priestess and the Priest. But what gave them away as Katie's parents was the resemblance. Katie had her mother's cheekbones and her father's nose.

'Meet Elise and Ronald, my parents,' Katie whispered to me.

They greeted Henry before proceeding to where we stood. 'Katie, what is going on? Who is this?' I could hear the resentment in her mother's voice.

I let go of Katie and took a step towards Elise. 'I'm here to fight for your daughter.'

Both her parents stared at me for a moment before Elise spoke up. 'How dare you! She is to be married to Henry, not some outsider that doesn't belong here. She has a reputation to uphold. Our lineage cannot be tainted by someone who isn't a witch.'

My eyes flashed red in anger, but I quickly calmed myself down.

Katie's parents took a step back. 'How can you love something like him? He's a d—' Elise glanced over at Henry. 'He's an abomination that doesn't belong here.'

Katie looked lovingly at me. 'I guess we will be a family of abominations together.'

Katie's parents looked at their daughter, confused, and

then looked at me with resentment. 'Family? Do not tell me you are with child,' Elise said.

At this point, Henry walked up to Katie. 'The wedding is off. I'm not marrying someone who's tainted with someone else's child.'

I scanned Katie's face to see her reaction as Henry walked away. She didn't seem bothered at all. I guessed she had told me the truth.

Elise shook her head and mumbled to herself before she spoke up. 'What do you see in him? He's evil. A demon. They can't be trusted.'

Katie gazed up at her mother. 'You're wrong. I see how hard Jax is fighting his nature, fighting to be good even though everything is against him. He didn't choose to be a demon, so why judge him for what he cannot help? Instead, you should judge him by what he does and what is in his heart. I love him and I want to spend the rest of my life with him.'

Elise crossed her arms. 'You can't be serious. Think about your reputation.'

Katie hesitated. 'If you don't let me be with him, I will run away. Imagine what that will do to your precious reputation.'

Elise shook her head. 'You can't honestly be considering that? This baby you're carrying is an abomination. It should not be allowed to be born.'

Katie hugged her stomach. 'If you do anything to this baby, I will curse you.'

I took a step towards Elise. 'And if you do anything to either of them, I will destroy this village.'

Elise studied me carefully. 'We could banish him,' Ronald said behind us.

Elise gave him a stare. 'And risk the wrath of a demon upon our village?'

I glanced at Elise. 'If you let us be together, I will obey your rules. Katie and our family is the only thing that matters to me. I am not a danger to you or your village unless you make an enemy of me.'

Elise became quiet and walked around me in a circle. 'His energy is weak. I don't think anyone would realise what he is.'

'If he's weak, why can't we get rid of him?' Ronald asked.

Elise let out a sigh. 'I didn't say he's weak. I said his energy is. I have no doubt he's powerful enough to carry out his threats.'

I ran my hand through my hair and cleared my throat. 'I'm standing right here.'

Elise cast me a look. 'How will we know you will honour your word?'

'I know right from wrong, and I care about people. I've been living in this village peacefully for several years. Besides, I love your daughter.'

Katie placed a hand on my shoulder. 'And I love him.'

Elise let out a deep breath. 'I guess we have no other choice but to agree. But there will be rules, and if you break any of them, we will banish you and you will never see Katie again. Now get out of the temple before it becomes more tainted than it already is.'

I gave Katie a smile before turning to her mother. It felt like we had won this battle. 'As long as I get to marry Katie and stay by her side, I agree.'

Living In The Village

After everything had been agreed and sorted, Katie and I moved into our first house a few days later. The house wasn't connected to the temple, as they wouldn't let me live there because of what I was. They were afraid I would kill them all in their sleep or taint the temple with my evil presence. Instead, it was a respectable distance away. It was a small white stone house, the same as all the others that surrounded us. It had a kitchen, a living room and a bedroom. Everything we needed – and the best part, it had Katie in it.

The weeks went by. I wasn't allowed to join any ceremonies – I wasn't even allowed in the temple – but I watched from afar. Katie was a powerful witch, but I'd never realised just how powerful her family was. The affinity for the elements had been passed down from generation to generation. They were the only ones in the village that could command all the elements.

Katie usually spent her days in the temple, so I would go over to Edmond and help out on the farm. On some days when Edmond didn't need me, I would pretend to go over there, but as soon as I got outside the village, I would turn into a crow and fly back to watch Katie work from afar. I wasn't supposed to use my powers, but no one other than Katie and Edmond knew I could turn into a crow. Katie had spotted me watching her on a few occasions. She wasn't pleased about it, but I think she was mainly worried for my safety. I told her I would be careful, and she seemed to leave the argument to rest.

A few weeks later, when Katie came home from work, she seemed annoyed. I wasn't sure why or whether it was something I had done. I embraced her with a hug and a kiss.

'What's wrong?' I asked carefully. Her body wasn't showing any signs of the pregnancy yet, but her hormones had been all over the place, and she had been experiencing major mood swings, so I trod carefully so as not to upset her any more than she already was.

'They won't let us have the wedding in the temple.' I could hear her voice breaking. I wasn't too bothered about where we got married, but I wanted her to be happy, and she had always dreamed about a wedding in the temple.

'It's okay. We'll find a way,' I said, trying to soothe her, but she wasn't having it.

'How can we have a wedding in the temple when you

aren't allowed to enter it?' she said angrily. However, she had just sparked an idea in my head. I wasn't allowed to go inside the temple, but they hadn't said anything about not being allowed to be close to it.

'How about we have the wedding right outside the temple?' I asked.

'What do you mean?' She seemed a bit confused, like she wasn't really following what I was saying. I explained it to her in more detail. I would be waiting at the bottom of the stairs, and she would get ready in the temple and walk down the stairs to meet me.

She shook her head. 'They will never agree to it.'

I shrugged. 'It can't hurt to ask. Technically we won't be breaking any of the rules.'

She hesitated. 'I don't know.'

'Why don't you go and ask them? No harm in that.'

She nodded and walked out of the door.

A few hours later, Katie came home with a big smile on her face. 'It took a bit of persuasion and a meeting with the elders, but they agreed. We will get married by the temple,' she said excitedly.

I gave her a big kiss. 'That's lovely news.'

'I'd better start planning. I want to get married before I'm the size of a cow.' She walked into the living room.

'You would still be beautiful,' I called after her.

She turned around and gave me a smile before grabbing some paper and muttering to herself about what needed to be done and who needed to be contacted. I was happy to see her so excited. I could easily have conjured everything she wanted, but as I wasn't allowed to use my powers, I didn't even remind her about it.

A month later, the day both me and Katie had been waiting for arrived. I couldn't believe it was happening. Today Katie would become my wife. It was a small ceremony – at least, in the scheme of things. Katie's parents didn't want to broadcast the fact that she was marrying a demon, even though most of the villagers had no idea what I was. They were just sceptical about Katie marrying someone who didn't belong to the village. Luckily for me, Katie didn't seem to care about that.

I stood at the bottom of the stairs leading up to the temple. Several of the villagers had gone inside to congratulate Katie and give her their blessing. Edmond had walked into the village to show his support for me. He rarely came to the village, so it meant a lot to me. Over the years that I had lived here, he had become a bit of a father figure to me.

My thoughts came to an abrupt stop as Katie walked down the stairs. She looked like an angel in her long white gown. I felt like the happiest being in the world. She had started to show, but not to the point where it was obvious she was with child unless anyone looked closely.

She joined me at the bottom of the stairs and her mother performed the handfasting ceremony. When it was all finished, we were finally husband and wife, and I couldn't have been happier.

Welcome To The World

Several weeks went by. I loved having Katie as my wife. As the birth of our daughter grew closer, I became more reluctant to leave her side.

One day, while helping Edmond repair a broken fence, my mind was preoccupied and I accidentally used too much force when hammering the wood panel. It broke into several pieces. Edmond made his way over to me and picked up the broken pieces from the ground. 'What troubles you? You haven't been acting like yourself lately.'

I scanned the area and conjured a new panel before meeting his gaze. 'It's just ... I'm worried about Katie and our baby. I keep feeling like something bad is going to happen and that I will lose them.'

Edmond gave me a reassuring smile. 'It's completely

natural to be scared.'

He handed me a nail and as we worked together on the fence, he told me a few stories of how it had been when his wife had been pregnant with their children.

'Do they ever come to visit?' I asked.

Edmond shook his head. 'I don't see them much since they moved away, but I know they are well, and that's all that matters.'

We finished fixing the fence and made our way back to the farm. Edmond placed his arm around my shoulders. 'Why don't you spend some more time with Katie? You won't have a lot of alone time after the baby arrives.'

'Are you sure?'

He smiled. 'Don't worry about me. I can manage the farm by myself.' I gave him a nod and he patted my back.

A few days went past during which I followed Katie around, watching her every move to make sure nothing happened to her. One afternoon, she looked up to the ceiling of the temple and caught me perched there. Her shoulders stiffened and a few seconds passed before she looked away and continued with her chores. Throughout the afternoon she gave me futile glares.

At the end of the day, I made my way to our home with heavy steps, knowing an argument was brewing between us. I took a deep breath and opened the door. Katie usually greeted me with a hug and a kiss, but as she walked over, she crossed her arms and stared me down. 'What do you think you're doing? What if someone sees you? They'll exile you from the village.'

I embraced her. Her tense body relaxed under my touch. 'But what if something happens to you and the baby and I'm not there?' I whispered into her ear.

She took a deep breath and rested her head on my shoulder. 'I'll be fine. It's too risky.'

'But doesn't it make you feel better knowing I'm nearby?' She nodded slowly. I gave her a kiss. 'Then it's settled. Besides, no one here knows I can turn into a crow. And the talisman will help keep my energy hidden.'

Another few weeks went by, and everything was going great. I woke up halfway through the night, Katie still sleeping soundly next to me. A feeling of unease engulfed me. Restless and unable to go back to sleep, I got up so I wouldn't disturb Katie. I walked over to the window and looked at the night sky. The stars shone brightly. If only I could go for a flight. But transforming in the village was too risky. Unable to shake the chill down my spine, I sent out my energies, but everything appeared normal. Where was this feeling coming from?

My gaze shifted to Katie and I heard her peaceful snoring. I settled myself down on a chair and let the sound soothe me. I must have fallen asleep, because the next thing I knew, it was morning and Katie was getting ready for her day.

'How about we just stay home?' I asked as she came back into the bedroom.

She shook her head. 'I can't. I have so much I need to sort out before the baby comes.'

I grabbed her hand and looked into her eyes. 'For me?' I pleaded.

She moved her hand away. 'I'm the High Priestess to be. I can't just ignore my duties when I feel like it.'

I positioned myself by the door when she was ready to leave. 'I can't let you leave.'

She took a deep breath. 'Jax, what is going on? You're acting weird.'

'I'm worried. I have a feeling something bad is going to happen today.'

'You've had a feeling something bad is going to happen for the last month. I'll be fine.' She gave me a kiss and left the house.

I stared after her until she disappeared from my view before rushing out of the village so I could turn into a crow and follow her around.

My senses were on high alert, but when it reached midday and nothing out of the ordinary had happened, I relaxed. Maybe I had overreacted? Unable to ignore the feeling in my gut, I continued to watch Katie carefully. She was in the last stages of the pregnancy, but the baby wasn't due for another week or so. She sat down on a chair to rest. It wasn't uncommon that she needed to have a break several times a day, but what caught my attention was the blood that had gathered on the chair.

Katie looked around, panic written all over her face. 'Jax, I need you.' Her voice came out as a whisper.

Within a second, I was by her side in my human form. I

grabbed her and teleported her to the healing centre. No one seemed to pay us any attention, so I started to shout. It didn't take long for someone to come to our aid after that, and as soon as they realised it was their High Priestess in training, more healers came to our aid. They took Katie from my arms and rushed down the corridor with her. I started to follow but was told to stay. They rounded a corner and disappeared from view. I paced the corridor, not sure what to do with myself. I thought about disobeying them, but the thought of being banished and having Katie and our baby taken from me was too much of a risk.

I stopped a healer walking past me. 'What's happening? Is Katie okay?' She glanced up at me without saying a word before hurrying away. The same thing happened every time I tried to ask someone what was going on.

Usually I wasn't bothered about being ignored. I'd grown accustomed to it during my time in the village, but I had no way of knowing how Katie was doing. I gave up and slumped down on a chair. A moment later, Katie's parents arrived. I was too distraught to show any courtesy towards them. I caught their gaze, but they looked away. A healer approached them and led them down the corridor. No doubt to the room Katie was in. Why was I not allowed to see her?

After what felt like hours, someone approached me. They cleared their throat, but when I looked up, they avoided eye contact. 'Katie has lost a lot of blood, and she is about to go into labour. She will not calm down and keeps asking for you.' The healer's lip curled before she turned away without another word.

I jumped out of the chair and followed her. This time when I got to the corridor, no one stopped me. I let out a breath of relief and rubbed my face.

I stepped into the room with shaky legs and a heavy heart, unsure what to expect. My eyes swept across the room. People were running around doing healing spells and preparing for the delivery of the baby. Katie's parents were seated by the wall. Her mother opened her mouth, but as my eyes found Katie's, everything else faded away. My throat constricted as I took in her appearance. She looked fragile, her face pale. It shocked me. She had always been filled with strength and determination.

Katie mustered up a smile that didn't reach her eyes. The next moment, I stood by her side. I placed a kiss on her forehead and the tension eased out of her. I took her hand in mine and told her everything would be okay.

A healer walked up to where I was standing. 'I'm not sure you'll be able to survive the labour. You have lost a lot of blood, but if we don't get the baby out now, you'll die,' she said to Katie, paying me little attention.

A numbness spread in my chest. I couldn't believe this was happening. I glanced down at Katie, tears burning in my eyes. I had expected her to look scared, but her face remained soft. Only her glossy eyes displayed how she was feeling. She met my gaze and a smile appeared on her face. 'Fate works in mysterious ways, and I have made peace with mine. There is nothing I would want more than to hold our baby girl and watch her grow up. But I can't sacrifice her life for the small possibility it may save mine.'

I nodded as tears fell down my face.

'Promise me you'll look after her,' Katie said as she reached up to wipe my tears away.

I took a deep breath to steady my emotions. 'You are my everything, and this baby is part of you – part of us. I will fight to the end of time to keep her safe.'

She squeezed my hand as silent tears trickled down her face. 'I love you,' she whispered in a trembling voice. A flicker of pain crossed her face. I'd opened my mouth to reply when someone cleared their throat. Katie pulled herself together, looking towards the sound. I followed her gaze, only now remembering that we weren't alone in the room.

'You need to leave now,' the healer told me. My gaze found Katie's again, her eyes wide.

'No. I'm not leaving,' I said sternly without taking my eyes off Katie. I knew she needed me.

'It doesn't work that way. You need to leave.' The healer took a step towards me. Anger and despair filled me, and I stared at the healer, willing my eyes to turn red.

'I'm staying.'

The healer lifted her hands in the air in front of her and backed away, mumbling something to herself. I turned my attention back to Katie.

The next few hours were filled with screams and shouts. I never let go of Katie's hand. I tried to give her my strength, visualising my energy healing her. I hated seeing her like this.

Eventually we heard the scream of our baby. Our daughter had finally been born. I gazed down at Katie. She looked even worse than before. Why couldn't I save her like I had the horse? Her skin was translucent, and if I hadn't been aware of her breathing, I would have thought she was dead already.

The healer brought the baby over so Katie could see her. She smiled weakly at the baby and then looked up at me. 'We made this.' She seemed so proud. 'I love you – always. I will find you in my next life. Our love has no boundaries. Even the universe cannot break our love for each other.' She gave me a kiss as the healer took the baby away to be attended to. 'Until we meet again,' she whispered to me before she took her last breath.

My legs stopped working and I fell to the floor. My heart shattered into a million pieces. I was in agony. Every part of me screamed. I was ready to give up, to take my life just so I wouldn't have to live without her. But then I remembered my promise to her. I had something to live for. Katie had sacrificed herself for our baby. Our beautiful baby girl. I named her Layla Fey Whitelake, because even in Katie's darkest moment, she'd still had faith. And had it not been for Freya, I would never have realised Katie was pregnant, and I would never have gone into the village to fight for her.

I spent the next hour by Katie's side, promising her I would find her again and tell her about everything when I did. I was reluctant to leave her body, but I needed to go and see our baby and make sure she was okay.

Because of everything that had happened, they wouldn't

let me leave the healing centre with Layla Fey. She was still too weak and needed constant care, so I spent all my time there, making sure she was properly taken care of. I could tell my presence made the healers uncomfortable, but I couldn't push myself to leave her. She was my life now.

Time To Say Goodbye

Two days later, the ceremony for Katie's passing was underway. Because it had to be held in the temple, I wasn't sure whether I'd be allowed to attend. I had begged Katie's parents to make an exception to allow me to say a proper goodbye. They'd reluctantly agreed to discuss it with the elders.

On the morning of the ceremony, I paced around the healing ward with Layla Fey in my arms, awaiting the verdict. Elise, Katie's mother, walked up to me. I bowed my head to show her respect.

'It has been decided. You will be allowed to attend the temple this one time.'

'Thank you,' I said with a grateful smile.

Elise stared at me with a pinched expression. 'It's what

Katie would have wanted.' She turned on her heel.

I glanced down at Layla Fey in my arms. 'We get to say goodbye to Mummy.' She made a cooing sound which warmed my heart. I was going to make sure she knew exactly how precious and special her mother was. The sound of someone approaching made me look up.

Elise cocked her head and gazed into my eyes with a hard smile on her face. 'Unfortunately, the baby will have to stay here. She's not strong enough to leave the healing ward yet.' She turned and walked away again.

My smile faded and my body became heavy. I put Layla Fey down in a cot and rubbed the back of my neck. I didn't want to leave her, but I needed to say my goodbyes to Katie. I watched Layla Fey sleep for a while before leaving her in the hands of the healers to attend the funeral.

The funeral of a witch was more of a departure ritual, as they believed death was part of life and should be celebrated. I wasn't sure what to expect, as no one had explained properly what it entailed. They had told me to attend quietly, keep a low profile and not draw any attention to myself. After all, I should be happy they'd even allowed me into the temple.

I turned up to the temple early as requested, before anyone else had arrived. I stopped in front of the stairs that led up to the entrance and took a ceremonial bath in the waterfall. Having followed Katie around, I'd learned that was the correct way to enter the temple before a ceremony. I wanted to adhere to their traditions as a way of cherishing

Katie. The bath was supposed to cleanse you and remove negative energy so it couldn't interfere with the rituals that were being performed.

After the bath, I walked up the stairs and entered the temple. White roses hung from the walls, and candles marked a path to the altar. In front of the altar was a large stone table on which Katie's body lay, draped in a purple robe. It was a witch tradition to put fire to the body to help the soul pass on to the afterlife while releasing the magic back into the world. I conjured a black rose and placed it over her heart. Tears fell from my eyes as hollowness swallowed me up from the inside. I took a deep breath and went over to the corner of the room, where I had been told to stay during the ceremony.

I sat there gazing at Katie's body but not really seeing it. Instead, my mind was filled with all the precious moments I'd shared with Katie.

The sound of footsteps brought me back to reality. Elise and Ronald were walking into the temple. They glanced around and gave me a nod before continuing. Not long afterwards, people started arriving to pay their respects to their High Priestess in training. They cast me looks, but no one approached me. They made their way to Katie to say their goodbyes.

Someone placed a hand on my shoulder, making me jump. 'I'm so sorry for your loss,' Edmond said with a sympathetic smile. 'It may not feel like it, but it does get easier.'

I gave him a nod. 'Thank you for coming. It means a lot to me.'

'I thought you could do with a familiar face. No one should have to face things like this alone.' He pulled a chair over and sat down next to me. We remained quiet as the ceremony started.

Elise, being the High Priestess, led the ceremony. She wore a purple robe that matched Katie's. There were eleven other witches, most of them in white robes, but there were four exceptions with robes of red, green, blue and yellow, representing the four elements. They followed the High Priestess as she walked in a circle around the stone table Katie was lying on. When she'd walked all the way around she stopped, and the other witches had formed a circle around the table. The witches representing the elements were standing at each cardinal direction, with Elise, representing spirit, standing at the top. Twelve was an odd number for witches, but if Katie was included, it made thirteen, which made more sense.

Elise started speaking. One by one she welcomed the elements into the circle and the witches of each represented element in turn lit a coloured candle and placed symbols of the element on the stone table next to Katie. There was an athame, a pentacle, a wand and a cup. According to Katie, these were the traditional symbols of the four elements, but there were also flowers, feathers, ash and seashells around her body. After the last symbol had been placed, Elise walked up to Katie and gave her a kiss on the forehead before putting an amethyst in its place. She used her magic to set fire to Katie's body as she spoke. 'Merry meet, merry part and merry meet again.'

The flames engulfed Katie's body. At first it was a normal-coloured fire; it turned pink, purple, blue and finally green. It burned brightly for a while before it started to die off. When the green flame finally disappeared, there was nothing left on the stone table. No athame, no wand, no candles, no gemstones, no seashells. And no Katie. My insides felt hollow and I blinked away some tears. Edmond gave me a reassuring squeeze on my shoulder.

The High Priestess lifted the goblet from the altar and raised it in the air. 'Blessed be.' She took a sip and passed it along to the other witches in the circle.

When the circle was closed and the ceremony over, food was brought out and everyone mingled and talked about fond memories they had of Katie. I had been told not to participate. Edmond brought some food over and remained by my side. A few people walked up and expressed their condolences. It surprised me, but having Edmond next to me probably eased their minds.

Edmond got up from his chair and gave me a hug. 'I'd better head back to the farm. I want to get the horses back in the stable before nightfall.'

I nodded. 'I should go back to the healing ward to check on my daughter. I've been away from her long enough.'

We were making our way towards the exit when Ronald came up to us with a puzzled expression. 'I need to speak to you.' He looked at Edmond. 'In private.'

I gave Edmond a nod, telling him it was okay, and followed Ronald to a nearby room. It looked like a storeroom. There were different types of herbs lying around, along with several bottles of wine and some ceremonial instruments. In the middle was a table with two chairs. He gestured for me to sit down before taking a seat opposite me.

Ronald shifted in his seat before speaking up. 'I don't know how to tell you this. I have some bad news about Layla.'

My gaze shot up to his face, but he avoided my eyes. He scratched his neck while glancing around the room. 'She died during the ceremony.'

My body went numb. In less than a week I'd lost part of my soul and the only piece I had left of her. I stared blankly into space as he continued. 'It was all very sudden. There was nothing the healers could do.'

It felt like I was being swallowed up whole. I tried to talk, to move, but my body wouldn't respond.

A moment later, Ronald came back with a cup of tea. I hadn't even realised he had left. He handed me the cup. 'Here, drink this. It will make you feel better.'

I brought the cup to my lips with shaking hands. The liquid warmed my numb body. I blinked back some tears. 'Can I see her?'

He rubbed his face and swallowed before clearing his throat. 'I will have to clear that with Elise and the elders.' He eyed the door. 'Let me go and check.' The door closed behind him.

Why was he acting strange? Was it because he was scared of being alone with me or were they hiding something? The room started to spin. I cursed under my breath. What was in that tea? I should have known there was something wrong. Katie's parents had never been nice to me. I needed to get out of there. I took a step towards the door and collapsed on the floor. Everything went dark.

I blinked a few times and looked around. Why was I in a storeroom?

'Thank the goddess you're awake.'

I followed the voice and my eyes landed on the High Priestess. 'What happened?' I pulled myself into a sitting position and rubbed my head.

'You fainted after you banished the creature that was hurting the villages.'

I scratched my chin. What was she talking about?

'Don't you remember? After your friend got killed by the creature, you helped us track it down and banish it.' The High Priestess looked at me, her eyebrows drawn together.

I ran my hand through my hair. My head was ringing, and I struggled to recall everything that had happened. I remembered that I used to work with a farmer called Edmond on the outskirts of the village, but for some reason I had been spending the last six months in the village.

'Edmond?'

The High Priestess nodded. 'Yes. The creature killed him. That's why you agreed to help us.'

I nodded thoughtfully. That made sense. I got up from the floor, grabbing hold of the table to steady myself. My head started to clear. 'I guess I should be off, then.'

The High Priestess gave me a smile and walked me out of the temple. She placed her hands on top of mine. 'We are very grateful for everything you've done.'

Back To Reality

My consciousness slammed back into my body. It took some time for me to realise I was back with Cassie by my side. 'I had a baby,' I whispered quietly, mostly to myself. 'A beautiful baby girl.'

Cassie turned to look at me. 'It was you. It was always you in my dreams. I wasn't sure, but it was actually you. It actually happened.'

What was she talking about? Then a light came on in my head. Cassie was Katie. Somehow, she must have experienced these memories of us too.

I gave her a hug. 'I found you.' I wasn't sure whether I was referring to the fact I had finally located Cassie or that I had finally found the missing part of my soul; either way, I was happy.

Holding on to Cassie, I looked around the area, trying to figure out where we were. Everything was dark. I conjured a light. The walls, floor and ceiling were made of stone. I glanced at Cassie. 'Do you know where we are?'

She shook her head. 'I don't know. I think it's some sort of basement, but there's no door. I've checked several times. I have no idea how anyone gets in here.'

I raised an eyebrow. 'People come and visit you?'

She nodded. 'Every so often, someone will walk in and offer me food and water. I've tried reading their minds, but the only useful information I got was that someone had told them I was important and not to be harmed.' Her shoulders slumped. 'I'm sorry I can't be more helpful.'

I stroked her face. 'Don't worry. Just take my hand and close your eyes.'

'Are you going to teleport?' she asked as she took my hand.

I nodded and concentrated on teleporting. Nothing happened. Somehow they must have blocked my teleporting ability. Time for plan B. I sent out my energy, expecting to feel a portal, but there was nothing. How were we going to get back?

I paced the small room. There must be some way out of here. I walked up to the wall and started touching every stone.

Cassie bit her lip. 'What are you doing?'

'The people visiting you must get here somehow. Maybe there's a hidden doorway or an area we can walk through.'

'Wouldn't you be able to feel that?'

I shook my head. 'They blocked my ability to teleport, so maybe they somehow blocked the door they're using too.'

While continuing my search, something started tugging at me. It felt like I was being pulled back with a rope. 'Cassie. Grab hold of me now,' I said with a raised voice. I met her halfway and embraced her. 'Don't let go,' I whispered in her ear as I gave in to the tugging sensation in my head. Everything around us started to spin. One moment we were standing in the basement and the next, we were falling. I strengthened my hold on Cassie. I wasn't going to lose her again.

A white light flashed around us before I hit the floor. Cassie landed on top of me.

'I'm so happy you're back,' Leah's voice sang out.

Cassie pushed herself off me and took her heat with her. Leah rushed forward and gave Cassie a hug. 'I can't believe it worked.' She squeezed her tightly before walking over to me and offering her hand.

'I told you it would work,' I said with a smile as she helped me to my feet.

Leah got her phone out. 'Mark and Seth should be here in a bit.'

I sat down on the sofa with Cassie next to me, squeezing her hand gently. Leah positioned herself on the other side of Cassie. She opened her mouth and closed it several times, probably because she was dying to know what had happened but at the same time wanted to give Cassie time and space to process everything she'd been through.

We sat there in silence until the door opened and Mark and Seth stepped in. Their gaze landed on Cassie, and they rushed over to embrace her.

'I'm so happy they got you back,' Mark said. He glanced over at me and gave me a nod.

We got Mark and Seth up to speed and explained to Cassie what had happened while she was gone. 'So that's what they were doing,' she said.

'Who was doing what?' Leah asked.

'The people in the robes. They were standing around Mark's bed chanting when someone hit me on the head and kidnapped me.'

Mark rubbed his forehead. 'But who are these people and why would they take my ability to shift?' He shook his head. 'It doesn't make sense.'

I shrugged. The witches had made me forget. Why would they do something like that unless they were hiding something? Was it a coincidence that I had been shown my past now?

'I think we need to look into the witches of Whitelake,' I said, and everyone's eyes landed on me.

Mark's brow wrinkled in confusion. 'I've never heard of them.'

Cassie gave me a look and pressed her lips together. 'In a previous life I was a Whitelake witch, but I died during childbirth.'

Everyone's eyes went wide. Cassie became flustered and quiet. I squeezed her hand and continued. 'It was a beautiful baby girl. I named her Layla Fey. Katie's father told me she died during the funeral of Cassie – or Katie, as she was called then. But they made me forget. I don't understand why, unless she didn't die.'

Leah got a distant look on her face. 'The name, Whitelake – it sounds familiar. But I can't recall why. How long ago was this?'

Her gaze met mine. I took a deep breath, trying to remember. 'It was probably two or three centuries ago in human time. Give or take.'

Cassie, Leah and I were deep in thought when Mark spoke up. 'What are we going to do about Cassie? She can't just walk back home.'

'She is not putting another foot near that house,' I said, a bit more forcefully than I had meant to. No doubt my eyes had started to change colour due to the turmoil of emotions I was experiencing.

Mark took a step back 'Chill, demon. I was just asking a question.'

Leah turned to Cassie, and her gaze went to my and Cassie's hands. I was still holding her hand, with no plan of ever letting her go. 'Maybe it's best if Cassie stays here – at least until we know what's going on. We still need to go back to the house, though, and act like nothing has happened. We can't let Abigail know we're involved – not if we want to find out what's going on and what her place is in all of this.'

Everyone nodded in agreement, and I let out a breath of relief. Leah pulled Cassie away from me and I reluctantly let go of her hand. She would be safe in the house, but I had just experienced the feeling of losing her once, and it was still fresh in my mind.

A moment later, Cassie came back to my side and took my hand again. My body relaxed at her touch. Leah, Mark and Seth decided to head back home, eager to see whether Abigail would give anything away.

Before they left, Leah came up to me and gave me a hug. 'Thank you for believing in me.'

I returned her smile. 'Thanks for getting me to Cassie.' Our eyes met, revealing a growing closeness, understanding and friendship between us.

RESEARCH

Cassie and I spent some time just being close to each other after the others had left. Her remembering her past life helped, and she forgave me for not telling her I was a demon. After living Katie's life, she understood why I had been so reluctant to tell her.

I was happy to have Cassie back, but I didn't want to push it. Cassie wasn't Katie, even though she technically was. I made the guest room into Cassie's room so she didn't need to feel like I was pressuring her. I spent most of the evening conjuring whatever furniture and other things she wanted for the room.

The next day I got a text message from Leah saying she was going to the library to see if she could find any information about the Whitelake name. She asked if I wanted to join her, but Cassie was supposed to be missing and I wasn't ready to leave her alone, so I told her I needed to clean the house.

A few hours later, Leah walked in through the door. 'How's the cleaning going?' She gave me a wink before proceeding to the living room. 'Where's Cassie?'

'She's resting.'

Leah gave me a nod and put her research down on the table. 'There wasn't much, but I found some records stating that there used to be a village of Whitelakes that vanished in the 1800s.'

Could that have been the village I lived in?

Leah pulled me out of my thoughts. 'I'd better head back to the house. Just wanted to drop off what I found. Abigail's been acting like everything's fine. I wonder if she'll mention anything about Cassie at dinner.'

I thanked Leah for her help. I felt so useless. I wished there was something I could do. Maybe Freya would have some words of wisdom, but I didn't want to leave Cassie on her own, especially not now when I finally had her back. She seemed to have recovered well from her kidnapping, but she still had moments of withdrawal. We hadn't spoken any further about her imprisonment. She hadn't brought it up and I didn't want to push her.

Cassie and I were sitting in the living room watching a film when the front door opened. Leah stormed into the living room. 'I can't believe her! Who does she think she is?'

Cassie got up from the sofa and gave Leah a hug. 'What

did Abigail say?'

'She said you'd committed suicide – that despite all the help you received at the facility, you hadn't been able to cope.' She threw her hands up in the air. 'How does she even come up with these things? I couldn't be around her anymore, so I excused myself and said I needed some time alone.'

I gave Leah a sympathetic smile. 'At least she didn't suspect you had anything to do with getting Cassie out.'

Leah had opened her mouth to answer when her phone made a sound. She checked it. 'There's a work emergency, so Abigail will be away for a couple of days. She asked Mark to keep an eye on me.'

I raised an eyebrow. 'So much for keeping up appearances. You would have thought she would at least pretend to be worried about you.'

Leah shook her head. 'Obviously not.'

'But we can use this to our advantage,' Cassie said.

'How?' both me and Leah said in unison.

'Abigail is going on a work trip. Maybe Jax could follow her in his crow form to see what she's up to. And we can have a proper look in the house. It may give us some more leads.'

'That's a great idea.' Leah looked over at me. 'I don't mind keeping Cassie company.'

I gave her a look of gratitude. I think she knew there was no way I would leave Cassie on her own.

Leah stayed the night, so I took the opportunity to stretch my wings. When the sun came up, I made my way over to Cassie's house. I got comfortable at my usual spot in the tree. It felt weird being back, especially knowing Cassie was safe and sound at my house.

Eventually Abigail left the house and got into her car. I followed her as she drove away. After a few hours of driving, she reached a city and parked her car. She walked into a seven-storey office building. I tried to follow her, but when she got into the lift, I admitted defeat. It would look suspicious for a crow to be seen in the lift. Instead, I kept an eye on the lift to see what floor it stopped at.

I debated whether to turn into a human and go to the same floor, but I had no doubt in my mind that Abigail would recognise me. Maybe it would be better to check the place out after she had left. I spent some time flying around the lobby, watching several humans come and go while pretending to be a confused crow trying to find its way out. Luckily for me the ceiling was quite high and there were some disoriented pigeons in the building as well, which helped me to look more inconspicuous.

After I had been flying around for a few hours, I still hadn't seen any sign of Abigail. I got out of the building and transformed back into my human form to text Leah with an update. I told her the name of the building and what floor Abigail had got out on. A moment later, Leah was texting me back. The company on that floor was called Whitelock Unlimited. I wondered if it had any connection to Whitelake; however, I didn't have to wonder for long, as my phone vibrated and showed another message from Leah saying that

Whitelock was an alternative spelling of Whitelake. She'd obviously had the same thought.

I flew up to the fifth floor to see if I could discover anything by looking through the windows. To my disappointment, it looked like a normal office building, with rooms containing chairs and desks. However, I couldn't detect any people inside. I sent out my energy and detected a force field, confirming that there was something strange transpiring. I just couldn't tell what.

I wished Leah was there to help. She seemed to be able to pick up much more than I could with the energy at the house. I sent her a text telling her I needed her expertise and asking whether she could get Mark, Seth and the rest of the wolf pack to look after Cassie.

She texted me back. 'Mark not enough?' The smiley face she put at the end of the text made me realise she was joking. She knew Mark wasn't strong enough to look after Cassie on his own without his ability to shift. Her text was quickly followed by another, telling me she was on it and would let me know when she had sorted everything out.

I wouldn't be able to check my phone as a crow, so I looked for an inconspicuous place to sit that would still allow me to observe the building. There was a small coffee shop on the other side of the street. I ordered myself a coffee and sat down by the window facing the office building.

An hour passed before I heard anything from Leah. She told me she had sorted everything out and would be able to leave. I swiftly found an alleyway where I could teleport to the house. I got Leah and made sure Mark and the wolves were around to look after Cassie before I teleported Leah and myself back to the city.

We arrived in the alleyway and made our way to the building. We found a sheltered area away from the crowd of people walking past. Leah closed her eyes and started to concentrate. After a while, she started talking. 'It's the same magic that shields our house.'

Leah opened her eyes, and I gave her a knowing look. This was not good. Abigail was obviously involved in something and knew exactly what was going on. 'Why don't we get back to the coffee shop and figure out our next step?'

Leah nodded and we made our way over. We ordered drinks and sat down.

'What do you think we should do?' I asked Leah. 'I'm tempted to just walk inside and see what's going on.'

She shook her head. 'We're better off waiting until Abigail has left. Imagine what she would do if we ran into her and she figured out what we're up to.'

I let out a defeated breath. 'I guess you're right.'

She gave me a smirk. 'Good. Let's get home and come back when Abigail has left. She's usually away for a couple of days, so no point in waiting around.'

An Alliance

I teleported us back to the house, but when we got there, it was empty. Adrenaline rushed into my body, and I jumped when Leah placed her hands on my shoulders. She gazed into my eyes. 'Calm down. The wolves wouldn't have wanted to come inside.'

I closed my eyes and nodded. She was right.

I followed Leah out into the back garden. There were still no signs of Cassie or the wolves. A repetitive banging rang in my ears and I rushed towards it. Leah followed behind. It led us into the forest and to the edge of the estate. Several people were there, whom I assumed to be wolves. Most of them were wearing nothing more than a pair of trousers, despite the chilly weather.

When we got closer, they turned and stared at us. I could

hear continuous growls coming from several of them, which stopped me in my tracks. One of the wolves made a sound and all the other wolves went quiet. He walked up to us with a strong posture. When he reached us, he looked directly into my eyes. There was no doubt in my mind that he was the alpha of the pack. 'Mark and Leah have assured me that you're different, which is why we have agreed to help.'

An overwhelming feeling of gratitude came over me. 'Thank you. That means a lot to me.'

He acknowledged me before he continued. 'I know we were invited, but we do not want to trespass on your territory, as we are known enemies. However, we are happy to strike an alliance with you as long as the treaty is respected.'

He gestured towards where the noises came from. 'To make it easier for us to look after Cassie when you are not around, we have taken the liberty of building a house where our territory meets. That way we can look after Cassie here while you try to unlock the secrets that have caused Mark to lose his ability to shift.'

I scanned the area. There was already half a wooden cabin between the trees. Knowing that they were building a house to look after Cassie filled me with confidence. They were obviously happy to help in the long run. 'When you've finished the exterior, I would be happy to supply the interior, and maybe Leah can provide some protective spells. That way the house will stay neutral.' I looked over at Leah as I said it to see if she would agree.

'Mark and Cassie are my family. I would be happy to

help,' she said with a smile.

The alpha looked over at Leah. 'Then it's decided.' He went back to the other wolves and continued to build the house.

I still hadn't seen Cassie, but as I looked around, I saw her walking towards us with Mark and Seth by her side. Our eyes met and she made her way over to me. I gave her a kiss. It felt amazing to be able to kiss her without any fear it might put her into a trance.

'Can you believe that they're building a house?' She sounded amazed.

'It is quite amazing.' I agreed with her.

'Don't worry, though; I'd rather spend time with you when I can.'

I pulled her in for a hug. 'Me too.'

Leah cleared her throat. 'Mark and Seth are going to stay with the wolves and help with the cabin.' I nodded in response.

Cassie, Leah and I walked back to the house. We filled Cassie in on what we had discovered.

'So we have to wait for Abigail to come back home before checking out the building?' Cassie asked.

I nodded. 'But you're not going.'

Her eyes narrowed and she crossed her arms. 'I want to help. My mind reading ability may come in handy.'

'I can't risk losing you again. Besides, they'd recognise you in a heartbeat.'

Leah opened her mouth to say something, but I cut her

off. 'It's better if I go alone.'

She shook her head. 'You need me. You know I'm better than you at detecting the magic in that building.'

I let out a breath. I couldn't argue with that. She would have an advantage over me, as it was her type of magic. 'Fine. But you'll do exactly as I say.'

She leaned back, a wide smile across her face. 'Aye aye, boss.' She glanced over at Cassie and laughter erupted.

Leah collected herself. 'So if you're supposed to be deadly with a sword, how come we've never seen you practise?'

I tapped my head. 'It's all in here. I spent many years learning how to fight. It doesn't just go away.'

Leah cocked her head with a raised eyebrow. 'Then why don't you teach us?'

I spent the evening teaching Cassie and Leah some simple fighting techniques. During a sparring session with Leah, she instinctively used her magic. I pretended to go in for a killer blow and the next second I was flying across the room, smashing into the wall on the opposite side. I hadn't been prepared for that. I could hear Cassie's worried voice. 'Jax, oh my god, Jax, are you okay?' She bent down so she was level with me.

I shook my dizziness away and sat up. 'I'm okay. It takes more than a bit of magic to get rid of me.' I rubbed my sore head. 'That's very impressive, though.' I glanced up at Leah.

Her cheeks were flushed and her arms were pinned against her stomach. 'I'm so sorry, Jax. It was instinct.'

'No worries.' I got up and patted her on the shoulder.

'Why do you think I trust you with Cassie?'

'I'm still here,' Cassie said.

I looked over at Cassie with a smile on my face. 'I know. You were great, but you don't have any offensive abilities yet. It puts you at a disadvantage.'

'It doesn't mean I'd go down without a fight.'

Leah nudged her. 'True, but the odds are better with me around.'

We gave up on the fighting after that; however, Leah gave us a demonstration of some offensive magic she had learnt. It was amazing to watch her throw fire, water and wind out of her hands. She had truly come into her own, and all she had needed was a small push.

When we were about to go and get ready for bed, Mark sent Leah a text asking if we wouldn't mind coming over to the newly built cabin. It was quite a walk, especially in the dark, so I teleported us over. The cabin looked finished from the outside, and a lantern hung by the front door.

Mark came out to greet us. 'I know there's still more work to be done, but I thought maybe we could go through what we need for the inside of the house. That way you can sort it out tomorrow.'

I gave him a questioning look before I realised that he didn't actually know I could conjure things with my mind. 'Why don't we sort it out as we go along?' I said with a smug expression.

Leah rolled her eyes and glanced over at Cassie, both knowing I could easily manifest the entire interior in a moment.

We followed Mark into the small wooden house. It was nothing special, but considering that they'd built it in less than a day, it was pretty impressive. There was a small hallway that opened up to a living room. To the right was a bedroom, though the wall between the rooms hadn't been put up yet.

I turned to Mark. 'What were you thinking?'

'Cassie will be spending time here, so maybe she should have a say.'

I looked over at Cassie. 'King-size bed? Sofa in the living room?' She nodded in agreement.

Mark made a shocked sound as the bed materialised out of nowhere. 'How do you do that?' I shrugged and continued to add things to the house.

'What about a TV and a microwave?'

I raised my eyebrows at Mark. 'If you can get electricity to the house, then sure. But it's pointless for now.' He seemed to take some time to consider it before agreeing.

Seth walked into the house and joined us. 'Wow, that was quick.' He looked around and turned to Mark. 'Would you mind if you and I stayed the night here? I don't want to go back to the house.'

I looked at Seth. 'Would you prefer two separate beds instead of sharing?'

His eyebrows drew together, and he glanced around the room. 'I don't mind sleeping on the sofa.'

Cassie walked up to him. 'Jax will happily sort out two beds. Come and watch.' She grabbed his hand and pulled him to the bedroom. I followed.

I removed the king-size bed with my mind and replaced it with two single beds.

'Wow, that's so cool.' Seth seemed very excited, and I couldn't help but smile at him.

'Would you like anything else?' I asked.

He frowned and turned to Cassie. 'Can he really make anything appear?' Cassie nodded at him with a smile. 'Can I have an extra blanket?' he asked innocently. I was sure he didn't need it, but I acquiesced to his request.

When I'd finished decorating the cabin, I teleported myself, Cassie and Leah back to the house. I said goodnight to them, but instead of going to bed, I turned into a crow. I needed to reflect on everything we'd discovered in regard to Whitelock Unlimited and Abigail, and flying was the best way to do it.

REMEMBERING THE PAST

I enjoyed my flight, knowing Cassie was safe in my house with Leah protecting her. It made me feel less worried, especially after the defensive display of magic Leah had manifested by instinct when we were sparring. I knew she still felt bad about it, but in all honesty, it was nothing. My fighting skills went way beyond some elemental magic.

There had been a war in the supernatural community. Freya had tried to solve it in a peaceful way for many centuries. She was a strong believer that everyone, no matter their origins, should be able to co-exist and live peacefully alongside each other – and amongst humans if we so wished.

Being raised by Freya had its advantages, and I had seen first-hand the beauty of different species living together in harmony. Freya's place – or more correctly, the surrounding area – had become a safe haven for supernatural beings that shared the same belief. If nothing else, I was living proof that nothing was ever black and white and that we aren't defined by what we are born into but by our actions.

Many powerful beings disagreed and retaliated against Freya. Luckily, she had many alliances and seemed to be holding her own. After I'd left the witch village, I felt lost and lonely. I begged Freya to let me join the fight so my life could have meaning again. She declined at first, so I took it upon myself to protect the beings on her land that had sought refuge. Seeing my determination, Freya eventually agreed and sent me to train with her trusted warriors to prepare me for battle.

It was safe to say we didn't lose the war; however, I wasn't so sure we'd won it either. After the fighting had stopped, I remained with Freya and helped her where I could. This involved going to school to evaluate a situation. That was where I'd met Nick, and the rest is history.

As the sun started to rise, I realised I'd got lost in past memories. I wasn't any closer to figuring out what to do about Whitelock, Abigail or Mark's inability to shift.

When I got back to the house, Cassie and Leah were in the kitchen, cooking breakfast. I walked towards them as Cassie came up and gave me a kiss before offering me some breakfast. We sat down at the kitchen table. There was a moment of silence. I guess no one quite knew what to say.

After a while, Leah spoke up. 'Abigail should get home today, so me, Mark and Seth have to go home soon to keep up appearances.'

I gave her a nod. I didn't like that they were going back to the house, back to Abigail, but they had all agreed it was the best way to stay in the loop.

I rubbed my neck. 'Do you want to check out the building this evening?'

Leah nodded. 'The sooner the better, I guess.'

'I wish you would let me come with you. I feel so useless,' Cassie said.

I reached over and took her hand. 'Just stay safe.'

After we had eaten, I left to take a nap. I had been up all night flying, and as we had no clue what we would be walking into, I wanted to make sure I was fully rested.

I woke up a few hours later and strolled downstairs, expecting to see Leah and Cassie, but the whole house was empty. My heart sped up in my chest. Had something happened to them?

I scanned the room and my eyes landed on a note in Cassie's handwriting stating she had gone for a walk in the woods. I let out a sigh. Between the protective spells in and around the house and the wolves patrolling, she shouldn't be able to get into any trouble, but I knew I wouldn't be able to relax until I had made sure she was unharmed.

I turned into a crow and took to the sky. It wasn't long before I spotted Cassie sitting on a rock with her sketch pad. I transformed back into my human form. Cassie looked up as I approached, a light blush on her face. 'I didn't mean to worry you. I just needed to get out of the house and get some fresh air.'

My gaze went to what she was drawing. It was a picture of us with a baby. I scratched my face. I hadn't realised how overwhelming it must be for Cassie with everything that was going on.

'Do you want to talk about it?' I sat down next to her and folded my arms protectively around her.

'It felt so real. I know it's not actually my baby, but I felt the same happiness Katie did when she saw the baby for the first time.' Cassie shook her head. 'It's silly really.'

I found her eyes and caressed her face. 'Your feelings are not silly.'

She closed her eyes and leaned into my hand. 'Maybe not, but we have more important things to worry about than me being upset at what was done to you and me – well, you and Katie. It must have been painful for you to remember losing her all over again.'

I had suppressed those memories since I'd got them back. It was something I'd deal with once everyone was safe. During my life, I had seen many people die. Being immortal had its downsides; however, what Cassie didn't understand was that I hadn't lost her. Sure, Katie had died, and it was horrible, but I had got her back. Cassie was Katie. They were the same caring soul, the same person I had fallen in love with, the piece of my soul that had been missing. Only this time fate had given me the opportunity to spend forever with her, because Cassie was an immortal being like me.

I gave her a passionate kiss, knowing I would never be

able to put all my feelings for her into words. 'I'm going to head back to the house and sort some dinner out. Leah should be here in a couple of hours.'

Cassie nodded. 'I'll see you back at the house in a bit.'

Beyond The Portal

Leah turned up a few hours later. She told us Mark and Seth were going to stay at home and hopefully that would keep Abigail from becoming suspicious. However, Mark had asked the wolves to meet us at the cabin.

I left Leah in the house while I teleported Cassie over. The new cabin didn't have any electricity, so I lit a few candles and waited for the wolves to turn up. I didn't have to wait long. After I had made sure they were happy to watch over Cassie, I returned to Leah.

'Are you ready for this?' I asked as I grabbed her hand.

'As ready as can be,' she said before I teleported us to the city and the Whitelock building.

When we arrived in the alleyway, the streets were almost empty. We walked up to the building and tried the door, but it was locked.

'What are we going to do now?' Leah asked.

I raised an eyebrow. 'You think a locked door is going to stop us?' I glanced around to make sure we were alone before teleporting us to the other side of the door.

Leah shook her head. 'You make it seem too easy.' I let out a chuckle as we made our way to the lift.

'It was the fifth floor, right?' Leah asked before pressing the button. I nodded and stepped into the lift with her. An empty feeling of anticipation appeared in my stomach, and I wiped my hand on my trousers.

Leah paced around in the small area. 'What do you think is going to greet us?'

'I don't know. But be ready for anything. And if we get caught in any crossfire, run and hide.'

She drew her eyebrows together. 'What about you?'

'I'll be fine,' I said with a reassuring smile.

Leah opened her mouth to argue as the lift stopped. She gave me a fleeting look, and I took a deep breath, readying myself for what to come as the doors opened.

We stepped out of the lift. Everything was quiet and deserted.

Leah put her hands on her hips. 'I thought there would at least be some people here. It's only eight o'clock. Doesn't anyone work late anymore?'

I gave Leah a stare to shut her up. It could be a trap. We walked along a corridor. Offices lined one side, separated from the corridor by a glass wall. All the lights were off, and no one was inside.

Leah tilted her head in the direction of an office. 'Should we check them out? There may be some important paperwork.'

I shook my head. 'Better to check out the whole floor first. Maybe send your magic out to see if anything's concealed. I got your back.' I conjured my sword.

Leah rolled her eyes. 'Aye aye, boss.' A smile escaped her lips.

I scanned the area and waited for her to do her thing. 'That's not a wall,' she said as she pointed towards the end of the corridor.

I walked up to it and placed my hand on where the wall was supposed to be. The energy vibrated around it, creating ripples on the surface. 'You're right. It's an illusion.'

'You mean someone created it to look like a wall?'

I nodded. 'Transformation magic is fairly common.'

'Then why have I never heard of it before?'

I shrugged. 'I don't know. Elemental witches think it's beneath them?'

I jumped as she jokingly hit my shoulder, and I gave her a stare. 'How about we concentrate on the task at hand?'

She straightened and looked at the wall. 'If it's just an illusion, do we just walk through it like it doesn't exist?'

'I guess. Technically there isn't a wall there.'

Leah grabbed my hand and closed her eyes before pulling me through to the other side.

A man jumped up from a desk. 'Who are you? You're not

allowed in here.'

He reached over his desk to get something. I lifted my sword, ready to fight, but Leah rushed over and blew some dust into his face. He collapsed on the floor.

I looked over at Leah in confusion. 'What did you do to him?'

A grin appeared on her face. 'You think I'd go into battle empty handed? It was ground up valerian root mixed with a bit of other stuff. He should stay asleep for a couple of hours. Come on, let's see what he was guarding.'

I glanced around the bare room and followed Leah to a solid wooden door at the end. There was no indication as to what was behind it, but there was something strange about it. 'I think it's a portal.'

Leah reached for the handle. 'Then let's see where it takes us.'

She opened the door, and I took her hand before stepping inside. Hopefully it wasn't an ambush.

A blinding white light engulfed us. When my eyes had adjusted, I scanned the area. We were somewhere outside. Silhouettes of houses could be seen in the distance. The place seemed familiar, but I couldn't figure out why.

'Where do you think we are?' Leah took a deep breath. 'The air seems lighter than normal. Do you think we're still on Earth?'

I shook my head. 'I don't know. I feel like I've been here before, but I don't know why.'

Leah hooked her arm in mine and pulled me towards the

houses. 'Then let's have a look around to see if it jogs your memory.'

We walked past several white rendered houses before we reached a temple. I stopped in my tracks, causing Leah, who was still holding on to me, to lose her balance.

'Oi, why'd you stop?'

'We're at the witch village.'

Leah's eyes went wide. 'You mean where you and Cassie lived?'

I nodded. 'Yeah, but it's different – more modernised.'

'Unless we've time travelled, it has been a few centuries since you lived here. Plenty of time for things to change.'

We approached the temple. A statue of three women in different life stages had been placed in the middle of the cleansing pool. I couldn't remember the witches worshipping any specific entity when I'd lived there.

Leah pointed at the statue. 'That's Hecate.'

I tried to remember what sort of goddess she was as Leah continued. 'She's the goddess of crossroads, called upon for protection.'

Why would the village need protection? I shook my head and started climbing the stairs that led to the entrance. My heart felt heavy as I thought about the last time I had been there. I pushed the memories aside and continued up the stairs. We entered the temple and looked around. There were no people around except an old woman in a black robe. She stood by the altar at the other end. A great amount of power radiated from her, but I had no idea who she was.

'You think it's the High Priestess?' Leah whispered to me as we got closer.

'I don't know. Whoever she is, she's powerful. Maybe it's Hecate herself?'

'Why would—'

The old woman stepped out in front of us. We froze on the spot, causing our heads to jerk back.

She tilted her head and studied us for a while. 'You are not supposed to be here, yet I feel like you have a connection to this place.'

I gasped and glanced over at Leah.

'Yes, both of you,' the old lady said.

I could understand how she may sense that I'd been there before, but Leah had never been there. Did that mean her ancestors were from this village? I opened my mouth to speak, but the old woman cut me off.

'Seems fate is on your side. I will leave you be for now. But heed this warning and go back to where you came from. You do not belong here. If I see you again, there will be consequences.' The woman disappeared in a cloud of smoke.

Leah turned to face me. Her eyes bulged. 'Well ... that was strange.'

I nodded. 'Yeah. I think we should do what she says.' I ushered Leah towards the exit.

'You think that was Hecate?' she whispered in my ear.

I didn't answer her until we had left the temple behind. 'I don't know. But I've never seen a High Priestess disappear into a cloud of smoke.'

'Hold on.' Leah turned around and put her hand on my chest to stop me from walking. 'What's our plan? We still need information.'

'We know Abigail's connected to Whitelock and that they are connected to the witch village where I used to live.'

'But what role does Abigail play in it all?'

I shrugged and glanced around. A few people had stopped what they were doing and were staring at us. 'I don't think we're going to find out here. Maybe we should try and get home.'

Leah followed my gaze. 'I guess you're right.'

I took her hand and tried teleporting away. Nothing happened. I didn't want to worry Leah, so I kept quiet, hoping we'd find the portal and get back the way we came.

We walked around for a while before Leah stopped. 'I think this is where we arrived.'

'I agree. Send out your energy to see if you can locate the portal.' I did the same, but without any success. We continued our search. Leah kept using her magic to try to find the portal, but to no avail.

She sat down on a bench with a sigh. 'This is useless. We're never going to find it. Why can't you just teleport us out?'

I placed a hand on her shoulder. 'I tried earlier. It doesn't work.'

She let out a defeated sigh. 'How are we going to get home?'

At the mention of home, an image of Edmond appeared

in my head. He was my home for a while. 'Let's check out the farm.'

Leah lifted her head with a frown. 'What farm?'

'The one I used to live on.' I pulled her up from the bench and marched in the right direction.

Leah struggled to keep up. 'Why are we going there?'

'I feel like we need to.'

Leah hooked her arm in mine. 'Lead the way.'

The stars shone brightly as we made our way to the farm. We passed a few fields, including the one where I'd first met Katie. The first rays of sunshine peeked over the horizon as the house came into view.

With Edmond being gone, I thought it had been abandoned after I'd left the village. But looking around, it was obvious someone lived here; why else would smoke be coming out of the chimney?

We knocked on the door. When no one answered, I pushed on the door handle, expecting it to be locked, but the door opened easily. The owner had kept some of the original features but mixed them with more modern things. We entered the room to the left, which used to be the living room. Someone had changed it into a bedchamber with several bunk beds next to each other. Who was all this for?

I sent out my energy and picked up on a few living beings. Somehow they had been cloaked. 'Hello?' I called out. 'We don't mean you any harm.' I gave Leah a nudge.

'We like to help if we can,' Leah continued. Quiet footsteps approached us from behind. We turned around and were met by a middle-aged woman. She had curly blond hair and warm hazel eyes. There was something about her eyes that made me feel like I knew her.

House Of The Hidden

The middle-aged woman stopped in front of us. 'Welcome to the house of the hidden. I'm Leaf.' There was a moment of silence as she studied us before she waved her hand, removing the concealing spell that had been placed over the house.

Several teenagers appeared in the room. A few cast us curious looks as they walked out of the room to leave us alone with Leaf.

'Why are you hiding out here instead of being in the village?' I asked.

'Isn't that the question?' Leaf said, giving me a sad smile. 'However, the more urgent question would be why are you here? You are clearly not from the village yourself.'

A feeling that she knew who we were entered my mind. I

looked her over. Something about her felt familiar, and my gut instinct told me we could trust her.

'My friend and I are looking for answers, but we seem to have stumbled upon more questions.'

She took a step towards us. 'What are the answers you seek? Maybe I can be of help.'

'We are trying to figure out why our friend lost his ability to shift.'

Leaf nodded with understanding. 'Then maybe the fates led you here, as I believe I have the answer. The young ones that live here had their magic taken as well. It was sacrificed by Hecate to keep the village hidden.' She let out a sigh and her eyes became distant as she continued in a low voice. 'You see, there was a demon living on these lands a long time ago, and the High Priestess and the elders were worried he would come back for revenge for what was done to him. He's immortal, and they took his child away from him and made him forget.'

A gasp escaped me as a tightness settled in my chest. They had done all of this, removing the village from the human realm to keep it hidden, because of me.

Leah placed a hand on my shoulder and gave it a reassuring squeeze. I gazed into Leaf's eyes. 'This demon you speak of. Did he happen to be living in this house with a farmer?'

Recognition shone in her eyes. 'Edmond. Bless his heart.'

How did she know who he was? I studied her a bit more closely. There was some similarity between this woman and the older version of Cassie. 'Katie?' I asked, even though I knew it couldn't be Katie. Katie had died and Cassie was proof her soul had moved on. 'Little Layla Fey?'

A sparkle appeared in her eyes and she slowly nodded her head.

Warmth spread through me. I couldn't believe my little girl was standing in front of me.

Leah raised her eyebrows. 'Are you saying this is your daughter?'

Leaf turned to Leah with teary eyes and a big smile. 'That is exactly what he is saying, my child.'

Leah shook her head. 'But you were born more than 200 years ago. How is this possible?'

'The fates work in mysterious ways; however, I am older than I seem. Due to my father's immortal blood, I do not age like a normal human. I was an abomination to my people, and they tried to sacrifice me. I escaped and ended up living here.'

I sucked in a breath and closed my eyes as they became tearful. She was alive and I had abandoned her. I had failed her. Guilt swallowed me up inside. As a father, I should have known she was still alive. I should have fought for her.

Leaf placed a hand on my shoulder and looked into my eyes. 'It's okay. You didn't know.'

I embraced her. 'How did you end up here?'

She wiped a tear from my cheek and gave me a reassuring smile. 'Edmond took me in, as I was still too young to care for myself. He wasn't afraid of my powers – he even helped me to control them. When he passed away, I wasn't sure what I was going to do, but the fates had plans for me. Some children stumbled upon this house. At first, I was worried they had come here to get me back to the village, but I later discovered the children had been stripped of their powers in the name of the goddess. I have been trying to figure out a way to reverse it ever since.'

I opened my mouth to ask about Edmond, but Leaf turned to Leah and continued talking. 'I watched as the children grew up and took a liking to a young man. There was something special about him. Even as time went on, he didn't wither away like the other children. We later fell in love and had a beautiful daughter. I could feel she was going to be a powerful witch, and I didn't dare to keep her here out of fear someone would come and take her. After a lot of preparations, I sent her away to the human world with her father to look after her. I never heard anything from them since that day, so I wasn't even sure I had succeeded.' She pulled some hair away from Leah's face. 'You are proof I made the right choice.'

Leah took a step back and turned to me with a frown. She stared at her hands before meeting Leaf's gaze. 'I'm your daughter?'

Leaf nodded. Her eyes glistened with unshed tears and a warm smile appeared on her face. 'The fates must have heard my prayers and sent the two of you to me.'

Leah shook her head. 'How is this possible? It makes no sense.' She backed away, arms crossed against her chest.

I reached out and placed a comforting hand on her shoulder as we stood there in silence.

Leaf let out a sigh. 'I know it's a lot to take in.'

I opened my mouth to say something but closed it again, still digesting everything that had been said. In my heart I knew the woman in front of me was my daughter and everything she had said was true. I was overwhelmed with joy and guilt. I'd never thought I would see little Layla Fey again, but she had been here all along. And the High Priestess had made me abandon her. The demon stirred inside me as my anger rose, but I pushed it down. I peered over at Leah. I would never have guessed that she was my granddaughter, but our growing connection finally started to make sense – as well as why Cassie and Leah were so close. They had not just grown up together, they were family.

Leah finally broke the silence. 'How do we get back home? We can't seem to find the door that we got here from.'

Leaf looked at me. 'For you, I believe it is fairly easy. Teleportation should work inside a connection circle. Let me go and get my tools.'

She left the room, leaving me and Leah alone. I ran my hand through my hair. 'This is crazy.'

Leah nudged me with her shoulder. 'Yeah. Who would have thought we were related?'

Leaf came back with a box of stuff. She placed it on the floor as Leah strolled up to her with an unsure smile. 'Why don't you come with us?'

Leaf's eyes became watery as she gave Leah a sad smile. 'I

wish I could. I would like nothing more than to get to know the woman you've become, but it's not my time to leave yet. Fate is still in motion, and I have a responsibility towards these children. However, I know someone who may be able to help you.' She looked towards the door. 'Sky, why don't you come inside? This is my father Jax and my daughter Leah.'

A girl around the same age as Leah walked into the room with a nervous smile. If it wasn't for her skin colour, the flush on her cheeks would have been obvious.

Leaf gestured towards her. 'Sky can help you get in contact with me again, but it's safer for everyone if you do not come back. The goddess is more than likely already aware you are here, and the High Priestess does not take kindly to outsiders, especially the kind that carry demon blood.'

'Are you sure you'll be okay?' Sky asked in a worried voice.

Leaf nodded. 'Don't worry, my child. The Fates have plans for me yet.'

Sky approached us slowly. 'Hi, I'm Sky. Leaf told me about your problem and how it seems to connect to ours. I've been researching how to reverse the spell for a long time, so she asked me to go with you to see if I can help.'

I gave her a smile. 'Thank you. Hopefully we can help each other.'

'It's all ready,' Leaf said as she stood back from the circle she had just created.

I hugged her tightly. There were so many things I wanted

to say to her. 'Are you sure you can't come with us?'

She cupped my face in her hands. 'Our time will come. Have faith. I do.'

I reluctantly let go of her and waited for Leah and Sky to say their goodbyes. When they were done, I took their hands and stepped into the circle to teleport us back to the house.

The Wrath Of Abigail

When we got to the house, I let go of their hands and left them behind to check on Cassie. I was excited to tell her what we had discovered. The morning sun warmed my body as I flew over to the cabin. Cassie was playing cards with some of the wolves. I approached her and gave her a kiss.

'How did it go? Where's Leah?' Cassie asked, biting her lip.

'She's fine. She's in the house with Sky.'

A frown appeared on Cassie's face. 'Who's Sky?'

I squeezed her shoulder. 'It's a long story. I'll tell you on the way back.'

She nodded and stood up from the chair. I thanked the wolves for keeping her safe.

While we made our way back to the house, I told her

everything that had happened.

'Leah's our granddaughter?'

I gave her a smile. 'Yeah, it seems that way.'

'That would explain why I've always felt like she's family.'

I raised an eyebrow. 'Don't you class Seth and Mark as your family?'

'Of course I do. But Leah and I have always had a special connection. This would explain why.'

When we entered the house, Leah came running towards us and gave Cassie a hug. Sky followed behind.

Leah turned around and gestured to Sky. 'Cassie, this is Sky. Sky, meet Cassie, the reincarnation of Leaf's mother.'

Sky approached Cassie with a shy smile. 'Everyone was always talking about the powerful Whitelake witch that fell in love with a demon while I was growing up. Do you still have your powers?'

Cassie shook her head, a pained expression on her face. 'I'm not the same person now. I'm not a witch anymore.'

Sky nodded and looked over at me. 'Leah filled me in on what's been going on. No doubt Abigail's a witch that's part of the movement that brings sacrifices to Hecate in exchange for protection.' I hardly had a chance to process before she started talking again. 'Let me meet this wolf that can't change. The quicker I know all the facts, the sooner I can try and fix them.'

Leah gazed at Sky. 'I don't think it's wise for you to go to the house right now. We're still trying to keep up appearances. Let me bring him here later.' She checked her phone. 'I should head back before Abigail realises I'm not home.'

She took a step towards the door but stumbled. I teleported to her side and grabbed her before she hit the floor. 'Leah, you are in no condition to go home. Maybe you should stay here?' I helped her up and led her to the sofa.

She shook her head and refused to sit down. 'I have to go home. Mark and Seth are there. Besides, it's our best shot at figuring out what part Abigail is playing in all of this. I'll be fine. I'm just a bit tired from being up all night.'

I rubbed my eyebrow. Her strong, determined gaze told me it was pointless to argue with her. I let out a sigh. 'Okay, but let me at least drive you home.'

She gave me a nod.

It surprised me that she hadn't turned down the offer. Our trip must have taken more out of her than she let on. She had been putting on a brave face, but humans were not designed to move between dimensions. Besides, she had been using a great deal of her powers trying to get us back. Not to mention the shock of meeting Leaf and learning she was her mother. Leah would need a lot of rest to recover her strength.

I led Leah to her car and got into the driving seat. On the way to the house, Leah leant against the door half asleep. After I'd parked up, I gave her a poke. 'Are you sure you don't want to come back with me to rest? I can tell you're exhausted.'

She straightened up. 'I'm fine.'

'I'd rather you were safe.'

'We can't let Abigail know we're on to her. Besides, Mark and Seth will be here.'

I ran my hand through my hair. 'Fine, but any problems, you let me know.'

She gave me a wide grin. 'Yes, Granddad.'

I shook my head, a smile playing over my face as I got out of the car and walked around to open the door for Leah. I escorted her to the house and she unlocked the door and said goodbye.

I waited for the door to close behind her before turning around and walking away. I hadn't gone far when the door opened again. Hoping Leah had changed her mind, I turned around. Instead of Leah, I was greeted by Abigail.

'So you are what has kept Leah away from her loved ones. Isn't it enough to have one suicide on your conscience?'

I jerked back. 'I'm just looking out for her. She's devastated over Cassie's death and so am I,' I said calmly, even though I knew it was nothing but lies.

'That is exactly why she should be with her family, not with someone who doesn't know the first thing about love.' She walked up to me until she was standing right in front of me. '*You* are not welcome here, demon.'

My eyes bored into her, and she gave me a satisfied smirk. 'Yes, I know what you are. I have known from the moment you first set foot in this house. You're an abomination that should never have been created. I was happy when you and Cassie broke up. It's just such a shame what you did to her. If she'd never met you, she would still be around. I should have told her about you, but I couldn't risk exposing myself. There would have been questions I'm not willing to answer.'

I clenched my fists to get my emotions under control. 'Then why are you telling me now?'

'You will never set foot here ever again. And you will not see Leah again either. I'll make sure of it. I don't know what game you're playing, but these are my children. Besides, who is going to believe a demon? All you do is scheme and lie. At least Mark had the intellect to see you for what you really are. Filth.' Abigail spat at me before she turned around and marched back into the house.

How I wished I could tear her into pieces. The thought of any of the others ending up as collateral damage made me reconsider. I closed my eyes and pushed the demon down.

I needed to get them all out of there without waking suspicion. I walked a bit further away before turning into a crow to fly back to my house. Cassie was in the living room when I arrived, and I told her what had happened. I asked her to text Mark, but she said he had already been in touch and told us to meet him by the cabin in an hour.

Sky wanted to come with us, so she would finally meet Mark. When we got to the cabin, we were greeted by some wolves, and I was surprised to see some of their children playing a bit further away in the woods. Gratitude swelled in my chest. They would never have allowed that if they didn't trust me.

Mark walked up to me and blocked the view of the

playing children. 'I heard everything Abigail said to you. I may not like you, but you have my respect and alliance along with the pack's. We need to come up with a plan to get Leah and Seth out of the house, but she's watching them like a hawk now. I'm not sure if she knows we know. Leah's in no state to do anything, so I couldn't get her out, and Seth didn't want to leave her alone.'

A crease appeared on Mark's forehead and he broke eye contact with me. He sniffed the air and glanced around. His eyes stopped at Sky. 'Hello, who are you?'

Sky locked eyes with him. 'I'm here to help you get your wolf back.' They seemed to get lost in each other.

I cleared my throat to get their attention. 'Mark, this is Sky from the witch village. And as you already seem to know, this is Mark, who lost his ability to shift due to something Abigail did to him.'

Mark turned back to me. 'I need to go. Abigail thinks I went to the shop. She'll be expecting me back soon. I'll let you know if anything changes.' I gave him a nod and he turned and walked away.

Cassie put her arms around me. 'We need to come up with a plan to get her out of there.'

I kissed her forehead. 'We'll figure something out.'

Cassie let go of me and hooked her arm in Sky's. We made our way back to the house. I walked quietly behind them. Guilt tore at my insides. Why had I let Leah go back? I should have listened to my instincts.

When we got back to the house, I led Sky to the third

bedroom and ushered her inside. 'What would you like?' I asked, waiting for her to tell me what she needed. She gave me a blank look.

Maybe I needed to clarify. 'This will be your bedroom. I can conjure anything you want. What would you like to have in the room?'

I conjured a bed, which made her jump as it appeared out of nowhere.

She glanced around the room. 'A desk and a wardrobe would be great.'

After I had conjured all the things she wanted, I left her alone in the room. Feeling exhausted, I went to lie down but struggled to sleep. Maybe I could teleport Leah out of the house, but what would happen to Mark and Seth if Abigail found out she was missing?

PATROLLING

The smell of food woke me sometime in the late afternoon. I walked downstairs and found Cassie and Sky cooking. I stood and watched them for a while from a distance. It looked like Cassie was teaching Sky how to make pancakes. After we had eaten, Sky asked for a scrying bowl.

'I thought you didn't have any magic?'

She gave me a sad smile. 'I don't, but I promised Leaf I'd let her know we had arrived safely.'

I gave her an understanding look. 'I'm sorry I won't be able to help you. I don't have the ability to scry.'

Cassie perked up. 'But I do.' A slight blush appeared on her cheeks. 'It's very new, so I don't know if I'll be able to get it to work, but I'm willing to give it a go.'

Sky gave Cassie a smile. 'Don't worry, I'll guide you

through it.'

I conjured a scrying bowl and left them to it. Hopefully they wouldn't be able to get into too much trouble. I stepped outside and took a deep breath, allowing the cold air to fill my lungs before I transformed into a crow and took to the sky.

I flew around the perimeter and into the wolves' territory. When I didn't notice anything unusual, I made my way over to the cabin to talk to the wolves. They wouldn't like me trespassing on their territory. It was one thing to be up in the sky, above the trees, but another to walk around on the ground. I turned back into my human form so I would be able to communicate with them. Even though we both had the ability of telepathy, they were two different versions and I wouldn't be able to talk to them mind to mind. They had a link between their pack where they could hear their alpha even over a great distance. I needed to be near the person I was talking to or else it wouldn't work.

When I approached the cabin, a big wolf occupied the entrance, his chest rising and falling in slow movements. I drew a bit closer. The wolf jumped up, teeth showing and hackles raised. I took a step back. The wolf became still and his fur receded, giving way to human skin; bones cracked as they rearranged themselves. A second later, a naked man stood where the wolf had been. 'I'm sorry, I didn't realise it was you.'

I shrugged. 'There's nothing to be sorry about. No harm done. Besides, I'm impressed by your quick reactions. It gives me confidence leaving Cassie in your hands when I can't look over her.'

The man bowed his head. 'I hope you don't mind. My daughter is in heat, but she has not yet found her mate, so I'm keeping her safe in the cabin from the other wolves.'

People gave demons a lot of grief, and in most cases it was warranted, but the shifters had their brutality too. Thinking about it, nothing was really black and white. There were always different shades of grey. Even the purest of beings had negative emotions, not to speak of their views of anyone less pure than them. Lily choosing Nick had turned her family against her. A light being like her couldn't possibly love something as evil and repulsive as a demon. She must have been hexed.

I gave him an understanding smile. 'You can use the cabin as you please, as long as Cassie is welcome when she needs it.'

'Cassie is a lovely girl and no threat to my daughter. It is an honour to look after her.'

I shook my head internally, remembering why I was there. 'I just came to check that everything's normal in your territory. After this morning, I don't want to take any chances.'

The wolf nodded at me and went quiet, no doubt checking in with the alpha. 'Nothing unusual to report,' he said after a while.

I gave him a grateful smile. 'Thanks.'

I turned back into a crow again and spent most of the

evening just drifting around. I went to Cassie's house, but everything seemed quiet. It had been a crazy week; losing Cassie, finding her, remembering the past, learning that Abigail was involved, meeting my daughter that I'd thought was dead, realising Leah was my granddaughter. I hadn't allowed myself to fully process everything yet.

When the sun started to come down, I headed back home to check on Cassie. I felt bad for not being there for her on an emotional level. I loved her, but I was restless with everything that was going on. At least I had her back. Maybe I should try to spend some quality time with her soon – just the two of us.

Cassie and Sky were watching TV. Sky flicked through the channels with her mouth open. I chuckled as I made my way over to give Cassie a kiss. I sat down next to her and wrapped my arms around her. She leaned into me with a sigh. 'Mark texted. Leah is still asleep. She hasn't woken up yet.'

I tried to reassure her. 'Leah used a lot of magic, and moving through different dimensions takes a lot out of you, especially if you aren't used to it.'

Sky glanced over at us. 'He's right, you know. Magic is beautiful, but it drains you, especially if you haven't learned how to control it.'

Cassie relaxed in my arms. I gave her a nudge. 'As soon as Leah wakes up, Mark will let us know, and we can proceed with getting them out of the house.'

Sky tilted her head. 'Surely Abigail will come after you when she realises they aren't coming back.'

Sky did have a point. But they would be safe in this house with me as long as the protection barriers remained.

We spent a few more hours cuddled up on the sofa before a gospel of howls echoed through the air. I jumped up, all my senses on high alert. I turned to Sky and Cassie. 'Stay here,' I said in a firm voice. I made sure the protection spells around the house were strong and working. I wasn't willing to take any chances, but at the same time I didn't want to bring Cassie with me in case I teleported into a trap.

In Between

When I arrived at the cabin, several wolves were there. They stopped howling when they saw me.

I turned to the shifter closest to me. 'What's going on?'

'Something's wrong. Mark and Seth are here ...'

As he spoke, Mark walked out of the cabin with the alpha and approached me in a stooped posture. His eyebrows were drawn together, his lips curled and his face pale.

My stomach tied itself in knots, and I took a deep breath to steady my racing heart. 'What's wrong?' If anything had happened to Leah, it would be on me. I'd let her go back against my better judgement.

Mark swallowed and met my gaze, his eyes haunted. 'Leah's gone. I got home and she wasn't in the house. When I asked Abigail about it, she told me Leah had been using her magic and that's why she was sick. I'm worried she'll make Leah lose her magic like she did to me. We need to find her.' Mark's voice was laced with desperation.

My body turned numb. This couldn't be real.

He rubbed his face. 'I think Abigail realised we know about her. Me and Seth were pretending to watch TV, but as soon as she went upstairs, we left everything and bolted. We can't go back.'

I collected myself and swallowed the lump in my throat. 'Thank you for letting me know. You guys are welcome to stay in the cabin. I'd offer you my house, but I know you prefer to be close to the pack. Just let me know if you need anything.' Mark gave me a nod.

I turned to the alpha, a numbness coating my chest and depleting me of any emotions. 'I need to make a trip. Would you mind getting your warrior wolves here while I get Cassie and Sky?' He opened his mouth to say something, but I cut him off. 'There's too much happening for me to feel comfortable leaving them alone in the house.'

The alpha gave me a reassuring smile. 'It would be my honour.'

I thanked him before teleporting back to the living room. Cassie and Sky weren't there. 'Cassie? Sky?' I shouted. The feeling of dread slowly suffocated me.

My body relaxed as they appeared in the living room from the stairs. I rushed over and wrapped my arms around Cassie. When I let go, she looked up at me with a furrowed brow. 'What's going on?'

I grimaced. 'Leah's missing. I need to talk to Freya so she can tell me where she is. I'll teleport you and Sky to the wolves. Mark can fill you in on what's happening.'

Cassie's eyes became watery. She bit her lip and grabbed my hand. Sky gave me a nod and took a deep breath before placing her hand on my arm. I teleported us to the cabin. Sky let go of my hand and walked off. I embraced Cassie and patted her hair. 'We'll get her back,' I said before giving her a kiss.

Cassie reluctantly let go and entered the cabin. I turned to the nearest wolf. 'Protect them with your lives.'

The wolf lifted his head in acknowledgement, and I teleported away.

I arrived at Freya's realm and turned into a crow to make the journey to her house. I flew as fast as I could, knowing every minute counted. My wings were beating hard against the wind. The sun shone brightly, even though it had been evening in the human realm. Freya sat on the porch, two cups of tea next to her. When I turned back into my human form, she stood up and moved to embrace me.

'I'm happy you found Cassie and that she is safe.'

Hearing Freya mention the word 'safe' made me even more impatient. I gave a grunt. 'Leah's missing.'

Freya looked me up and down, obviously sensing my distress, but stayed quiet. She sat back down on the chair.

I cocked my head. 'Do you know where she is?'

She ignored me and picked up her drink. I paced back and forth in front of her.

'Why don't you sit down and have some tea?'

I shook my head and stared into her eyes. 'This is not a social visit. Do you know where she is?'

Freya took a sip of her drink. 'She's in between.'

I let out a loud breath. 'Did you know she was my granddaughter?'

Freya gave me an apologetic nod. 'It was not my place to tell you. Sometimes we need to find things out for ourselves. Create our own path.'

I stopped in my tracks, the blood boiling in my veins. How could she have kept this from me? Not only had she withheld information, but she also wasn't very forthcoming about how to find Leah. How was I going to get her back? I clenched my fists in an attempt to control my anger.

Her gaze met mine. 'Your connection to her is strong. Your heart will guide you,' she said in a calm, soothing voice.

'Freya, I do not have time for this,' I said between gritted teeth. 'Just tell me where to find her.'

She took a deep breath. 'Patience, my child. Come and have a seat. The tea is getting cold.'

'I don't care about the stupid tea.' I swept the cup off the table. It broke into several pieces as it hit the ground.

Freya raised her voice. 'Sit and calm down.' The sound vibrated through the air.

I was so stunned, I did as I was told. She hadn't raised her voice at me since I was a kid.

A new teacup appeared in her hand. She handed it to me with a smile and cleared her throat. 'How did you find

Cassie?'

I took a sip of the tea and reeled in my anger. 'With Leah's help.'

'Well then. You will be able to find Leah with Cassie's help.'

My frustration burned in my veins. I knew she could sense my emotions, but she ignored them. Why could she never speak in words that made sense? 'But Cassie isn't a witch anymore,' I yelled at her.

Freya let out a sigh. 'I'm well aware, Jax.' She sounded annoyed. It caught me off guard, as she usually had lots of patience with me. I was walking on thin ice.

She looked me in the eyes. 'You need to look inside. She's a part of you and the three of you are connected.' I opened my mouth to ask for more information, but she cut me off. 'I must be off now – business to attend to. I will see you soon.' Freya disappeared in front of my eyes. I knew she had the ability to teleport, but she had never done it in front of me before. She also hadn't given me a kiss goodbye. That wasn't like her. I wonder what she was up to. Something must be going on.

I left Freya's and made my way back to the house in a hurry. Would I be able to find Leah in time?

When I got to the cabin, I scanned the area. Everything was quiet except for a few wolves walking around in the dark. I opened the door and found Cassie, Sky, Mark and Seth asleep on the sofa.

Magical Connections

I walked over to Cassie and gave her a kiss on the forehead. She stirred and opened her eyes to meet my gaze. 'What did Freya say? Does she know where Leah is?' she asked, chewing her lip.

'She said that she was in between.'

Her hand went to the necklace. 'What does that mean? How will we find her?'

'It means she's in between two realms, probably in some sort of pocket dimension. Freya said to follow our hearts and use our connection to Leah to find her.'

Cassie frowned at me. 'That doesn't make sense.'

'But you are related.' Sky let out a yawn. We must have woken her up.

I looked over at Sky with a raised eyebrow. Did she know

something I didn't? 'Does that make a difference?'

She tilted her head back and gave me a smile. 'Of course it does. You should be able to sense her with a bit of magic.'

I let out a sigh. 'Magic we don't have. You forget that none of us are actually witches.' Why couldn't she grasp that without Leah, we didn't have any magic?

She narrowed her eyes at me. 'Magic is all around us. What about the tree Leah created?'

I wasn't following. To be fair, I didn't even know Sky knew about that. 'What about the tree?'

'It's infused with Leah's magic, so you should be able to use it to locate her. Especially as she's from your bloodline.'

Sky's words left me with more questions than answers, just like Freya's. I took a deep breath and unclenched my teeth. All that mattered was getting Leah back. I gave her a nod. 'Okay. How do we do that?'

'You could try to eat the apple and visualise finding her.' She looked down at her feet. 'Depending on your connection, it may work.'

She didn't seem confident, but it was the only idea we had. I pushed my sleeves up. 'Okay. Let's try it.'

Sky got up from the sofa and I grabbed their hands ready to teleport. 'Can't we just walk instead?' Sky asked.

'It's dark. Besides, it's quicker this way.'

I dropped them off at the house before collecting one of the apples that was hanging on the tree Leah had created. It had helped us before in finding Cassie, so maybe luck would be on our side.

Sky told us what to do and me and Cassie sat down on the floor. We shared the apple and took each other's hands before closing our eyes and concentrating on finding Leah. It was different from when I had been looking for Cassie, but my subconscious seemed to know what to do.

It was almost like watching a film, being able to move freely while following a little light, only it was happening in real life. I followed the light with my mind as it moved outside, making its way towards Cassie's house. It went inside and moved through the house and down to the basement to the hidden door, which we had established was a portal. From there the light bounced back from the wall over and over again. It didn't seem to be able to cross the barrier. After a few attempts, I lost my concentration and opened my eyes. 'She's in the basement of Cassie's house, but on the other side of the portal.'

Cassie fixed her gaze on me and wrapped her arms around herself. 'I couldn't locate her, but she's feeling scared and worried.'

It amazed me that Cassie had been able to feel her feelings, but it did seem to come naturally to her. Even with the telepathy, she picked up feelings and pictures much better than words.

I got up from the floor and headed towards the door. 'Let's go get her.'

'Wait. Running into the house without a plan would be foolish,' Sky said.

I stopped in my tracks and turned around. 'You're right.

We need a plan.'

Cassie put a hand on my arm. 'Let's go back to the cabin and talk to Mark and Seth. Maybe the wolves will be able to help too.'

When we arrived back at the cabin, we woke Mark and Seth up and told them what we had discovered. While we were trying to come up with a plan, Cassie spoke up. 'Abigail thinks I'm dead. Maybe we can use that to our advantage?'

Mark shook his head. 'She knows you're not dead. You may catch her by surprise, but what are you going to do?'

Cassie opened her mouth, but I cut her off before she could get a word out. 'Mark's right. Besides, I'd rather have you here, where I know you're safe.'

She pressed her lips together and stared into my eyes. 'That's not going to happen. She's my family, so I'm going to help get her back whether you want me to or not.'

My muscles went rigid and I clenched my jaw. She was just as stubborn as Nick, which meant I wouldn't have a chance at persuading her otherwise. I let out a breath. 'Cassie and I will go to the house.' I glanced over at Mark. 'I think you, Sky and Seth should stay here where it's safe.' Mark gave a grunt but didn't argue.

Cassie leaned her head against my shoulder. 'Ready to go?'

'You still don't have a plan,' Sky said.

'If we go now, we'll have the protection of darkness and maybe Abigail will be asleep.' I was exhausted after all the flying, but I knew I wasn't going to get any rest until we had rescued Leah.

'Wouldn't it be better to wait until she leaves the house?' Sky asked.

I nodded. 'Probably.'

Cassie took my hand. 'We can wait her out by the house.'

I teleported us over. 'You think she's gone on another work trip?' I asked, gesturing to the empty driveway.

Cassie shook her head. 'I don't know, but at least she's not home.' She fished out her keys as she approached the door. 'Ready?'

I shook my head. 'Not really.' There were just too many things that could go wrong. Cassie walked into my embrace. 'We'll be okay. I have faith.' She stood on tiptoe to give me a kiss.

I let out a sigh. It was now or never.

We entered the house but avoided turning any lights on so as not to draw attention. The house felt eerie and quiet as we crept around in the dark. We made our way downstairs to the basement. I threw my energy out so I could locate exactly where the portal was.

Cassie and I tried several things in an attempt to get through the portal. None of them worked. My frustration rose, and I slammed myself into the wall to try and break it down. The wall shook but remained standing. It obviously didn't work. I hadn't thought it would, but it did make me feel better.

I took a deep breath, ready to throw myself into the wall again, when Cassie grabbed my arm. 'Stop. It isn't working.'

'Do you have any better ideas?' I snapped back.

Her eyes became watery. Shit. I hadn't meant to upset her. I caressed her face. 'I'm sorry ...'

She shook her head and wiped her face. 'I want her out as much as you do, but brute force isn't working. We need to think of something else.'

I let out a loud sigh and closed my eyes. I had no idea how we could get through the portal and rescue Leah. Why had we not considered this major problem?

A voice in my head made itself known. Both Freya and Sky had said to use our connection to Leah. It gave me an idea. I wasn't sure it would work, but I had been told to listen to my heart.

I walked up to the wall and placed my hand on one side of the portal. 'Cassie, come here.' I held out my other hand to her and grabbed hers when she got closer. 'Put your hand on the other side of the portal.'

She wiped her hand on her trousers before placing it on the wall. 'Like this?' she asked.

I gave her a reassuring nod. 'Now concentrate on Leah and on breaking through the wall to get to her.'

She closed her eyes, her forehead creasing from concentration. I turned towards the wall and did the same.

At first nothing happened, but slowly the wall became more and more transparent. There was a gasp, and a second later Leah became visible on the other side of the wall. She walked towards us, somehow understanding what we were doing. She placed her hands over ours and started chanting.

The transparent wall began to crumble. The stairs on our side creaked and I lost my concentration. Someone was walking down the stairs. I turned away from the wall, my senses on high alert as I prepared myself for battle. I wasn't going down without a fight.

Abigail's eyes narrowed as she stared at me with a hard expression. 'You.' Her lip curled. 'The witches won't let you get away with this. They will hunt you down.'

I conjured my sword and moved into a fighting stance. 'Good. Let them try.' I wanted blood for what they had put me and Cassie through. 'They took my daughter away from me, so they deserve what's coming to them.'

Abigail's eyes widened as the realisation of who I truly was sunk in. Her face went pale as she shook her head. 'It can't be.' Her voice was trembling. 'You're not supposed to remember.'

I raised my eyebrows. 'I guess the fates had other plans for me,' I said smugly.

Abigail took a deep breath, her eyes moving past me. I followed her gaze. Cassie had somehow managed to get Leah out of the portal, and both were standing in the room. Cassie pushed Leah behind her defensively.

Abigail shook her head. 'I should've known,' she mumbled. 'What are you doing here?' Her voice was cold, devoid of any emotion.

Cassie pressed her lips together. 'I'm here to get my granddaughter.'

Abigail's confusion was obvious. At first she just stood

there quietly, like she was trying to digest everything. Then, suddenly, before I even had a chance to react, she threw out a blast of energy from her hand towards Cassie and Leah. Adrenaline pumping through my body, I teleported in front of them to try to stop the blast, but it all happened so fast.

A deafening sound echoed through the basement and the walls shook from its impact. My stomach dropped. I struggled to breathe as my eyes searched the room for Cassie and Leah. They were nowhere to be seen. Had they managed to escape? Were they safe?

Together Again

Abigail let out a laugh and I turned towards her, weapon ready. Anger pulsed through my veins. She had tried to kill the people she'd spent the last decade looking after. Beings she was supposed to care about.

Cold spots appeared on my skin, turning black. My body was transforming into my demon form. I fought against it. If the demon inside won, instinct would take over and I wouldn't be able to control my actions. I gritted my teeth, willing myself to stay human. Losing control wasn't an option. 'I'm not going to let you get away with this.'

Abigail rolled her eyes. 'With what?'

I glared at her in silence. Part of me, the demon, wanted to rip her into pieces for what she'd done, but my logical part knew we needed her if we were to figure out a way to get

Mark and Sky's magic back.

She took a step back. My red eyes were reflected in hers. 'We're doing these kids a favour. Without us, they would be wandering the streets alone without any idea of what happened to them. Most of them would easily get into trouble. We take them in and turn them into functioning adults. By the time we harvest their powers, they've learned to live without them. At least, that's how it has been for the last 150 years.'

Her words made my blood boil. How could she believe taking someone's magic, someone's identity, away from them without their consent was doing them a favour? It didn't make sense. An icy feeling penetrated my core, chilling me to my bones. The demon inside was becoming restless. I didn't like being a demon. I had always struggled to accept that part of me, but I'd learned to live with it. I would be fuming if someone took my powers away. They were a part of me. The good and the bad.

Abigail watched me warily. I cocked my head. She deserved to die for what she'd done. What would the repercussions of killing her be? I shook my head. That was the demon talking. A life should never be taken out of revenge. An eye for an eye only led you down the wrong path – the path of anger and hatred.

An energy bolt flew past me, nearly hitting me. I fell into a fighting stance as Abigail hit me with one energy bolt after another. I blocked them with my sword, which vibrated from their impact. I continued to fight defensively. The adrenaline pumped through me, and I knew that if I were to strike, I would let the demon inside me out and kill her. But I needed to end this fight. I needed to find Cassie.

I got knocked back, a burning sensation in my leg. I looked down. I'd been hit by one of Abigail's energy bolts. My feet turned into talons, and feathers the colour of midnight grew out of my skin as hatred built up inside me. I tried to calm myself. To fight it. But it was too late. I didn't have control over my body anymore.

I strode towards her, sword held high. Her energy bolts did little to stop my advance. They didn't even affect me anymore. All they did was push me back with the impact they created.

Abigail's smile faded and her body trembled. I watched in slow motion as the demon raised his sword. He was going to kill her. I used all my willpower to suppress him and thought of Cassie and my love for her. At the last moment, I got control of my body and knocked Abigail unconscious with the hilt of my sword.

I took a deep breath and pushed the demon back, allowing me to return to my human form. I was desperate to make sure Cassie and Leah were unharmed, but I needed to deal with Abigail first. I swung her over my shoulder. Where should I take her? She needed to be contained somewhere her magic wouldn't work and where she couldn't cause any problems. Nick's dungeon would do.

I landed in his living room with a bang.

Nick came running down the stairs, fire in his hands,

ready to throw it in a second. When he realised it was me, he extinguished the blue flames. 'What is this?' He looked at me and then seemed to notice the body I was carrying.

'This,' I said as I dropped Abigail on the floor, 'is Cassie's foster mom. She's part of an organisation that been stealing the powers of supernatural beings for a long time.'

Nick's eyes flashed to black.

'You can't kill her,' I said quickly when I realised what his intentions were.

'Why not? It sounds like she deserves it.'

'She has information we need. I've got a shifter that can't shift because of her, and a whole group of witches have lost their magic too.'

Nick nodded. 'I see. And Cassie?'

My breath got caught in my chest. I wasn't sure where she was or whether she was injured, but she had managed to escape – that much I was sure of. 'She's safe.' I rubbed my head. 'She managed to escape before the fight.'

Nick gave me a probing glare before walking over to pick Abigail up. 'I'll take her to my dungeon. I expect that's why you brought her here.'

I nodded as my mind filled with memories of when I'd taught Nick to create pocket dimensions. He had been inspired by Dungeons and Dragons.

I thought about waiting for him to return, but I still didn't know where Cassie and Leah were. I walked out of the house and teleported back home. I hoped they would be there, but I was out of luck. I sat down and took a deep breath. The worry weighed me down, making it hard to think. I closed my eyes and concentrated on Cassie's energy. Her smile, her strength, her love. At first I struggled to sense her, but as I dug deeper, our energies connected. She was in the clearing where Leah used to practise her magic. I teleported over but was knocked down by a blow to the head before I even had the chance to look around.

'Oh my god, Jax. I'm so sorry. I didn't see that it was you. Are you okay?'

I opened my eyes. Cassie was bent over me. I pulled her down on top of me and gave her a big kiss. I couldn't believe we'd all made it out safe.

She let out a laugh. 'I guess this means I'm forgiven.'

Leah cleared her throat somewhere to one side. I let go of Cassie and got up. Leah ran towards me. She looked like a mess, but at least she seemed unharmed. I gave her a tight hug. 'I'm so happy we found you. I should never have let you go back there after everything that happened.'

'It's not your fault,' she told me. 'What happened to Abigail?'

'I took care of her.'

Leah's eyes went wide. 'As in …?'

I shook my head. 'No. I dropped her off at Nick's very much alive.'

Cassie put her arms around our shoulders. 'I don't know about you guys, but I'm cold and dirty and could really do with a hot shower right about now.'

I gave her a smile. 'Your wish is my command,' I said

jokingly as I grabbed hold of them and teleported us back to the house.

Leah and Cassie went upstairs to have a shower, while I teleported myself over to the cabin to inform the others of what had happened. Mark looked up as I entered. 'It looks like someone dragged you from hell, mate.'

I gave him a tired look. 'Cassie and Leah are safe.'

Seth perked up. 'Can we go and see them?'

'Sure. They're in the house. I can teleport you if you want.'

Seth seemed a bit unsure and glanced over at Mark. Mark shrugged. 'It's up to you. You can go with Jax if you want.'

Seth's eyes darted to me. I thought he was going to decline, but after a moment of silence, he walked over to me and asked me to take him to the house.

I glanced over at Mark, mainly to double check he really didn't mind. He gave me a nod. 'Me and Sky will meet you there in a bit.'

When Seth and I arrived at the house, Cassie had finished her shower and was sitting on the sofa in the living room. She got up and rushed over to give Seth a hug.

Seth looked around. 'Where's Leah?'

Cassie had started to answer when Leah strolled in. Seth ran over and gave her a big hug. I smiled at them. Leah and Cassie were home and safe.

I went over to Cassie. 'I'm going to go upstairs.'

'You want company?'

I shook my head. 'I'll be fine. I'm just exhausted. Besides,

Mark and Sky should be here soon.'

She gave me a kiss and I walked up the stairs. I was in desperate need of a shower and some sleep. I went into my room and undressed. My eyes went to the burn on my leg. I had not only failed Cassie, I'd lost control and allowed the demon to take over. What would have happened if Cassie and Leah had still been there? Would I have tried to kill them too?

Their laughter from downstairs made up my mind. If I couldn't control the demon inside me, they would be safer without me. I opened the window and turned into a crow. I was ready to leap into the sky when Cassie stormed through the door.

'What do you think you're doing?'

It's better this way, I said to her mind.

'No, it isn't.' She went over and closed the window.

I turned back into a human, tears burning in my eyes. 'I'm a liability to your safety. I lost control. The demon inside me took over and I almost killed Abigail. What if it had been you? I would never have forgiven myself.'

Cassie shook her head. 'But you didn't. And I know in my heart you would never hurt any of us. You just need to believe it yourself. Besides, you said you'd always be there for me.'

I opened my mouth to tell her that I didn't deserve her love, her trust, but she cut me off. 'Come on. Let's go downstairs. We still need to figure out how to get Mark and Sky's magic back.'

ABOUT THE AUTHOR

Cecilia has always been interested in writing and spent many hours writing poems and short stories throughout her teenage years. She has always had an interest in fantasy, mythology and witchcraft.

As she grew up, the writing got put on ice as she followed her true passion – Animal care. She moved from Sweden to England, where she completed her Bsc (hons) degree in veterinary nursing and started working full time at a 24 hour hospital. She later moved to Cambridge with her partner and two dogs, hoping to get a better work- life balance.

It wasn't until the lockdown came knocking on everyone's doors that she picked up her writing and fell in love with it all over again. It started off as one book, but by the time she finished the first draft of her young adult fantasy novel, she knew it would be a series.

www.ingramcontent.com/pod-product-compliance
Lightning Source LLC
Chambersburg PA
CBHW032155190726
48290CB00005BC/1570